**W9-BRW-028**

## SHE THOUGHT, SHE HALF-HOPED, HE WAS GOING TO KISS HER RIGHT THERE AND THEN.

For Maureen had spent most of the night staring at Julien's lips, wondering how they would feel pressed against hers.

Instead, he grinned and leaned forward until his warm breath caressed her ear. "The next time I come over, I'll bring you a dress. A dress you can wear for me."

"I won't put it on," she told him. And for the first time in her life, Maureen batted her lashes.

Julien smiled at her. "Yes, you will."

"And why would I be doing that?" she asked, her heart hammering in her chest.

"Because it is want I want."

"And what about what I might be wanting?"

"Oh, that can be taken care of right now," he whispered into her ear. And without a moment's hesitation, he did exactly what she wished and kissed her.

SEP     2010

*Dell Books by Elizabeth Boyle*

BRAZEN ANGEL
BRAZEN HEIRESS
BRAZEN TEMPTRESS

SEP 2010

# Elizabeth Boyle

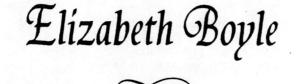

# Brazen Temptress

A DELL BOOK

Published by Dell Publishing
a division of Random House, Inc.
1540 Broadway
New York, New York 10036

This novel is a work of fiction. Names, characters, places, and incidents either are the product of the author's imagination or are used fictitiously. Any resemblance to actual persons, living or dead, events, or locales is entirely coincidental.

If you purchased this book without a cover you should be aware that this book is stolen property. It was reported as "unsold and destroyed" to the publisher and neither the author nor the publisher has received any payment for this "stripped book."

Copyright © 1999 by Elizabeth Boyle

All rights reserved. No part of this book may be reproduced or transmitted in any form or by any means, electronic or mechanical, including photocopying, recording, or by any information storage and retrieval system without the written permission of the Publisher, except where permitted by law.

The trademark Dell® is registered in the U.S. Patent and Trademark Office.

ISBN 0-440-61376-0

Printed in the United States of America

Published simultaneously in Canada

To the sisters of my heart, Darcy Carson, Melinda Rucker Haynes, DeeAnna Galbraith, and Lisa Wantajja. Truer support, better critiquers, and more laughs will never be found outside your circle of friendship. Thank you.

# Chapter 1

London
1813

"These acts of predation must cease!" The judge's voice boomed throughout the oak paneled courtroom. The black-robed magistrate of the Admiralty court continued his high-pitched rail at the ragtag group of prisoners standing before him. The tattered lot shuffled their feet, the chains binding them together rattling as if in punctuation to the judge's rambling dissertation on their fate.

In the last bench near the doorway, the Lord Admiral shook his head. "Leave it to Porter to use such a toplofty speech on an illiterate pack of thieves," he whispered to his companion, Captain William Johnston.

"Practicing for his turn in the House of Lords, I'd wager," Captain Johnston replied. Porter's father had been poorly of late, and it was well known that Porter was pulling at the tide for the old man to stick his fork in the wall—leaving him free to resign from the Admiralty bench and assume his father's title and seat.

If only Captain Johnston could be so lucky to have a dying father—at least a wealthy titled one.

Instead, he was the fifth son of a poor fisherman who had barely a net to cast out, let alone a title. No, Will Johnston, unlike his well-connected friends, had through his own talents risen to the rank of captain in His Majesty's Navy.

Still, what was a captain without a ship? A poor excuse for a sailor marooned ashore on half pay, that's what he was.

He barely listened to the proceedings before them, for he knew that Porter loved the sound of his own voice and the poor buggers would be half dead before they ever saw the hangman.

He was almost as anxious as the smugglers to learn what Porter had in store for them. For when they were done, he'd learn his fate as well.

The Lord Admiral hadn't dragged him down here to Porter's courtroom if it wasn't for some reason. Peter Cottwell, Lord Admiral of His Majesty's Navy, didn't do anything without a reason. Will held out a tenuous hope that Peter didn't need a favor, rather that he was about to extend one.

A ship. The Lord Admiral had the largesse and the power to grant one. And Will needed a ship.

Almost as much as he needed a drink. Shifting in his seat, he crossed his arms over his chest and held back the shakes threatening to reveal his poor condition to the very man who could give him what he wanted.

He'd kept his promise to his dear Mary and not taken a drop this morning before his meeting with the Lord Admiral. The Lord Admiral. Will glanced over at the man beside him, his pressed and crisp uniform glittering in sharp contrast to the wrinkled tatters worn by the prisoners.

A real laugh it was to see Peter Cottwell strutting about in an admiral's uniform. An admiral! Why he, Cottwell, and Porter had been nothing but frightened boys when they'd first sailed together some forty years ago on the *Faithful*.

Now look at them—Peter was an admiral, Porter, a respected magistrate, and Will, a tired, broken captain.

Still, Peter wouldn't have called him down here to meet with Porter if it wasn't to toast Will's new ship.

The image of the beautiful lady rose up before his weary eyes. Beneath his feet he could almost feel the pitch of the deck as the bonny new ship danced with the waves, the sun in his eye as he charted a new course, the smell of tar and pitch and new paint filling his nostrils.

Never mind that a war raged out on those seas. A man could forget about his thirst when such things surrounded him, ruled his life.

"The merchants are all up in arms, not to mention some rather high-ranking investors in the House of Lords. Why, after that damned pirate de Ryes sunk the *Greco* and the *Joyful*, he sailed right up into a Scottish harbor and demanded the villagers provision him out of the government stores. Damned cheek, these

Americans. Need to be taught a lesson," the Lord Admiral remarked.

"So I've heard," William murmured. He had no desire to go out and seek fame and fortune by hunting down the likes of de Ryes. No, he just wanted a nice packet to sail. Steady work, commanding a packet. No worries about privateers seeking their fortunes against you. Just back and forth between England and some far-flung port with a cargo of Admiralty missives about requisitions and promotions.

The Lord Admiral shot a scornful look up at the prisoners before them. "If I don't find a way to stop de Ryes, I'll be spending my retirement scrubbing barnacles off the nearest prison hulk. And you right alongside me, my friend."

Captain Johnston looked up, startled out of his own hazy dreams. He was already on half pay, and even that he knew was only through the generosity of his old shipmate, the Lord Admiral.

But go after de Ryes? He licked his lips and thought about the bottle of rum he had hidden in his study back home.

*De Ryes.*

The notorious American privateer had sunk far better sailors than Will, and now the Lord Admiral thought to send *him* out into that fray?

"De Ryes?" he said, hugging his chest tighter to keep his voice from shaking like an old woman's. Will might need a commission, but not one that would leave him in an icy Atlantic grave.

"Aye, de Ryes. That's why I asked you to join Porter and me. I need your help. 'Tis rumored de Ryes has full run of the *ton*, as well as his own contacts in the Admiralty. He's right under our nose, and I can't find him to save my life. Our lives."

"De Ryes, in London?" Will shook his head. "Who'd believe the man would have so much nerve?"

"Aye. It's why he's able to take his pick of only the best prizes, the most important ships. He knows their cargo and when they are sailing."

"And how do you expect us to help you find him?" Will ventured. While his wife, Mary, was the daughter of a viscount and still had some rank in the *ton*, their financial situation had limited their social connections. The type of society that would give de Ryes access to such highly secret information could come only at the top levels. A level Will couldn't afford.

"Milord, no one knows what the man even looks like," he said cautiously.

"Don't milord me, old friend. In a case like this, it's Peter, like it was on the *Faithful*. You and Porter are my oldest friends. I need your help. I thought we'd share a pint, like we used to, and perhaps we could, between the three of us, come up with a plan to catch this rascal."

Will saw his ship of dreams sink under the waves, dashed by the desperate tones he heard in Peter's voice. There would be no ship, not today.

Besides, he knew the Lord Admiral and how he worked—the crafty sea dragon had called him down here for a reason. Perhaps he even had a plan, one he needed Porter and him to implement, to do his dirty work.

A better man, Will knew, would have been insulted

by these games, but a better man wouldn't be on half pay and beholden to the likes of Peter Cottwell.

Something he would be for the rest of his days.

He sighed and closed his eyes for a moment. Mary had been so proud of him this morning when he'd left their little house, full of promise of the riches that would at last be theirs.

How could he tell her, once again, that he'd failed?

Up at the bench, Porter cleared his throat. "I pronounce that each able-bodied member of this crew be immediately transported for indefinite service in His Majesty's Navy. And you, Captain Hawthorne, fate has a different course for you. I order that you be hanged by your neck until dead."

*Captain Hawthorne?* Will's gaze jerked up toward the bench. He hadn't heard that name in . . . well, long enough for him to have almost forgotten it.

Almost.

He perked up in his seat to study the prisoner at the end of the row.

*Hawthorne.* It couldn't be the same man. Too slight, and too straight for a man in his sixties. Will glanced over at the Lord Admiral to see if the name affected him in any way, but Cottwell sat with his usual ramrod posture and unruffled features.

As if he'd known the prisoner's name all along. A shiver of unease trembled over Will's already shaky limbs. 'Twas as if Peter had gathered them together to remember—to remember what they owed him.

No, Will concluded, he'd heard Porter wrong.

Captain Hawthorne indeed.

It was this damned lack of drink—it was making him hear things.

"Do you have anything to say, Captain?" Porter asked the prisoner.

Though the man's back was to them, Will watched the prisoner rear back and spit directly at Porter's bench.

"A curse on you, you bleeding pig." The words rang forth with the same vengeance as the gesture, only it was the unmistakable voice of a woman who spoke.

Will blinked and looked closer. It was easy to see how he'd missed her—dressed as she was as a common sailor, the oversize coat and tight knit cap hiding any evidence of a female shape.

"I ain't no pirate, and neither are my men," the woman continued. "We're innocent traders, I tell ye, innocent."

Porter's face colored to a mottled red. "I'll have no more of that from you, Maureen Hawthorne. Traders indeed! Smugglers and marauders would be a more apt description, but it doesn't matter to me what you call yourself; you'll find the same fate in His Majesty's courts." Porter reached for his gavel and pointed it directly at his prisoner. "You're a scandal to your fair sex, and hanging will serve as an example to the rest of your kind that this court will not tolerate pirates, be they a man or," he said with an eloquent pause, "a woman." He turned to the idle guards standing at either side of the lot. "Take them away."

As the Captain and her crew began their low shuffling procession out of the courtroom, Porter rose from his seat and nodded to his audience.

"Milord, I didn't expect you until next week," he said to the Lord Admiral, his voice rising over the rattle of chains.

The Lord Admiral bowed his head slightly, then stood. "This de Ryes matter has gotten out of hand. I need your help if I'm to find him."

The line of smugglers came to an abrupt halt, the rattle of chains falling momentarily silent as Maureen Hawthorne turned her sharp gaze on them.

The color of her eyes tugged at Will's heart. Like the waters off a faraway Caribbean island. Warm and deep and clear.

And familiar. Too familiar.

"De Ryes?" the woman said, her voice dropped to the low angry growl of an alley cat. "What do you know of that murdering scum?"

The Lord Admiral drew himself up to his full height, a move that sent many a seaman and hardened naval officer alike scurrying under the nearest pile of ropes.

But not this woman. All it garnered from her was a cocky lift of one dark brow.

"Madame," Cottwell said in his most formal and annoyed tone. "This is an Admiralty matter and not your concern."

She laughed, laughed right at the Lord Admiral with the same reckless disregard that she'd shown when she'd spit at Porter. "So de Ryes is giving you a hard time, is he? He's got no soul, that one, and sails with the devil at his side. You'll not catch de Ryes, milord. Not you or that one," she said with a toss of her head toward Porter. Then her knowing glance fell on Will.

Her eyes held him in a wary trance.

She couldn't be related to that Hawthorne, he tried to tell himself, but her eyes, the color haunted him.

Years slipped away, and he was once again in a courtroom looking into a pair of eyes that blamed him, cursed him. And now they beheld him once again.

No, he told himself. This lass couldn't know what he'd done. He washed the thought away. It was an idea worse than a life without rum.

But the girl still studied him as if she sensed his fears. "Or this one as well," she finally said, her gaze never leaving his. "He looks like the only course he's going to chart is to the nearest gin shop. He'll need a drink before he'll find de Ryes—that is, if he can still sail a straight line."

She was right. Will didn't need a drink, he needed an entire bottle. And he hadn't charted a straight line in nearly fifteen years.

Cottwell glared at the guards, who finally got back to the task at hand and prodded their prisoners forward.

But Maureen Hawthorne was not done. "You'll not find de Ryes, milord. Not without someone who's seen his face. Someone like me." She grinned and followed the guards out of the courtroom, whistling a particularly bawdy Irish ballad.

The Lord Admiral's arm swung up, halting the procession. "What do you know of de Ryes?"

She glanced over her shoulder, her mouth turned up. "Enough to catch him. Enough to know what he looks like."

The entire courtroom stilled, as if this woman had

just offered them a long-lost Spanish treasure trove of gold.

"And how would that be?" the Lord Admiral asked.

It was her turn to rise up to her full height. "I used to be his wife."

# Chapter 2

A nondescript black carriage lurched and rolled out from the gates of the Admiralty court behind the elegantly trimmed carriage of the Lord Admiral. Inside the rough conveyance rode Captain Maureen Hawthorne, still shackled but closer to freedom.

The deal she'd wrangled and argued out of the Lord Admiral would have made a fishwife proud. Then again, she hadn't been a smuggler most of her life, raised with bounders, pirates, and thieves, not to know how to get the best of a bargain.

But this, this was like finding an unguarded Portuguese merchantman loaded with New World bounty. She'd gained her freedom and that of her crew—at least for now.

And all she had to do was see that her husband finally received the hanging he so rightly deserved.

She crossed her arms over her chest, the irons on

her wrists clattering almost as loudly as the creaks and groans of the old musty carriage as it bounced over the poor London streets.

While she had no love for the Royal Navy and their high-handed ways—her arrest, imprisonment, and sham of a trial still ringing in her ears—she'd own up to this much: She and the Lord Admiral, for all their obvious disparities, had one thing in common—both of them wanted nothing more in life than to see that buggering pirate de Ryes swing from a hangman's rope.

So she had to make a few concessions in her usually unrelenting bargaining style.

Concessions she'd live with just fine once she and her crew and her ship were back out on the high seas where they belonged.

Smiling to herself, she closed her eyes and enjoyed a delicious daydream of watching de Ryes kick and swing as his last breath rattled from his throat.

She hoped he turned down the offer of a hood. She truly wanted her gleeful face to be the last thing he saw in this life.

Only too soon the carriage came to a halt, and Maureen found herself being hauled down from her rolling prison to stand in front of a typical London house in a generally clean and modest neighborhood.

Used to the fresh sea air and the constant motion, Maureen always felt more than a little uneasy on land. And standing in this block of tidy little houses, one stacked against the next, she felt all but closed off from the gray sky above.

Not that the house at number sixteen didn't have a familiar feel to it, she realized, glancing at the lace curtains in the windows. The sheer drapes, the pansies in the window boxes, and the poorly made Grecian columns on either side of the door were not so unlike her Aunt Pettigrew's house just up the Thames in Greenwich. A house she'd come to tolerate for the five years her father had decided to civilize her by marooning her ashore with her mother's only remaining English relation.

She looked again at this house. While clean and neat at first glance, a closer look showed the paint chipping from the window frames and the chimney leaning perilously away from the house, all signs of an unmentionable and underlying poverty behind the crisp white curtains.

The other houses up and down the block showed the same signs of wear, as if the entire street was resigned to its fate—almost spinsterly in its outlook, as if it knew the long years ahead weren't going to be any kinder than the last ten or fifteen had been.

"Welcome to my humble abode, Captain Hawthorne," Captain Johnston said, sweeping up the steps in the familiar rolling gait of a man who'd spent most of his life at sea. He glanced back at her and then just as quickly looked away, with something akin to panic behind his hooded glance.

Why did he have the feeling he knew her? Knew her better than she knew herself?

The guard at Maureen's elbow gave her a rough shove, and she stumbled forward.

"There now," Captain Johnston told the man, "that is no way to treat a lady."

" 'er, a lady?" The grinning oaf laughed.

"You'll treat Miss Hawthorne with respect," Captain Johnston repeated. "Or you'll be reassigned to guarding prison hulks. It's your choice."

The man shrugged, but his next push wasn't as forceful. "Come along with ye, *miss*."

Maureen studied her newfound champion as he retreated into his house, following the path cut by the Lord Admiral. For a moment she'd seen past the ravages of alcohol and years of disappointment lining Captain Johnston's face. Once again he'd been a captain, a leader, a man others followed.

"Lucy?" he called out. "Where are you, girl?"

A maid appeared from a doorway and bobbed her head. She smiled politely at the Captain and the Lord Admiral until her gaze fell on Maureen. The girl's eyes widened with horror, while her mouth fell open like a day-old mackerel.

"Tell her ladyship that we've got company."

The girl just stood there staring at Maureen.

"Lucy!" he barked. "Off with you. Tell your mistress we've got company."

"Yes, Cap'n," the girl stuttered, backing down the hallway, her gaping features never leaving Maureen's disheveled appearance.

They were here, Maureen knew, to see if Captain Johnston's wife, Lady Mary, would be willing to play a part in the charade the Lord Admiral proposed—a ruse to turn Maureen into a lady who could move amongst the *ton* and ferret out de Ryes.

Once she'd found their man, she and her crew would have their freedom. A more than fair bargain, in Maureen's humble estimation.

As she passed through the open doorway into the ordered world of Captain Johnston's home, a house ruled by the smell of lemon oil and beeswax, of polished candlesticks and faded but clean carpets, she couldn't help but wonder about the woman who held sway over this small corner of London, a place far removed from the rough-and-tumble world of the sea.

She glanced up to find herself staring at the portrait of a much younger Captain Johnston and his smiling bride. The young demure woman in the picture hardly seemed the iron-willed matron capable of turning Maureen and her rough ways into a lady society would accept.

Lord knows, Aunt Pettigrew had tried and failed.

Maureen could only hope Captain Johnston's Mary was made of sterner stuff.

"Madame," the young maid said. "The Cap'n is home and asking that you attend him in your parlor."

Lady Mary Johnston glanced up and noticed the odd look on the girl's face. "Is there more, Lucy?"

The girl nodded. "His lordship is with 'im. The one with the great bushy eyebrows and . . . and . . . they brought with 'em a . . ."

Mary held up her hand to stave off any more. "Thank you, Lucy. Will you see that refreshments are brought in immediately? Something appropriate for a celebration and for a man of the Lord Admiral's tastes."

Lucy sniffed. "There ain't nothing in the house but them cakes," she said with a nod toward the sad plate of stale cakes on the table, "and the cordial yer aunt sent last Christmas."

Never quite resigned to her reduced status, Mary nodded for the girl to get to work.

Well, cordial and day-old cakes it would be, but now that William had a commission again, their days of this hideous reduced state would be over.

His half pay barely covered their expenses, so full pay would be like a small fortune. And if he was able to take a prize while at sea, perhaps a small ship or one of the highly prized new American frigates William had been talking about, they would be able to afford to entertain their friends and family in the style Mary could only dream about.

She rose slowly from her nuncheon, folding her napkin and setting it precisely beside her unfinished plate before proceeding down the hall toward her favorite room. At her feet trotted her ever-present companion, Baxter, a pug dog William had bought to keep her company. His flat nose wrinkled and twitched in every direction as he led his mistress down the hall.

Their house in Cheapside had been part of her mother's dower holdings and, thankfully, had been left to her despite her family's unhappiness over her unsuitable marriage to William Johnston. Mary had always loved the bright and cheerful little house. And even though it wasn't situated in the most fashionable neighborhood, it still held a quaint charm.

The sunny rooms, the old-fashioned regal furnishings with their glossy coats of wax, castoffs from her father's estates, gave Mary a sense of still belonging to the *ton*—though she'd given up every inch of her rank and social standing when she'd eloped over thirty years ago.

With William going back to sea again, her dreams stretched beyond the niggling embarrassment of such poor refreshments to visiting her family and being able to afford the new clothes such visits would require.

It was one thing to spend an afternoon with her old friend Lady Dearsley. Effie didn't care if Mary wore the same made-over gown year after year, only that she listened with rapt attention to the lady recall all the recent scandalous antics of the *ton*.

Mary's family was another matter. Appearances and fashion always ranked higher than amiable companionship.

As she turned the corner toward her parlor, the strong scent of the sea assailed her. It caught her unawares and brought back happier memories of William returning from a long voyage, fresh from his ship and so eager to be in her arms.

She hadn't cared then how he smelled; she was just happy to have him back on dry land. She'd never thought that being a captain's wife would mean so many lonely hours, but then again she'd never dreamed her family would turn their backs on her and leave her, as William often said, marooned.

From the parlor, boisterous male voices rose in discussion. A ring of triumphant laughter followed.

William had his ship! It must mean that. They'd gone down to the pool to see his new ship and now were back to tell her the good news.

But as she drew closer to the room, she realized the

odor overpowering the subtler scent of beeswax was not just the sea but something more odious.

She frowned and looked down at Baxter. Oh, she shouldn't have fed him those kippers this morning—he'd had another one of his accidents.

Steeling herself against embarrassment, she entered the parlor with her sunniest expression pasted to her face.

"My dear Lord Admiral, what a delight it is to—" Her voice fell to a staggering halt as she discovered the true source of the stench in her home.

With a quick glance she noted William standing sheepishly by the fireplace. At the other end of the mantel stood the Lord Admiral, his posture as straight and sure as it had been thirty years earlier when he and William had been young hot-blooded captains in their sharply pressed and starched uniforms.

But it was the bundle of rags perched on her best chair that stopped her in her tracks.

Though dressed in the rough clothes of a seaman, the ragtag person before her was most definitely a woman, though what age and what she looked like was hard to tell. It was her eyes, like the aquamarine ring Lady Mary's grandmother had given her, that gave her away. And there were her lashes, too long and full to belong to anyone other than a woman. But the comparison to her fair sex stopped there, for the little baggage appeared to have been dipped in filth and deposited into their parlor without any thought for the carpet or the furnishings—threadbare though they were.

"What is the meaning of this?" Mary demanded, directing her comment at the Lord Admiral, knowing full well this was his doing, for William would never think of bringing such a person anywhere near their home.

"My lady," he began, clearing his throat and shuffling about much as he had the first time he and William had called at her father's house all those years ago. He shook his head and continued, "Mary, I need your help with this girl." Mary's eyes must have grown wide with alarm as the scandalous implication of his request hit her. All too quickly, he started sputtering, "No, it's not like you think . . . she's not . . . it's just that she's critical to the Admiralty, and we need her to . . ."

Baxter let out a small, threatening growl.

The girl ignored the dog. "What this mackerel-mouthed fool is trying to tell ye, milady," she said with an insolent shrug toward the Lord Admiral, "is that 'e wants you to make me into a lady."

Mary's mouth dropped open, and she looked to her husband for confirmation at this outlandish proposal.

William nodded mutely.

"A lady?" she managed to whisper, before she sank into the closest chair. Her gaze fluttered up to William's flushed face.

The Lord Admiral knelt before her. "Mary, it's been a long time since I've asked anything of you, but on this we need your help. This woman has the power to identify a heinous criminal who has taken refuge amidst the *ton*. With your help and your sensibility, she could make a brief entrance into society and complete her work. I wouldn't ask this of you if there wasn't so much at stake."

"Certainly you must be joking?" Mary's gaze returned to their other guest, who sat with one leg propped up on the arm of the chair and her arms crossed over her chest. She turned back to the Lord Admiral. "Why don't you take her to your house? Priscilla has a much better chance of launching her than I ever would. You know I've been out of society for years now."

"My dear cousin hasn't your . . . your nerve, Mary. Besides, this venture requires delicate handling," he said, leaving out what Mary knew to be the truth of the matter—Priscilla would never keep her mouth shut or allow such an obvious piece of baggage into their stately Pall Mall house. There was also the other reason—the Lord Admiral's daughter and only child, Eustacia, was making her entrance this Season.

The last thing the widowed Lord Admiral would want was to have anything mar his precious daughter's entrance and acceptance by the crème de society.

The Lord Admiral rose and cleared his throat. "I think it would be more convincing if you were to present her as a long-lost cousin perhaps or a godchild in need of sponsorship. Few would doubt your kindness or your veracity."

Mary wasn't all that convinced. "Surely you aren't asking us to take her in? To have her live with us?" This she directed at her husband.

William shrugged, obviously still unable to speak.

That wasn't the case with their other guest.

"This is a cracker idea if ever there was one." The woman got up, and Mary was loath to even look at the damage done to the needlepoint cushions. "There ain't no way none of the quality is going to take me for a lady, and I don't think I cotton to spending time with the likes of those blokes either." She crossed the room and held out her grimy paw for Mary.

To Mary's utter shock, manacles hung from the girl's narrow wrists, bound together with a short chain.

A criminal? This girl was a criminal?

Too stunned to even consider what she was doing, Mary took the proffered hand, her eyes riveted on the sturdy iron links.

Calluses closed around her own manicured fingers, and the woman pumped her arm enthusiastically, while the chains rattled their own grim tune.

"Sorry for bothering you, milady. They thought you could help me and that I could help them in turn. I can see from your face, this is a bleedin' crazy idea. Me a lady!" The girl laughed, a bitter little sound, as if being a lady was akin to getting to heaven.

Up close Mary could discern the girl's face, which before appeared buried under the striped stocking cap and mop of dark hair. There was structure there and perhaps even a dash of nobility behind the sunburn and freckles spattered across what might be a fair complexion.

"Take me back to the gallows, milord. I'll hang for my deeds, as I should." The girl sighed and braved a smile for Mary's benefit—and a poor smile it was.

There Mary saw it—hope, resignation, and a sisterhood of suffering. All of it passed between them in those few fractured seconds.

Mary had known all those feelings. Hope that her marriage to William would be successful, resignation at the loss of their only child—stillborn while William had been away at sea—and the slow suffering through the years of poverty.

And something else lurched through her heart, reopening a long withheld instinct. Why, this poor girl was obviously motherless! She could only wonder what indignities and shameful dealings the poor thing had had to endure out there, out in the world of rough and ill-mannered men.

Having dropped the woman's hand and retrieved her handkerchief to stave off the foul odor that had only grown more intense with her proximity, Mary found she now needed it to dot at the tears coming to her eyes.

"The gallows? Hanging? What is this creature talking about?" She looked accusingly at her husband.

William shuffled his feet. "This here is Captain Maureen Hawthorne, Mary."

*Hawthorne?* Mary's gaze swung back to the girl before her.

It couldn't be. She stared into the eyes that had held her attention before and now saw why they looked so familiar. The girl had her father's eyes and coloring.

William continued, drawing her attention and shock away from the creature before her. "She was convicted of smuggling this afternoon in Porter's court. His lordship has agreed to grant her a pardon in exchange for the information she can provide, but if you don't think she'll make a fitting lady, at least one that you can pass off for a night or two, then she's scheduled to hang in the morning."

# Chapter 3

When Julien D'Artiers entered a London function, every matchmaking mother in the room found herself at sixes and sevens as to what she should do. Their matronly hearts told them to shield their daughters from his roguish attentions. However, the mercenary desire to see their precious darlings married to a rich man nearly always left them pushing their awkward little debutantes into his rakish path.

Tonight at Almack's it was no different.

He entered the sacred rooms, his cynical gaze roaming the room as if in search of likely sport. The sought after acknowledgment passed over the most eligible young misses, both pretty and rich, as if they were just another lot of overpriced cattle at Tattersall's.

With haughty disdain he made his entrance, as if he'd just have to make do with tonight's selection.

How he'd secured vouchers to these hallowed halls was a wonder, but then again, his charm and wealth seemed to open doors wherever he went, despite the sordid tales trailing in his wake.

One of the matrons turned to another and whispered the latest of these *on dits*: It was rumored his last mistress had thrown herself into the Thames in despair over his philandering ways!

The other woman nodded. Everyone had heard the story, though it wasn't quite the Haymarket tragedy some were making it out to be.

The silly chit, an actress of some repute, had been fished out of the filthy water by a passing ferryman, not moments after her ridiculous stunt. And she hadn't been foolish enough to wear any of the expensive jewels Julien had showered upon her.

But still, the first woman insisted, to drive a woman to such lengths, the man was a monster in the very least.

Albeit a very rich one.

That was the other element of mystery about Julien D'Artiers: Where had he acquired his seemingly unlimited wealth?

And such wealth. He'd been known to stake an entire room of players at White's. He'd also been known to be generous to the Society for the Betterment of Girls in Need, a sign that he was neither pernicious with his funds nor unfeeling toward those in dire circumstances.

"Of course," as the well-to-do matron put it, as she shied her daughter out of his path and out of earshot, "he wouldn't have given so generously to the Society if his conscience didn't prick him so roundly over all the girls he's ruined."

Julien, on the other hand, always found the reshuffling of the room as he entered a party a true testament to his hard-won reputation. It didn't take him long to spy his latest prey, preening behind her fan, while her straight-backed chaperone looked more than undecided about his attentions.

He didn't worry about the other woman's opinion. Her spoiled charge was used to getting what she wanted, and there was no doubt she wanted Julien.

And he wanted her.

Though not for the reasons the coddled little baggage thought.

To his dismay, as he started to make his meandering foray to the chit's side, his sisters bore down on him, in tandem and with matching expressions of grim determination on their faces.

Only too late, Julien realized it might have been wiser to go to White's, rather than spend the evening at Almack's.

But business was business, and Almack's was where his quarry was, fluttering her fan and glancing at him with hopeful eyes.

He turned to conceal his presence, but it was too late. Lily and Sophia were on either side of him, their arms linked to his and their firm grips confirming something he'd learned long ago.

His sisters were a force to be reckoned with.

"What is this nonsense about some actress?" Lily demanded, referring to his heartbroken and Thames-

soaked mistress. Before he could draw a breath to answer and explain that he'd had nothing to do with the
bird-witted creature's theatrics, his eldest sister, Sophia,
launched in.

"Julien, why is it that every day I find yet another
irate father in my drawing room demanding the family
make amends for the disgraceful way you've treated his
daughter?"

He would have preferred to ignore them both, but
he owed some measure of his acceptance in the London
*ton* to their high standings. Few dared snub the brother
of the enchanting Sophia, Marchioness of Trahern,
or the lovely Lily, Viscountess of Weston, and risk
losing their much coveted positions within the sisters'
gracious and prestigious social orbit.

Right now, however, Julien wished he were an only
child.

Sophia steered him toward the punch bowl, where
the crowds were lighter. "I'll not be put off, Julien. I'll
have the truth from you."

"The truth?" He laughed heartily. "As if either of
you knows how to tell the truth."

They both shot him censorious glances until he
broke out laughing at their outrage. "You've become
quite the pair of virtuous paragons, haven't you?"

"I quite resent that, Julien," Lily said. "Sophia and I
may not always have been honest in the past, but we
have positions now, families and reputations to consider. Things you seem to care little about."

Julien shook off her words. She was right. He didn't
worry about those things. Yes, he loved his sisters and

his nieces and nephews, but a family, a family of his own? That was too far removed from his life to even consider.

No, the ties that bound his sisters' hearts would never entangle his.

Still, her words rattled around inside him. In the spot, he supposed, where he was rumored to be heartless.

He nodded to the servant behind the bowl and then handed glasses of punch to his sisters. "You are both right. I'm a cad, a reckless scoundrel. The fact that either of you still acknowledges me is a veritable wonder."

Sophia wrinkled her nose over the lukewarm brew. "Don't even try your oiled charms on me. I won't be put off any longer, Julien. Why do you persist in these antics? It's scandalous. Why can't you be like most men your age, married and happily settled?"

*"My age?"* Julien shook his head. "You make it sound as if I have one foot in the grave."

"You may find more than just one foot in a grave if you don't stop dallying with every miss, mistress, and matron from Edinburgh to Penzance," Lily told him.

"Penzance?" he said. "I don't recall ever going to Penzance."

Both his sisters looked ready to explode, when his unlikely rescue came in the form of Lady Jersey, one of Almack's illustrious patronesses.

"Julien! I'm so glad you received the vouchers I sent over," Lady Jersey said, edging aside Lily and slipping her hand into the crook of Julien's elbow. "The minute I heard you were back in town, I had them delivered immediately. Wednesday nights have been quite dull without you."

Julien grinned at his sisters. He knew they'd been whispering in the ears of all the other patronesses to have him blackballed, but they had yet to exert any influence over Lady Jersey.

As long as he remained in the lady's good graces, offering her tidbits of gossip and making her feel as if she was making headway in reforming his rakish ways, she'd more than likely continue to assist him in his dangerous game, albeit unwittingly.

"Lady Trahern, Lady Weston," Lady Jersey said. "Do you mind terribly if I abscond with your delightful brother? He is in such demand of late, and I have so many people begging for introductions." She smiled sweetly and, without waiting for their assent, pulled Julien away.

There were few women in the *ton* who could have pulled off such a maneuver and dared risk the ire of two of London's leading hostesses, but Lady Jersey was a patroness of Almack's. Neither Sophia, who still had two daughters in the Marriage Mart, nor Lily, whose eldest daughter would be coming of age in a couple of years, wanted to find themselves without vouchers.

Julien tipped his head to his sisters and followed Lady Jersey.

"This isn't finished, Julien," Sophia called after him.

"I don't think it ever will be, sister dear," he said over his shoulder. He turned to Lady Jersey. "I should call you Lady Galahad for coming so gallantly to my rescue."

"They looked positively dreadful," she said. "Whatever were they scolding you about?"

At this Julien smiled. Sally might be a friend, but she was also an incorrigible gossip. Why should he have thought that her rescue would come without a price?

"The usual," he told her. "Julien, get married," he said, mimicking his eldest sister's severe tones. "Julien, stop breaking so many hearts. Julien, you are a disgrace to our family name."

"Oh, but you are." Lady Jersey laughed. "You are a terrible rake, and that is why I love having you here. It is the one place where you must behave."

"Are you so sure?" He wiggled his eyebrows and then narrowed his gaze until it came to rest on a group of young girls, which included no less than a duke's daughter and the heiress of a highly respected marquis, whose lineage was said to go back to the time of William the Conqueror. The circle of misses all broke into nervous giggles or deep red blushes at his bold regard.

"I could be quite uncivilized at any moment," he whispered into Lady Jersey's ear.

Her eyes grew wide. "You wouldn't! Not after I gave you the vouchers and promised the others that you were perfectly respectable. Why my reputation would be—" Her words faltered as she studied him for a moment. Then she playfully swatted him in the arm with her fan. "You dreadful cad. I should accede to everyone else's wishes and give you the cut direct, but I just can't. Not yet. Not as long as you continue to enliven these frightfully dull evenings."

"Ah, the terrible woes of being the arbiter of good company," he said, his gaze falling back to the gaggle of young girls. "So are you going to introduce me to yonder flock, or will I have to do something scandalous and approach them on my own?"

Lady Jersey scoffed. "I'd be careful there. Too well connected for your taste," she warned him. "Their fathers won't take it lightly if you toy with their affections."

"Never fear, I have designs elsewhere tonight, but I want my quarry to wait a bit longer." He knew this bit of information would delight Lady Jersey.

"The poor girl. You'll probably send her and her chaperone home with a case of vapors. But I'm dying to find out who this newest victim of your affections is to be, so of course, you wily cad, you've tricked me into helping you once again."

If Lady Jersey was affronted, it was hard to tell by the gleam in her eye as she steered Julien toward the clutch of waiting girls. "You are the worst, Julien D'Artiers, the worst."

They stopped before the open-mouthed group of girls. All stared wide-eyed at Julien, as if they expected him to devour one of them as an evening snack.

Lady Jersey made the introductions, ignoring the dark looks from several of the matrons at the sidelines. One mother hustled up and hauled her protesting daughter away before the fateful introduction could be made.

The others grinned with malicious delight at their friend's misfortune.

Julien bowed low to his new conquests. "Ladies, it

is an honor to meet you. I can see I've been away from London far too long."

They tittered behind their gloved hands and wavering fans.

"Now, tell me, which of you are spoken for, so I don't have to meet any angry betrotheds at dawn? It's been at least a month since I've been in a duel, and I fear I might be rather rusty."

This delighted the girls, and they all shook their heads.

"Not one of you is betrothed?" he asked. "Have the young men in London gone blind?" He winked at the girl at the end, a Lady Annabelle, if he remembered correctly.

Lady Annabelle's face turned bright pink and then went white, as her legs started to give out beneath her.

Julien knew all the signs only too well. It happened at least once a night when he was in attendance at Almack's. He immediately stepped forward and caught the unsteady girl in his arms.

"Oh, Mr. D'Artiers, you saved me," she whispered, while the other girls surged forward, offering their fans and advice, ranging from burnt feathers to a good pinch. Each one seemed pea green with envy at not having thought of the stunt first.

Lady Jersey rolled her gaze heavenward.

He carefully righted Lady Annabelle and smiled at her. "I think you should be steady now."

"Oh, yes, quite fine," she said, her words ending in a soft little sigh. It was said her father, the Marquis of Sandre, had numerous investments with Lloyd's. Lady

Jersey's introduction might net some added dividends to his plans for the evening.

"Oh, Mr. D'Artiers," Lady Annabelle said. "May I ask another favor of you?"

"Anything."

"A personal question. A matter we were discussing before you came over."

Several of the girls looked at their daring friend with alarm. Julien could only guess what their diabolical schoolgirl minds had been concocting. "What is it?"

Lady Annabelle smiled, her long golden lashes fluttering with all the coquetry of a high-priced mistress. "Is it true that no lady has ever held your heart? That you've never loved anyone?"

Her daring took him aback, used as he was to the truly inane chatter of young girls in their first Season. Even her friends appeared stunned, silenced and aquiver like a group of birds having spotted a hawk on the wing.

"That happens to be two questions, my Lady Annabelle," he told her, trying to think of a way to extricate himself. But at his side Lady Jersey seemed to be just as taken with the question as the girls.

"Yes, Julien," she said. "Do tell. You did promise the girl anything, after all."

"Has a lady ever caught my heart?" he repeated.

"Oh, yes, have you been in love?" another girl begged.

"No, never," he lied.

All at once their faces fell into dismay. "I can't

believe that," Lady Annabelle said. "Everyone falls in love once, especially when they are young. You were young once, weren't you, Mr. D'Artiers?"

Beside him, Lady Jersey was doing a miserable job of holding back a most undignified outburst of laughter.

After Sophia's jab about *men his age* and now this pointed comment from a girl barely old enough to pin her hair up, Julien was starting to wonder if nine and twenty really was as old as everyone seemed to be implying today.

"Well, let me think," he said. "That was such a long time ago."

The girls immediately began to look hopeful.

He didn't know whether it was the blue eyes of one of the girls or the rapt expressions on their faces. Or maybe it was Lily's words about his lack of family ties. Or his advanced age. But something inside him, something he usually held so tightly in check, gave way.

"Yes," he started slowly. "I did love someone once."

"I told you," the girl with the blue eyes told her friends.

"What happened to her?" This barely audible question came from a shy girl at the opposite end of the gathering, far from Lady Annabelle's more boisterous companions. No one seemed more surprised at this inquiry than the girl herself. She blushed and stepped behind one of her taller friends.

"She was lost to me. Drowned."

His admission brought the inevitable onslaught of memories he always fought to shut out. The sound of battle—cannon fire and shot whistling through the rigging overhead. Shouts of agony. Wood splintering around him.

*Don't jump,* he'd cried. *Please don't jump. Let me explain.*

On the edge of the railing stood a woman. A dagger in one hand, the other clutching the rigging.

Her gaze, angry and hard, bore into him with more searing heat than a red-hot piece of shot.

*Don't do this,* he'd told her. But she'd leapt into the churning water before he could cross the deck to stop her.

Leapt to her death, the waves closing over her, reclaiming their own.

"Drowned," the girl with the blue eyes said. "How dreadful. Was it a boating accident?"

*A boating accident?* How calm and peaceful that sounded compared to the truth. "Yes. A boating accident," he said, not wanting to look into those blue eyes.

Feeling a pall fall over his audience, he knew he needed to change the mood. Better to lighten their hearts and remove the chains from his. He leaned forward and whispered in a conspiratorial tone, "That is why I never take sea voyages or travel over water."

They nodded solemnly, until the far reaches of his words stopped them.

"Surely you jest," Lady Annabelle said. "You must cross a bridge occasionally."

"Only very sturdy ones," he told them solemnly.

They all laughed, like happy little songbirds once again.

"Mr. D'Artiers, what did she look like?" the duke's

daughter asked, preening in her elegant gown and tossing her perfectly coiffed curls. Not one of her friends
missed for a moment the implication of her question:
Their vain friend wanted to know if she favored the
missing love of his life.

"Oh, yes, what did she look like?" several of them
asked at once, happy to get to a subject they all were
well versed in.

*What did she look like?* He'd almost forgotten. The
years had erased so many of her nuances from his
memory—the way she walked, the sound of her voice,
how her hand felt clasped in his. These details had
slipped away, but he had never forgotten her eyes.

Eyes the color of the waters off a forgotten cay in
the West Indies. Eyes that looked right down to a man's
soul. Eyes that still scorched his heart with anger as
they had the last time he'd looked into their stormy
blue depths.

He shook off the maudlin thoughts, teased from
him by a clutch of romantically inclined girls.

"Oh, Mr. D'Artiers, what did she look like? Surely
you must remember what she looked like," Lady
Annabelle persisted.

And when he looked up, he glanced around the
circle of enraptured faces, all eagerly awaiting his
revelation.

"What did she look like?" he said. "Well, she looked
like . . ." His voice trailed off as his gaze rose beyond
the perfect English misses in front of him, and he
found himself staring across the Assembly room at the
latest arrival and her matronly escort.

Tall and stately in her demure white muslin gown,

the lady was as out of place as a swan among seagulls. The haughty tilt of her chin and the bored expression on her face told everyone who looked at the lady that she wasn't here by choice.

Julien opened his mouth, like a fish out of water sucking for air. The sight before him had to be a trick of his eyes, an apparition born of his tale to the girls.

But as she moved closer, his memories sprang to life. She continued forward like the sea breeze that had fostered and nurtured her most of her life. Her hair, though well contained in the latest fashionable style, still held the dark, rich essence of ebony.

Unlike the other misses, with their downcast glances and shy manners, this woman entered the room as if it were a dockside tavern, head held high, eyes alert for danger, her shoulders thrown back in a daring manner.

It couldn't be her, he tried to tell himself. After all, she was wearing a dress. The woman he'd known and loved had conceded to wear a dress only one other time.

On the day he'd married her and made her Maureen Hawthorne de Ryes.

# Chapter 4

Maureen entered Almack's with no small measure of impatience. She'd spent the last month cooped up in the Johnston house, enduring numerous fittings, lessons, and countless other indignities. Used as she was to the freedom of the sea and being the commander of her own fate, she found her prison, regardless of its comforts, unbearable.

The only thing that kept her sane was the one thought, the one driving desire.

*Find de Ryes. Make him pay.*

She'd waited eight long years to see this happen. And now, perhaps even tonight, she would see her long-sought revenge finally come true.

She had wanted to start weeks ago, but the Lord Admiral and Lady Mary had made it clear that Maureen was under no condition to be presented to society until she demonstrated the ladylike behavior necessary to move amongst London's finest.

The Lord Admiral's rules were very clear. She would follow Lady Mary's instructions to the letter. She would not venture out into public until it was determined that she was suitably prepared; this included walks in the park or visits to dressmakers and other shops.

When Maureen had balked and told him she'd rather take the gallows over this high-handed treatment, she found him intractable.

To Maureen's further dismay Lady Mary had taken to her new duties like a newly promoted squadron leader, eager to do battle and prove her worthiness, especially with the Lord Admiral's considerable purse at her disposal. And where her Aunt Pettigrew had given up, Lady Mary only dug her aristocratic heels in deeper and made Maureen's life a living hell.

Lessons in serving tea. Curtsying. How to enter a room. How to dance. How to hold a fan. Conversation that neither began with such salty phrases as *blasted*, *lazy sod,* or *bloody* nor included any other of the colorful expressions with which Maureen usually peppered her speech.

Much of it she remembered from Aunt Pettigrew's endless lectures, but remembering and putting into practice notions she hadn't considered in over ten years were another matter.

No, becoming a lady, Maureen decided, was akin to being keelhauled—without the advantage of drowning halfway through the punishment.

The only thing that bore her through more than one painful hairstyling session or visit from the pin-wielding seamstress was the thought of watching de Ryes's miserable carcass swing through the air.

*The wretched bastard. The scurvy sod-kissing . . .* Mentally she cursed his hide with every phrase she was now forbidden to use out loud.

"Don't you dare scratch," Lady Mary whispered to her as they walked down the steps.

Maureen lowered her hand, wondering for the thousandth time at Lady Mary's unerring ability to perceive when she was about to commit another social gaffe.

But the lady's command did nothing to alleviate the blasted itching from the ribbons at her sleeves. Or stop her slippers from pinching her toes.

"So this is your blessed Almack's," Maureen commented. "Not much, is it?"

Lady Mary looked at her as if she'd just blasphemed the pearly gates. "I will have you know that it is only by a miracle that you are seeing the inside of this place. Many other young ladies," she said, "are home tonight and would give anything to be in your shoes."

What Lady Mary had left out of her censure was the word *deserving*. Deserving young ladies. Well-bred young ladies. Not ladies who climbed rigging, lived with sailors, and smuggled brandy and tea for a living.

The vouchers to Almack's had been hard won, Maureen knew, but their arrival the day before had made even the unflappable Lady Mary break into a gleeful smile of pride and almost, if Maureen dared say it, a small jig.

This again had been the Lord Admiral's doing, but Lady Mary couldn't have cared less. To return to Almack's, Maureen surmised, was as close to gaining entrance to heaven as could be found in the dirty and clogged streets of London.

She looked around the Assembly room and wondered what all the fuss was about. Well-dressed young ladies stood on either side of the dance floor, shadowed by matronly figures who watched their every move. Young bucks, in their dandified fashions and prancing mannerisms, stalked through the eligible young misses like lions grazing through a field of nervous antelopes.

"Poor wenches," she muttered, looking at her female counterparts, trapped as they were in this prison of muslin and manners.

Lady Mary shot a hot glance over her shoulder.

"I was saying, is it always so poorly attended?" Maureen said, struggling to cover up her lapse in speech. "What did you think I said?"

Lady Mary's expression was one of disbelief, but she wasn't about to launch into a tirade of reproofs. Certainly not within the hallowed halls of Almack's.

Maureen gazed about the room, taking it in as she had so many other establishments, locating the exits and entrances, gauging and weighing the patrons as friends or enemies.

But she stopped herself when she started to calculate the most defensible position in the place—this wasn't, after all, a dockside tavern in some rough Carib port town.

She doubted the fashionable of London considered an evening's entertainment incomplete if it didn't end with a good knife fight.

Not that she wasn't carrying hers, just in case. . . .

Maureen smiled to herself. She was sure Lady Mary would go into a fit of vapors if she knew Maureen had stolen her prized dagger out of the Captain's sea chest. When she'd spied one of the Lord Admiral's lackeys delivering her personal effects to the Captain a few days after her arrival at the Johnston house, it had been only a matter of timing and picking the poor lock on the chest to retrieve her weapon, as well as the coins she kept sewn in the hem of her coat.

She'd felt somewhat better about her situation after that. With her knife and a few bob, at least she wasn't as helpless as the blushing creatures daintily mincing around Almack's.

Besides, concealed as the dagger was beneath her skirts, she decided what Lady Mary couldn't see was probably acceptable.

Beyond the dancing there seemed to be a refreshments table, in which no one appeared all that interested. Rooms beyond held gambling, Maureen knew, from Lady Mary's descriptions, but those areas were off limits to decent young ladies.

If she knew de Ryes he wouldn't be prowling the dance floor with these vapid misses but rather playing some high-stakes game with someone's life and welfare hanging in the balance.

So it was time to find him before he had the chance to ruin any more lives.

Her gaze swept the room again, passing over the elegantly dressed men, and she wondered if after all these years she would recognize him.

Of that she had no doubt. His face, his features, his

every nuance were burned into her memory. For years she'd retraced every moment from their first meeting to their last, not wanting to forget even the smallest detail.

Even now, as her thoughts wandered to that day so long ago, the day he'd first set foot on her father's ship and claimed to be a friend, she wondered why she hadn't seen through to his evil intent.

No, how could she forget him? The man who'd murdered her father.

# Chapter 5

West Indies
1805

Maureen had been watching the ship following them for nearly seven hours. Her father had tried to call her down from the rigging, but she'd refused time and time again.

And he knew better than to argue with her when she set her mind to something.

She gazed out over the waves separating them from their shadowy counterpart. How could she explain it? The ship matching their movements held an eerie fascination she couldn't account for. Not to her father, not to herself.

She knew her father's lack of patience was behind his orders to the crew to slow their pace enough for the other vessel to catch up with them. He never liked a cat-and-mouse pursuit. He chose when and where he was going to be confronted, and he'd decided to do it before sundown.

And so it was in the last hour that she'd spied the other vessel's name.

The *Destiny*.

The words sent shivers down her spine, chilling her sun-kissed skin.

As if the name called to her across the waves, whispered to her that this encounter was about to change all their lives, *their* destiny.

A premonition, she knew, was nothing more than her Irish half getting the better of her. If she'd been full Irish, like her father, she might have understood the odd sensations rippling down her spine as the *Destiny* let down two longboats, each filled with half a dozen sailors, who then bent their backs to the task of rowing toward the *Forgotten Lady*.

She shook off her forebodings with the good sense inherited from her mother's proper English bloodlines and brought her spyglass up to her eye so she could watch the longboats' approach.

"They've no weapons, father," she called down. "At least none that I can see. Nor is there any smoke or activity around their cannons. If they mean to fight, it isn't right away."

Her father nodded. As the captain of the *Forgotten*, he had a duty first to his ship and his crew. Caution when sailing these days was the first and foremost rule of the sea. With England and France back at war, the Dutch and Spanish had flocked to the seas to take advantage of the hostilities by sending out their own privateers, while the brash and cocky Americans picked at the leftovers. All this left a ship with no country, like the *Forgotten*, with few friends.

But Captain Hawthorne and his crew liked it that way. Loyalty unto themselves. It was a lesson Captain Hawthorne and his men had learned from experience, and they'd weaned Maureen on that notion from the time she'd started toddling around the deck—a lesson that made her all that much more wary at these strangers' approach.

She tipped her glass toward the back of the first longboat, looking for the man in charge of this expedition. But it was the sailor at the last oar who caught and held her attention.

*Her destiny.*

The words haunted her again, as if her Irish blood refused to give up its banshee refrain.

The ocean swelled, lifting the longboat up and then down, hiding it for a moment from her view. The instant the sea rose again, her eye was trained on the man at the last oar.

"Oh, my," she whispered. *He's incredible.*

It was the only word she could think of to describe him. Considering she was inured to the company of men, the sight of one—even one with his shirt open—should hardly hold any surprises for her.

But this man gripped her attention like no one else ever had.

His muscles moved with the oar and the sea as if they were a mere extension of the powerful forces pulling the waves this way and that.

His hair, tied back in a queue, glinted coppery lights under the hot Caribbean sun. The shirt on his back strained at his shoulders and arms. The white fabric, bleached from the sun, appeared stark against the dark tan of his forearms.

Out of nowhere she wondered how many women those arms had held and how it would feel to be caught in their grasp.

Immediately aghast at such a daring notion, she dragged her attention away from his limbs, but still she found herself mesmerized by the raw determination in his grasp of the oar, the set of his jaw.

There was something about this man that wasn't quite as it seemed to be.

More Irish nonsense, she thought.

Despite her disgust with herself, she looked again at the approaching man. This was no ordinary seaman. No wharf rat or prison refugee.

All of a sudden, as if he sensed her watching him, he looked directly at her and flashed a grin. A brilliant, knowing smile that nearly toppled her from her perch high above the deck.

She yanked the glass away from her eye and clung to the ropes like a dizzy London miss at her first party.

"Damnation, Reenie," her father bellowed from the decks below. "Have you got too much sun? What do you see, girl?"

"I don't see anything," she shouted down, annoyed at her uncharacteristic loss of concentration. What was the matter with her, gawking at a sailor like some cheap doxy?

Ignoring the man who'd held her gaze, she made a quick assessment of the other longboat and its inhabitants. Satisfied nothing was amiss there, she looked back at the *Destiny*, searching for any signs of a trap, signs of an impending battle, anything that would give her a clue as to what these strangers wanted.

But aboard the *Destiny*, like on her longboats, it appeared to be business as usual.

Who were they? They, like the *Forgotten*, flew no flag, so she studied them for any clues.

Glancing over the other ship's decks and then at the sailors, she decided they were too tidy for Spanish and their clothes in too good shape to be Brits. They also looked well fed and well provisioned, which could only mean they'd left a friendly port recently. Their ship, a frigate, had similar lines to the *Forgotten*, as if it had come from the same Baltimore shipyard where her father had purchased his vessel, not two years earlier.

"I think they're Americans," she called down to her father. She took another glance.

Below, her father paced the deck. "Get down, then," he called to her. "I may need you."

What he wanted was her to be out of the rigging, out of the easy pickings of any sharpshooters. At least down on the decks she could hold her own against any scoundrel.

Ignoring the tugging desire to take one last glance at the sailor in the first longboat, she stowed her spyglass in her belt, and with the skill born of years at sea, she clambered down the lines and dropped to the deck next to her father.

The longboats were just drawing alongside the *Forgotten*.

Captain Hawthorne was quietly issuing orders to his men. Armaments had been stowed about the deck for just this sort of emergency, and the men, moving about as if nothing was unusual, started to pull back the ropes and canvas concealing the muskets and cutlasses.

"What do you think they want?" she asked.

Her father scratched his beard and looked out at the other ship. "I don't know, but I suppose we'll soon find out."

The first longboat bumped into the side of the *Forgotten*.

"Ahoy, sir," a deep rich voice called out. "May we come aboard?"

Captain Hawthorne lumbered over to the railing. He pushed back the wool cap covering his gray and balding head. A large man, he crossed his arms over his barrel chest and spat just over the heads of the men in the longboat. "And why should I grant you that?" he asked. "You've slithered after us for the last seven hours, with nary a sign that tells me if yer friend or foe. I'll be more willing to let ye aboard if ye can bother to tell me who ye are and what ye want with me ship."

Maureen moved to her father's side and looked down at the longboat next to them. To her shock it was the sailor at the last oar conducting the negotiations.

In the time since she'd climbed down from her lookout post, he'd donned a tricorn hat and a black jacket, and now he stood in the bow, one hand clasped to a rope hanging from the side of the *Forgotten*.

This close, the unmistakable green of his eyes

glowed with a strange intensity, like the sight of spring-fed meadows and trees after a long journey on the winter's gray seas. The shadowy cut of his jaw, bearing a day or two's worth of dark stubble, only accented the strong lines of his mouth and chin.

*Your destiny,* the wind and waves seemed to hush and whisper to her.

She drew back from the railing, as much in shock as from an unfamiliar feeling of breathlessness.

"My name is Captain de Ryes, and I have a business proposition for you."

*Captain de Ryes.* His name rolled silently over her tongue as she tried it out.

Her father made a rude noise in the back of his throat. "I've heard of ye, but I have no time for yer kind of trouble."

"I have no mind to make trouble for you or my ship," de Ryes said smoothly, his deep and slightly accented voice teasing Maureen's ears with a hint of something that made her want to blush.

*Blush?* What the devil was the matter with her?

De Ryes continued his negotiations. "What I want is to expand my business opportunities. And I know you can help me."

Maureen glanced at her father, then over the rail at de Ryes. He looked too young to be the trouble her father obviously thought him to be. Why, he couldn't be more than three and twenty, just a few years older than herself.

"And just how could I be helping ye do that?"

"I want to join the Alliance. And I want you to sponsor me."

The statement stilled everyone aboard the *Forgotten*.

While it was common knowledge among the men aboard that the *Forgotten* sailed under the loosely held fraternity of the Alliance, few spoke of the connection. Known membership in the brotherhood—considered by most governments nothing more than a group of ruthless pirates—could leave a ship open for attack. That is why the captains who belonged kept the names of their members a closely held secret from the world outside their less than legal realm.

While being publicly labeled a pirate would mean death to any captain and crew, for ships like the *Forgotten*, which sailed without the protection of a flag and navy, the Alliance was the better of two evils.

The captains knew they could count on a fellow member to sail with them in protective convoy. They had trade agreements with less than honest customs agents and merchants, who ignored their lack of tax stamps and duty forms. When a fellow ship was in danger, a member of the Alliance offered immediate aid, no matter the peril. And if one captain obtained information about a particularly rich prize or convoy, he could count on his brethren to sail with him and share the profits without stealing him blind under the cover of night.

Yes, some of the members were less than honest, perhaps even as ruthless as the pirates of old whom they had inherited the Alliance from, but membership was granted to few and open only to those they trusted.

And now this handsome stranger wanted to join.

Maureen let out the breath she'd been holding. The man certainly had iron in his anchor to sail up and ask to be let in the Alliance just like that. With hardly an introduction.

"Did you hear me, sir?" he called out again. "I've a mind to join the Alliance."

Captain Hawthorne laughed. Loud and hard. "The Alliance, you say. And what would I know about them thieves?"

It was de Ryes's turn to laugh. "Because your hold is full of silks, provisions, and ammunitions taken from a Portuguese ship bound for Lisbon. The *Forgotten Lady*, the *Avenger*, and the *Scarlet Mistress* were seen dividing up her goods not five days ago." The man scratched his chin. "Or perhaps you didn't know that Captain Jacobsen and Captain Smyth were members when you offered to help them?"

Maureen's hand slid to her knife. She could see other members of the crew moving toward their weapons as well.

"And how would you know this?" her father asked.

"Because I was searched by the man-of-war that was supposed to be guarding that merchantman two days ago, and lucky for you I speak enough Portuguese to send its captain hunting for you and your crew in the wrong direction." He paused, his once welcoming green eyes shifting to cold stone. "The way I see it, you owe me a favor, Captain Hawthorne. A big one."

Her father studied the man below him and then turned in her direction. "What say you, Reenie? Do we let him on board and hear him out, or do we fight our way out of this?"

She should have told him to blow the bastard out of

the water, but she glanced back down at the man in the longboat, and his gaze met hers.

He smiled at her, only slightly, but the kind that hinted he would like to come aboard if only to meet her.

In that moment she was charmed, and trapped. She didn't want him anywhere near her, for his presence unsettled something inside her she'd never known she possessed. Still, all she could do was nod her assent to her father and stand back as her destiny climbed aboard the *Forgotten Lady*.

# Chapter 6

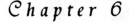

Julien's heart hammered in his chest.

Maureen at Almack's, let alone alive. *How could this be?*

He all but forgot the clutch of enthralled misses encircling him in adoration. He forgot Lady Jersey at his side. He automatically moved toward Maureen, following his heart to where she stood poised at the entrance of the Assembly Rooms.

Yet even as his foot itched to take another step, he stopped himself.

What the hell was he thinking?

He couldn't approach her—not unless he wanted to find himself gutted and hanging from the nearest lamppost before the night's end.

While first all he saw was the brassy, willful girl he'd fallen in love with all those years ago, he looked again and found that time had touched what his memories held dear. She was still breathtakingly beautiful, but then, nothing could have ever marred that.

Her raven hair, her wild Celtic features—even trapped as they were in the confines of fashion—made the surrounding society misses seem more mousy, more plain than they had moments ago. Her body had grown and changed, taking on fuller lines, giving her movements a maturity and sureness that made every other young innocent in the room look like a nervous filly.

But then again, she wasn't a young girl anymore, or even innocent. He'd seen to that.

He turned his back to the damning evidence from his past.

How could it be that after all this time, all these years, she was the only woman in the world he'd ever wanted and at the same time be the very one who could bring about his complete ruin?

Still, he couldn't help himself; he glanced back in her direction.

"Who has caught your notice, Julien?" Lady Jersey asked.

"My what?" he said, looking toward the patroness.

"Your attention, my dear. Am I to assume that our late arrival is your newest lady love?" she said with a nod toward the steps. "I should have known. She appears quite enchanting. And she's rich as well, if the rumors are true. Yes, I do believe I've found your next scandal."

Julien knew he needed to divert the lady's focus immediately. The last thing he needed was Lady Jersey's tongue wagging the next day, making her titillating speculations in every fashionable salon, parlor and morning room in London as to Julien's interest in Maureen.

"Hardly," he shuddered, gathering up his best Corinthian disdain. "She looks to me to be at her last prayers. And rich? Doubtful. That dress hasn't been in fashion for ages. Why, if I was to venture a guess, I'd say she must be coming on the tenth anniversary of her first Season. Wouldn't you, ladies?"

The girls around him laughed maliciously, delighted to discover that the beautiful and unknown newcomer held little interest to one of London's most discerning rakes. Especially if she was as rich as the knowledgeable patroness intimated.

Beside him, Lady Jersey didn't appear so convinced. "Are you sure you aren't confusing the young lady with her companion?" she said, tapping her fan to her chin. "I do believe that must be Lady Mary Johnston, though I've never met her. Lady Cowper mentioned the Lord Admiral had twisted her arm to grant Lady Mary and her goddaughter vouchers."

"The Lord Admiral, you say," Julien commented, arching one brow, all the while feeling his mouth suddenly going dry. "Whatever would he want with such an ill-favored girl?" He waggled his eyebrows at his young audience. "Perhaps he is looking for a stepmother to keep his dear Eustacia in line," he said, referring to the Lord Admiral's daughter, who'd recently made her entrance into society. Beautiful, well-mannered, and spoiled beyond repute, she was quickly becoming the Season's newest toast, especially considering she was in line to inherit her father's barony and rich Kent estates.

The girls all laughed at his comment. Julien could tell none of them liked the Admiral's daughter. With her perfect manners and haughty ways, he suspected, Eustacia Cottwell had few bosom-bows.

"Julien, you are too wicked," Lady Jersey said, drawing the conversation back. "The Lord Admiral re-marrying some chit of unknown breeding? Why, it is preposterous. No, it is as I've heard. A favor to an old shipmate. Her father, a naval hero or some such non-sense, brought home a pile in prize money, then up and died and left the girl a fortune. No matter. She has no family connections—even with Lady Mary's pa-tronage, she will be considered by most as little better than a chit."

The lady and the girls around him nodded know-ingly. Money was one thing, but breeding and lineage, they were everything.

Even as Lady Jersey continued to supply him with the information he needed, Maureen confirmed his worst fears by her actions.

First she spoke to the older woman at her right, Lady Mary, who in turn nodded her head across the room. Maureen's gaze followed the woman's gesture until her searching stopped with an almost impercep-tible flinch.

Julien swung nonchalantly around and found her gaze resting on no less than the Lord Admiral himself.

The Lord Admiral championing Maureen? Mau-reen, a long-lost heiress? Indeed.

Maureen taking her place in society was about as

likely as him heeding his sisters' advice and settling down and getting married.

Looking across the room, it suddenly hit him: If Maureen was still alive, that meant they were still married.

*Married.* Wouldn't his sisters find that amusing— that is, once they got done scolding him for hiding the fact that he had been secretly wed all these years.

Julien took a deep breath, this time to clear his head. Turning on one heel, he put his back to his long-lost *wife* and uttered a quick apology to his young admirers.

"So am I correct?" Lady Jersey asked, her fingers winding around Julien's arm. "That this is the one you have designs for."

"No, not at all. I've other plans for tonight." He bowed to the circle of girls and then to Lady Jersey before taking his leave. Slowly, he circled the room, careful to keep himself out of Maureen's line of vision.

No easy task, he knew, considering she could spot a sail on the horizon long before a lookout did.

Still, as he made his way through the Wednesday night gathering, he tried to tell himself that this was all an uncanny coincidence, a wry twist of fate.

Yet there the Lord Admiral was, now having crossed the room to greet Maureen, bowing over her gloved hand, bidding her welcome to London's inner sanctum. His beefy arm swept wide over the crowd as if to offer her the pick of the *ton*, the gold braid and buttons on his sleeve glinting in the candlelight.

Oh, she was there to pick all right. Pick the one

man only Maureen Hawthorne de Ryes could identify for the Admiralty.

But Julien D'Artiers hadn't taken his place among London's finest simply because of his sisters' connections, nor through his charm or his rakish antics. He'd gained his social standing through a cunning and calculated course.

The same skills he'd now use to ferret out Maureen's true reasons for allying herself with the Lord Admiral.

Still, it was a sight, he mused as he watched the old sea dragon fawn over her as if she were the daughter of a duke. And as the evening progressed, Julien came to the only possible conclusions for the Lord Admiral and Maureen's unlikely alliance.

She hadn't forgotten him. Or forgiven him.

"I thought he'd never leave your side," a deep, familiar voice whispered in Maureen's ear as she gazed at the departing back of the Lord Admiral. "Shall we dance?"

Before she could protest, the man who seemed to have miraculously appeared at her side took her hand and led her out onto the middle of the crowded dance floor.

He spun her around so she faced him, and her breath caught in her throat.

*De Ryes.*

She opened her mouth to call out his name, to betray him, but at the same moment the music swelled to life and drowned out the words that were already dying in her throat.

With a polite, wry smile—the type one expected

from a polished rake—he took her hand in his and began to lead her through the complicated steps.

That smile, the flash of white teeth, the teasing glimmer in his eyes, and the roguish turn of his lips caught her heart unawares.

Her mind might be screaming his name for all to hear, but her heart stopped her tongue.

As the music continued he said nothing more, though his gaze never left hers, following her as if he expected her to vanish at any moment.

She kept the same close watch on him.

To her discerning eye he looked different and the same, and she didn't know which she distrusted more—the newly acquired haughty demeanor or the vague hint of boyish charm that clung to the edges of his veneer.

His rich chestnut hair still gleamed, though instead of his pirate's queue, he now wore it trimmed fashionably short. The only other change was a smattering of gray starting to take hold at his temples.

He looked almost tame in his fancy clothes and stylish manners, but she didn't let that fool her for one second. He still moved through the waters like a shark, with intent and grace and wile.

As she turned and whirled through the maze of dancers, she came face to face with him again, only to discover she found him as handsome as she had the first day she'd met him.

"Have we met, Miss . . ." he asked politely.

"Miss Fenwick," she told him, providing the name the Lord Admiral insisted she use in public. He'd said

he didn't want to risk anyone making a connection between her and a recently convicted smuggler.

"Well, Miss Fenwick, may I say you look vaguely
familiar."

"Stow it," she whispered as she moved past his
shoulder. "Did you think I would forget you?"

"Well, yes, I assumed you had," he said, his voice
taking on that lazy drawl she'd once found so spine-
tingling. "But then again, I thought you were dead."

"That would have been quite convenient for you,"
she told him. Even as she said it, she would have
sworn de Ryes almost missed a step, but he covered it
quite well.

When next they crossed paths in the course of the
dance, it was his turn to whisper in her ear. "I never
thought of your death as convenient, Reenie. Even
when I thought you lost, I never stopped loving you."

*Reenie.* Her father's nickname for her. She hadn't
been called that since—well, since forever. He and
de Ryes were the only ones who'd ever used that lost
and beloved name.

Hearing it again almost drowned out the rest of his
statement.

*I never stopped loving you.*

In that moment she felt herself falling prey to the
same wild rush that had raced through her the first
time he'd said those words to her. Oh, she'd believed
him then, believed him with all her heart.

That was then.

Obviously, the man still had no shame. He'd never
loved her. Never. He'd used her, her father, their ship,

their crew, everything they valued to gain his own means.

And then he'd cast her away like rotting flotsam.

How dare he think his overplayed charm would save his neck now!

"I'm not the same green girl you chiseled with your sweet words and lies," she told him. "I'm here to see you hang."

"Hang?" He shook his head. "Now, *that* would be inconvenient."

His grin flashed only for her, and it struck at her traitorous heart.

*Damn, why does he have to still be so handsome?* His hand cradled her elbow as he led her through the set, the warmth of his fingers coiling into her flesh like the same treasonous tendrils creeping around her heart.

Well, at least he'll look good enough hanging from a rope, she told herself, suddenly finding she needed more reasons to see him dead. "You've made quite a name for yourself since we last met," she managed to say.

He shrugged.

"Piracy, thievery, some might even say treason," she said lightly.

His eyes narrowed. "Be careful, Reenie. Have you forgotten there is a war on? There is always extra room at a hanging for one more pirate."

"Ah, yes, the war," she said. "Then they should have room to hang you twice. Once for piracy and a second time for spying. That is why you are here, isn't it? To spy?"

His hand closed around her arm with all the strength

of a man used to the hard labors of the sea. He might be dressed in the frippery of a dandy, but the man underneath remained an untamed creature of the sea. "You would do well, madame, to hold your tongue."

"I've every right to see you get what you deserve," she shot back, freeing her arm with a quick twist. "And I vow I'll see justice done."

"Justice can be rather fickle these days," he told her. "Take your Lord Admiral, for instance."

She swung her gaze up. How did he know about the Lord Admiral? "I haven't the vaguest notion as to what you mean," she bluffed, using the same words and tone she'd heard Lady Mary use with a merchant who'd arrived to dun her for the unpaid grocery accounts.

"The Lord Admiral. Your good friend, your champion, your sponsor. Now, there's a fellow who could stand to see some justice."

"I don't know what you mean," she repeated, unwilling to say anything more, to give him any more information than what he had obviously already gathered.

"I don't suppose you do. Have you ever asked him about your father?"

"My father? What has he to do with the Lord Admiral?"

"They sailed together. As boys. And then in the same squadron as captains."

The music swelled, and they were separated by other couples. When they came back together, she shook her head at him. "My father never sailed with the British navy."

Julien studied her. "You don't know." His voice was a mixture of incredulity and wonder. "He never told you."

"Perhaps it was because you killed him before he had time to." For a second she could have sworn he flinched with something akin to guilt, but she told her- self it was only a wild hope.

As if Julien de Ryes ever felt anything akin to guilt for his nefarious deeds.

"It's just that," he said, almost to himself, "I find it amazing no one ever told you."

She knew he was stalling, trying to distract her from carrying out her plans, but her curiosity prodded her to ask, "Told me what?"

"Your father was a captain in the British navy, long before you were born. He was betrayed by one of his fellow officers, charges were trumped up, and he was court-martialed."

Again she shook her head. "That isn't true. He would have told me."

"It is true. But what should concern you at the mo- ment is who betrayed him."

She laughed, as if he'd just offered some out- rageously flirtatious compliment. "First I'll deal with his murderer, then I'll worry about the minor offenses."

For a few more movements, they said nothing to each other. The dance was starting to wind down, and soon she would be rid of him.

In more ways than one.

Julien broke the silence by saying, "The Lord Ad- miral must have something on you. You wouldn't be in

London for any other reason." His gaze searched her face with such intensity that she looked away.

"I think seeing you hang is reason enough."

"Must be, to get you into a dress," he joked. When she glanced back at him, he told her, "No, Reenie, you're lying. There's more to this than meets the eye. I saw you enter the room; I saw your face when you spotted him. He is no friend and no ally. Whatever he's promised you, don't trust him."

"You don't know what you are talking about. Do you think your lies will distract me?"

"Distract you? I'm trying to save you. If you turn me in now, I won't be able to help. Let me fix whatever is wrong, and then you can betray me. I owe you that much."

The sincerity of his words trailed along on the last notes of the dance, stopping her for a moment.

As the couples began milling apart, Julien faced her. "Don't trust him, Reenie. Your father did, and it nearly cost him his life. I won't have that happen to you."

"You're lying," she said.

"No, I can prove it." He ran his hand through his hair, a movement that used to tug at her heart. "Ask yourself, Reenie, how did· an Irish-born pirate like your father meet an English lady like your mother? Don't look at me like that; I remember everything you told me about yourself, your family. You told me yourself your mother was highborn. Well, your father was as well, and English to boot, no matter what type of Irish malarkey he tried to pass off. Ask that aunt of yours, the one you lived with. She'll tell you the truth."

He glanced over to where the Lord Admiral was now approaching them like a frigate under full sail. "But whatever you do, don't trust that man. It won't prick his conscience to betray you any more than it did when he consigned your father to life on a prison hulk."

With that he bowed over her hand and then crossed the floor, cutting a smooth course directly for the door.

Her instincts clamored for her to stop him, to call out for the officers the Lord Admiral had planted throughout the room to catch him, but she couldn't.

Everything about him called to a place in her heart she'd thought safe from ever seeing the light of day again. His stance, the throw of his shoulders, his very gait . . .

Maureen turned her gaze from de Ryes, torn between the past and the present and everything she loved.

How was it that no one else had seen or questioned the rolling movement in his motions? The commanding bearing he lent his fussy London clothes? Or the hawkish way he watched the horizon, even if it was only the far wall of Almack's? His very presence screamed of the sea, of a man who'd lived through battle and survived, who'd ridden through a hurricane, who knew how to chart a course with nothing more than his eyes and instincts.

But then again, she was surrounded by fools. Dancing, prancing, pretentious fools hiding behind their own fragile facades.

Herself included.

"Well, have you seen him?" the Lord Admiral demanded. "I'm not paying for all this for you to start husband-hunting. I want you to find de Ryes."

She glanced over at him. His disparaging tone did nothing to improve her humor. So instead of answering him directly, she said, "I thought I would be able to see more of the crowd from the dance floor."

"Harumph," he snorted, taking her by the arm and leading her back toward Lady Mary. "Your behavior out there looked more like that of a Thames-side doxy. Remember, you are supposed to be a lady, but I doubt even Lady Mary could instill that in the likes of you. That comes with breeding, and don't forget it."

"I won't," she said, bristling at his reproach.

"So is he here?" he repeated.

She turned around and faced the man who held her life and the lives of her crew in the balance and, against her better judgment, lied. "No, I haven't."

If at first she didn't regret lying to the Lord Admiral, as she turned and watched Julien meld into the departing crowd and then disappear from sight, she wondered how she'd let herself trust *him* once again, even after everything he'd done to her.

And as the evening progressed, her doubts about letting de Ryes go only grew. She should have known better than to trust him.

Just as she should have known not to fall in love with him in the first place all those years ago.

# Chapter 7

"How long are you going to moon over this railing like a lovesick calf, lassie?"

Maureen looked up to see her father walking toward her. "I'm not mooning," she told him, turning her back to the ship moored alongside them.

"You've been watching him for a fortnight now. And don't shake your pretty head at me; I've seen you. I've also noticed you've taken to washing your face and combing your hair when we have company for dinner."

The *Forgotten Lady* and the *Destiny* sat moored in the quiet bay of an unmapped cay. There had been too many British ships of the line prowling the waterways of late, so they'd taken to this hideaway to wait out the passing patrols. The extra days had given both ships time to make some repairs and time for the crews to get to know each other.

"I would bet that if you were to wear that dress he brought over for you, you would look quite fine tonight," her father said nonchalantly.

"I won't wear a dress for him or any man," she said, scuffing her bare foot across the decking. "If he can't like me for who I am, then I've no use for him."

"So, it's that way, is it?" her father asked, scratching his beard.

"What way is that?"

"You're afraid you'll look foolish in such a fine bit of rigging."

She closed her mouth tight and stalked down the deck away from him. She knew she looked like an indignant cat, but she didn't care.

Leave it to her father to get to the heart of the matter.

It was true, she would look foolish in that dress. She wished wholeheartedly that de Ryes had never given it to her.

Flopping down on a coil of rope, she scowled at the sailors who glanced in her direction. She'd not listen to their teasing. Why, the entire crew knew she had a dress now. It had been five years since she'd worn one. Ever since the damned thing had come aboard, there wasn't a man on the *Forgotten* who hadn't been pestering her to put it on.

As if she could. She'd carefully opened the tissue-wrapped bundle and laid the wretched thing out on her bunk, gawking at the expensive silk and delicate laces, afraid her callused and tar-stained hands would leave snags and smudges all over the fine fabric.

To get away from their amused looks, she climbed to her favorite perch in the rigging, where usually she found a strange peace. This time all she found was her gaze wistfully glancing over at the *Destiny*.

Damn de Ryes. How had he gotten so thoroughly under her skin?

No, she corrected herself. Julien. His name was Julien. He'd asked her to call him that the day after they met, but as yet she'd only whispered the intimacy of his Christian name to the wind or in the quiet darkness of her cabin.

She could no more call him Julien to his face than wear the gown he'd chosen for her. She turned her face into the breeze and let the soft Caribbean wind wash over her cheeks and hair.

Oh, it was a terrible muddle.

The fact that the man left her tongue-tied and confused only added to her misery.

She'd sat mutely through most of the dinners her father had hosted for Julien and his officers. It hadn't taken but a few hours in his company to realize that Captain de Ryes was no average sailor. The man had all the telltale markings of a gentleman, the type used to the company of ladies.

Real ladies.

Still, she could have listened to him talk for hours about Paris before the Revolution, of Charleston society, of wealthy Virginia families, of the antics of the London *ton*—subjects that before had held little interest to her.

This was a man who straddled the sea and the ballroom.

She'd tried to do the same once, live in both worlds. At the age of ten her father had marooned her with her Aunt Pettigrew in Greenwich. Until she was fifteen, she'd lived with her aunt, studied music, learned the lessons a lady held dear. But every spare moment she could slip away from her aunt's neat and tidy house, she'd found herself donning her sailor's breeches and jacket and stealing down to the Thames to watch the ships sail past the busy Greenwich docks. Each flap of a sail, each creak of oak, every clank of an anchor left her longing to feel the wind in her hair, the hemp ropes twisting in her hands, and the stinging kiss of salt on her lips.

So when her father had come to visit her after nearly five years, she'd sneaked after him in the wee hours of the morning, climbing aboard the *Forgotten Lady* via the anchor line. And when she was discovered two days later, long after they were well away from the English shore, she'd told her irate parent she would never set foot in England again.

Her home was the sea.

But Julien's life was different. That she knew. And she couldn't help but think there was no room in it for her.

Still, she loved the little attentions he gave her, drawing her into the conversations, asking her questions about sailing, bringing her small presents.

Gifts a man brought a lady.

First it had been a tortoiseshell comb. To hold her hair out of her eyes when she was on lookout duty.

Next came a blue ribbon, which he claimed matched her eyes.

Why a man kept such trinkets about, Maureen could only speculate, but she was sure they were meant to entice a lady into doing unspeakable things.

She'd accepted his gifts and wondered how long she'd have to wait for the unspeakable part.

And a few nights ago, as he'd been about to leave the *Forgotten* after a long evening of dining, drinks, and tall tales, he'd caught her in the passageway, just the two of them.

She had thought, half-hoped, he was going to kiss her right there and then. For she'd spent most of the night staring at his lips and wondering how they would feel pressed to hers.

Instead, he'd grinned and leaned forward until his warm breath caressed her ear. "The next time I come over, I'll bring you a dress," he said. "A dress you can wear for me."

"I won't put it on," she'd told him. And for the first time in her life, she'd even batted her lashes.

He grinned at her, his gaze roaming from the top of her head down to her bare feet. "Yes, you will, Reenie."

"And why would I be doing that?" she'd asked, her heart hammering in her chest, her legs suddenly feeling like the cook's bread pudding—wobbly and not too set.

"Because it is what I want."

"And what about what I might be wanting?"

"Oh, that can be taken care of right now, you little sea witch," he whispered into her ear. And without a moment's hesitation, he'd done exactly what she'd wished and kissed her.

His lips had touched hers almost reverently, the gentle pressure sending shivers down her spine and arms. Her mouth sprang open in a soft sigh, and his arms wound around her neck and waist, pulling her closer to him.

She'd never been kissed before, not like this.

As if he knew, he kept his kiss contained, but she could feel the fire in his blood burning just beneath the surface. He wanted her, and not just for kissing.

The notion startled her, yet she felt her own body melting to his, answering for her untried heart, begging for his touch and kiss.

One of his hands slowly stroked the small of her back, while the other worked its magic at the nape of her neck. He'd pulled the ribbon from her hair, the blue one he'd given her. Her hair, which she'd so carefully arranged, came tumbling down in a wild mess.

She thought to protest but heard the sigh of delight in the back of his throat as he pulled his fingers through the long coils.

She swore right there and then to never tie her hair up again. Not if de Ryes was around.

And just when she thought she could no longer stand the torment of his touch, when she thought she would lose all reason and turn as wanton as any dockside baggage, the door to her father's cabin began to creak open.

They broke apart like guilty children caught stealing tarts. Julien backed down the corridor into the shadows, where he could remain unseen.

"Is that you, Reenie?" her father called out.

"Yes, sir," she replied, smoothing out her shirt and pulling her hair back.

"Haven't you got this watch?" He stepped out of his cabin and into the hall, eyeing her with a speculative glance.

"Yes, sir," she said. "I was just going up." She motioned toward the ladder.

"Well, get on it, lassie. I need my best lookout up there. There's a moon tonight, and I don't want to be taken unawares."

"Aye, sir."

He nodded to her and turned to go back into his cabin.

"Sleep well, papa," she called to him.

"I'll see you in the morning," he said over his shoulder. "And Reenie, tell de Ryes there to go back to his own ship." With that he'd chuckled and closed the door.

# Chapter 8

During the carriage ride home, Maureen stared out the window and wondered at her own stupidity, while Lady Mary prattled on about their triumph at Almack's.

"And both Lady Wilcott and the Dowager came over to me to ask about you. I hadn't seen Eliza since . . . well, since before I married the Captain. But oh, she looked jealous when we were interrupted seven times by young men seeking introductions to you. How many requests to dance did you turn down?" The lady didn't wait for Maureen's reply, rather continued with barely a pause. "Fourteen by my count. The Dowager almost went into apoplexy over your success, especially when my friend, Lady Dearsley, came over and pointed it out. Oh, the Dowager tried to tell me that it was because her granddaughter is too modest to draw attention to herself, but then, one look at Miss Wilcott tells the entire story, doesn't it? The poor girl favors her father's side of the family—an exact replica of the old Dowager." Lady Mary sighed. "You outshone everyone."

Maureen let the curtain fall back into place and smiled at the lady, her memories of the evening far different.

She could hardly call the night an unqualified success. She'd let de Ryes go.

How could she have been so foolish?

"And did I tell you we've been invited to a soiree Friday night? The invitations are quite exclusive. Oh, this is exactly how I always imagined it would be to have a—" This time the lady's chatter stopped abruptly, as if she realized how close she'd come to revealing such a secretly held desire.

Maureen knew what she would have said if she'd finished her sentence.

*. . . . to have a daughter.*

But Maureen wasn't her daughter, not even the goddaughter everyone thought her to be.

How she wished she could join in Lady Mary's triumph, forget who she was, forget de Ryes. Pretend she was nothing more than a daughter riding home from her first entrance into society. Have a woman like Lady Mary beaming across at her with motherly affection and pride.

But that was not to be. Those dreams weren't meant to be a part of Maureen's life. How would she even know what motherly regard felt like? Her own mother had died of yellow fever when Maureen was but three.

And Aunt Pettigrew, well, she was a dear soul, but she hadn't a maternal bone in her body.

Now, as Lady Mary's make-believe fell away, Maureen regretted the loss of a mother she'd never known, much as Lady Mary's face told her that her newfound "godmother" feared the day when this masquerade would end.

But Maureen never underestimated Lady Mary's resiliency. In a matter of moments, the dear woman had settled back in the seat of the hired carriage, as if the cracked and stained leather were royal velvet, obviously choosing to return to her revelry in her new social position. "Now, tell me about dancing with Julien D'Artiers."

"With whom?" Maureen asked, her ears perking at the sound of Julien's name, connected as it was to the unfamiliar surname.

"Julien D'Artiers. The man you danced with. I thought you were going to turn down all your offers, so imagine my surprise when I saw you out on the floor with *him*."

*Julien D'Artiers.* So that was de Ryes's London name. At least he'd kept the Julien part. She wondered if D'Artiers was his real name or another *nom de guerre*.

"Yes, well, Mr. D'Artiers left me little choice."

Lady Mary clucked her tongue. "I suppose I should be furious that he didn't seek a proper introduction before he whisked you out on the floor. From what Lady Dearsley has told me, there seem to be no limits to what that man can do to rules and appropriate conduct and get away with. Why, it is scandalous." The lady looked anything but horrified, more like delighted.

"Is he as wicked as they say? Whatever were you two discussing?"

"Nothing of consequence," Maureen said. "I found him quite annoying and told him so."

"Oh, how delightful," her companion said, rubbing her hands together. "Why, he's considered the catch of London, and if you turn your nose up at him, why, you will be the next Original before the week is out. You'd never catch that dull Miss Wilcott calling Julien D'Artiers annoying."

"I hardly think the Lord Admiral is doing all this so I can become the *ton*'s next Original." Maureen didn't like the direction in which this conversation was headed.

But even worse she didn't know if she liked Julien being considered a catch. Not that she cared, but they were after all still married. Obviously, such a small fact didn't matter to him. The heartless cad!

Then again, what would his beloved *ton* say when they found out who he truly was?

An American privateer and spy.

She smiled to herself. The idea of toppling him from his lofty perch only added to her satisfaction. It also meant he wouldn't be very hard to find when it came time to betray him.

*When?*

What was she thinking? One night at Almack's, one dance with Julien, and she was becoming as fanciful as Lady Mary!

This wasn't a matter of biding her time. She had the lives of her crew to consider. While they were locked in the cold and damp hold of her ship, eating whatever scraps their guards deemed worthy fare, she was partaking of three meals a day and sleeping on a feather mattress.

First thing tomorrow she would send a message to the Lord Admiral and tell him she had, indeed, found Captain de Ryes and be done with the entire business.

But even as she made up her mind, Julien's warning about the Lord Admiral haunted her.

*... don't trust that man. It won't prick his conscience to betray you any more than it did when he consigned your father to life on a prison hulk.*

Her father in the Royal Navy, much less courtmartialed or ever having spent time on a prison hulk? Why, it was too ridiculous to even consider.

No, Julien was lying. As he'd lied about everything he'd said tonight, including that he'd never stopped loving her.

As if he ever had to begin with.

The arrogant bastard probably thinks I won't have the courage to do it, she fumed. No wonder he walked out of Almack's as if he hadn't a care in the world.

Oh, hand him over she would, first thing in the morning.

"Ah, yes," Lady Mary was saying as the carriage rolled to a stop in front of her little house. "Tonight was a triumph that will be envied by every mother in Almack's and all the ones unable to get their daughters vouchers. You were the only one with whom Mr. D'Artiers chose to dance. Whether you like it or not, you've been chosen. Tomorrow morning will find us buried in invitations, just you wait and see."

*   *   *

Maureen settled into her bed, but sleep appeared as likely as de Ryes owning up to his sins in the morning paper.

*Julien de Ryes.* She crossed her arms over her chest. *The wretched, base-born fiend.* Soon she'd be well rid of him.

Still, she found it wasn't so easy to dismiss him from her thoughts. His words whispered over her, as if he lay beside her, held her close.

*Reenie, . . . I never stopped loving you.*

Pulling a pillow over her head, she tried to muffle the devilish murmurs.

Instead, she found herself back at Almack's, dancing with Julien. His hand cradling her elbow, caressing her like a secret lover. The enticing sound of his voice edging past her sensibilities and calling to her long-unmet needs.

And if her tortured thoughts couldn't get any worse, she saw herself stroking the breadth of his shoulders encased in his perfectly tailored dark jacket.

Her wayward imagination carried her from Almack's, far away to the West Indies. She stood on that distant beach, pulling his coat away to reveal the muscles and strength of a man who sailed the seas.

A body she'd touch and claim and kiss—

Blast and curse, she thought, tossing the pillow aside and flopping back and forth until she found a somewhat comfortable spot.

She wondered what the rest of the peevish little misses at Almack's would think if they saw Julien naked, as she had? Would they be as reckless as she had been and throw themselves at him?

With that disturbing thought, she yanked the counterpane up higher under her chin and studied the waterstained ceiling overhead.

She had too much to do tomorrow to spend the night memorizing the blemishes in the Johnstons' leaky ceiling. She needed to sleep.

Tossing once more, she turned to her tried and true method of falling asleep—planning Julien's hanging.

The images always gave her comfort and usually brought on a restful night's sleep before she could even get to the crack of the rope as it went taut over his jerking body.

So pushing aside the images of soft Caribbean breezes, whispered words, and gentle caresses, she followed the cart hauling de Ryes to Tyburn. She joined in with the cries and insults slung by the bloodthirsty crowd, jeering with the best of them. She watched him, clothed in tatters, mount the stairs.

Coming to her favorite part, she reveled as his features whitened and then grayed with an unholy fear as he beheld the rope before him, the instrument of his final reckoning.

Even as his knees buckled and she watched with delight as the hangman's assistant prodded him none so gently forward, she felt the welcome oblivion of sleep spread over her, the restful respite that always came in knowing that justice would be done.

But this time in her dreams, she found something entirely different.

*She found memories.*

# Chapter 9

Maureen lay tucked in the bowsprit of the *Forgotten Lady*. With the ropes cradling her back, she stared up at the clear stars twinkling in the night sky. Anchored close to shore, she could hear the soft hiss of the gentle waves as they lapped against the white sand beach of the palm-studded cay. There was only the barest sliver of a moon, so the stars glittered like diamonds against the inky backdrop.

She let her thoughts float upward toward the heavens and then let them tumble down like the mercurial path of a falling star.

"Julien," she whispered to the night sky. "Julien, come to me."

Since he'd kissed her in the passageway she found herself unable to sleep without succumbing to such wildly erotic fantasies; she wondered if she had been bewitched by some strange island spell.

*Julien holding her. Julien kissing her. Kissing not just her mouth, but her neck, her shoulders, her breasts.*

Even in the cool air, her cheeks burned hot at the wild notions.

As she'd done too many times to count in the last few days, she turned her gaze toward the *Destiny*. Like the *Forgotten Lady*, she sat moored without lights. There were too many ships about to risk lighting lamps on such a dark night. Ships possibly hunting for members of the Alliance.

But even in the shadows Maureen could trace the sleek lines of Julien's ship, until she swore she could make out the window of his cabin.

She wondered what type of room he kept. Full of pirate splendor, with plump couches, chests of treasures, and velvet pillows awaiting his latest mistress? Or, like the Americans he favored, functional and sparsely furnished?

Now she wished she had been able to accept his invitation to dine with him tonight but her father had put his foot down and said no before she could utter a word.

She couldn't fathom why her father had suddenly seemed to change his opinion of Captain de Ryes—at least when it came to her visiting his ship.

"I'll not have ye over there alone, lass," he'd told her sternly. "Not until we know his intentions."

And Maureen knew better than to challenge her father when he made such an adamant decision. Especially when his tone clearly stated that he'd brook no resistance on her part.

Just what intentions her father had been inferring she didn't ask. She knew only too well what she hoped for.

More of Julien's kisses.

A wave sloshed against the ship, and she watched its movement as it rolled from the bowline across the water until it touched the *Destiny*.

There in the shadows of the other ship, she saw movement, a boat being lowered quietly, and a single occupant rowing toward her.

She smiled slowly, hugging her arms around herself. *Julien!*

Rolling onto her side, she watched his silent progress across the narrow channel between them. He'd obviously wrapped his oars with cloth to muffle their sound, for if she hadn't seen him, she certainly would never have heard his approach.

She glanced up at the watch on the deck and the man in the mizzenmast. Neither seemed to have noticed Julien's approach.

Her father would have their heads if he knew. Not that she was going to tell him about this obvious breach.

"Maureen," Julien whispered as his boat came up underneath her position. "Climb down. Come with me."

She resisted the urge to leap directly into the rocking boat below her. "My father said I couldn't go over to your ship alone. I gave him my word."

Julien grinned up at her. "I know. That's why we are going ashore."

At this Maureen nodded. She hadn't promised not to go ashore alone with Julien, and in a flash she clambered down a line to join him.

In a few quiet strokes, he took them out from under the shadow of the *Forgotten Lady* and closer to shore.

"Why aren't you wearing the dress I gave you?" he teased.

" 'Tis too fine."

He'd taken them down shore from where the two boats were moored, just out of sight of the watch. The rowboat bumped up against the sand, and she jumped out automatically and grabbed the line to pull the boat in farther.

"Perhaps that dress is too fine," he said with a small laugh.

She stopped herself and realized that most ladies did not leap from the boat until it was safely ashore. Hardly the action of the type of woman he was probably used to.

Maureen was glad for the darkness, for she knew she was blushing. She was a fool to think a man of breeding like Julien de Ryes would ever want anything from her that he couldn't get for a few gold coins at any dockside.

Hell, being such a handsome devil, coins were probably unnecessary.

They walked along the sandy beach for a few feet, Maureen stalking ahead and Julien following with a blanket in hand.

"Maureen, look at me," he said to her. "I like it that you can handle a boat, that you don't go into vapors at the sight of maggots, that you can climb rigging and trim sails better than any man aboard your father's ship or mine."

"But I'm not a lady," she whispered.

"Oh, but you are. That dress may not seem right now, but one day you'll wear it and put every other woman to shame. I would bet if you arrived in London, you would be dubbed the newest Original. Not a debutante in town could hold a candle to you. You have a fire in your soul that makes you more of a woman than any amount of finishing school or silk gowns can add."

"I doubt that. I was in London for a time, and no one seemed to notice me."

"I would have."

Even in the darkness she could see the intensity of his gaze. It burned over her, and for a moment she saw that to him it mattered not that she was a sunburned, rough-edged lass in breeches, not a lady, manor-born and dressed in pale muslin. He didn't care that her hair smelled of salt water, not roses, or that her hands and feet were rough with calluses and black with tar, instead of soft and smooth as satin.

He loved her. Loved her for who she was.

As if he sensed the conclusions she'd come to, he pulled her into his arms. "I didn't risk going against your father's wishes to bring you here just for some lark. I can't stop thinking about you," he whispered breathlessly into her ear. "You are unlike any woman I have ever known. I want you, Maureen. You, not some simpering society miss. I want you now, tonight, always. I would have you next to my side for the rest of our lives."

His words pushed away all her insecurities, all her doubts.

*Always. I want you always.*

She didn't care that it wasn't a proposal of marriage; she'd never expected one from any man. But to know that he wanted her, wanted to share his life with her, was enough.

She pressed her lips to his eagerly, sighing as his mouth closed over hers. They sank to their knees in the sand, and for a time all they did was kiss.

She opened her mouth to him, as he had opened his heart. His tongue caressed hers, loved her, just as his words had, and she felt the rising heat of desire coil within her heart and burn through her veins.

His hands, just as rough-hewn as hers, caressed her as if she were made of porcelain, first pulling at the cord that held her braid, then gently separating the bound strands until they flowed freely through his fingers.

She pulled away from his mouth, her head tilting back. She wanted what she'd dreamed of—his mouth touching her. And he seemed to sense her needs, for his lips plied and teased her neck, while his hands pushed her shirt away from her shoulders, exposing them to the cool night air.

The heat of his lips burned her skin. If her dreams had nearly driven her to madness, then the reality of his touch pushed her over the brink.

Without shame or care she pulled at the ties on her shirt and opened it further. "Kiss me. Kiss me here," she whispered breathlessly.

At first she thought she'd gone too far, been too

brazen, for all he did was stare at her exposed breasts. Then, slowly, he reached out and cradled one in the palm of his hand, his fingers winding around the softness until they touched the hardened peak of her nipple.

She sucked in a deep breath. His touch sent hot currents coursing through her blood. His fingers teased and stroked her fevered flesh. If that weren't enough, he unleashed a new fire by placing his lips on her.

As he began to suckle, she arched her back and moaned softly. Her dreams had only hinted at such ecstasy, at such hot, driving passion. His other arm wrapped around her back and drew her closer. The wet heat of his mouth washed over her, and when he pulled back for a moment, she realized just how hot it was, for the cool air sent a shiver over her fiery flesh.

He tipped his head over the other breast and loved it the same way, lapping at the nipple, suckling and teasing it until it rose again to a hardened peak.

Beneath him, she writhed and twisted, not wanting him to stop but wondering how he would ever put out the inferno raging within her.

He rose with a grin. Gone were any of the boyish features she'd fallen in love with, for the man staring at her held only desire and need in his eyes.

Need for her.

She wanted to make him feel the same torture he had inflicted on her. She pulled at his shirt, nearly tearing it from his back. In the same frenzy, she found hers being pulled over her head and tossed beside his.

For a moment she paused, not sure what to do next. Carefully, she reached out and touched his face, her hands grazing over the smoothly shaved ridge of his jaw, dropping to run over the thick muscles in his neck and shoulders.

How could a man feel so much like iron and yet touch her with such a gentleness?

His eyes were closed as she continued her explorations. She nearly stopped as she came to the top of his breeches. Like her, that was all he had on. And once those garments were gone, Maureen knew there would be nothing to stop the natural desire between them.

Not that she could even think of stopping now.

She opened the breeches slowly, one button at a time. Each a chance for him to end this madness, to tell her he'd made a mistake. But the telltale hardness beneath, straining as much to be free of the buttons as she was to see them opened, told her that she'd never hear him utter a word to halt her.

Finally, the last button opened, and without even stopping, she pushed his breeches down, and then pulled them free from his body.

She glanced shyly back in wonder at his legs, long and lean, and then upward, farther, to where his hard, thick manhood awaited her.

How she wanted to touch him, to love him, as he had loved her, but she didn't know how. Just then Julien reached for her and pulled her down into the sand with him, closing his mouth over hers and kissing away her doubts.

His fingers once again found the hardness of her nipple, teasing it again, stroking the flesh around it, and rubbing it between his forefinger and thumb.

She followed his example and reached for him, allowing her fingers to close around him. It was his turn to moan, deep and full of an unearthly longing—one she understood. She stroked and caressed him, growing more bold with each movement as she watched his reaction, felt the arch of his hips and the sway of his body moving in concert with her touch.

"Not so fast, Reenie," he whispered raggedly. "You'll unman me before . . ." His voice, husky and deep trailed off leaving her raging imagination to finish his declaration.

He pulled back, and then he reached for her own breeches. Unlike her, he didn't hesitate to undo them, and they were gone before she had a chance to reconsider.

In that moment it seemed everything around them stilled. The whisper of breeze, the rise and fall of the gentle waves. He stared at her, his face masked in the darkness so she couldn't tell what he was thinking.

Slowly, on his knees beside her, he whispered, "You look like some fey beautiful creature, lost from her watery cove, come to steal my heart, Reenie." Beside her now, he brushed back a wayward lock of her hair. He continued to touch her, here and there, until his fingers wound over the gentle mound below her stomach. He touched her lightly, opening her to his explorations.

Suddenly, the sensations she'd felt before faded as the intensity of his touch focused on her very need. He stroked her slowly, his fingers drawing lazy circles over her. Her hips rose under his spell, dancing to catch the cadence of his touch.

She opened her mouth to cry out when he found

the very center of her need, but he'd covered her mouth with his, stealing her cry in a breathless kiss.

His finger moved deeper toward her center, tentatively dipping inside her. She felt her body open and close around him, and then his hand slipped away. He moved so he now lay over her, his manhood rubbing insistently at the spot where his fingers had been moments before.

"I want you so bad, Reenie, but I have to know this is what you want," he said. "I want to make you mine, but I have to know you trust me."

Maureen opened her eyes. "I trust you, Julien. Please, make love to me. Make me yours forever."

It was the first time she'd ever called him by name.

"It might hurt a bit," he whispered. "At least at first."

She heard his warning, but she didn't care. What was a bit of pain amidst so much pleasure? She reached for his hips and pulled him closer.

Slowly, he entered her, and though for a moment it did hurt, the pain was as he said only just for that moment. Used as she was to the hardships of the sea, Julien's gentle breaching of her virginity hardly seemed more than a minor bump.

Especially once he began to move within her.

She sighed softly as the rapturous longing returned. Like the waves lapping at their feet, Julien stroked her with the same rhythmic tide. It started like the first winds of a gale, then moved over her like the rush of a September hurricane.

She couldn't breathe, she couldn't think, letting her hips rise and fall, matching his movements. She climbed higher in the storm, as if caught by the wind and carried up into the very heart of the tempest, tossing with the wild wind until she reached the very top of the clouds. There, her breath caught in her throat, the cry on her lips frozen as she could only wonder at the sensations breaking over her.

Julien, too, seemed to share in her awe, for his movements suddenly became frenzied. His mouth closed over hers, claiming her again, closing off his own ragged cry of release.

The beach grew still except for the never-ending rise and fall of the waves and the hammering of Maureen's heart. She looked up at the star-trimmed sky, Julien's arms wound tightly around her, and wondered how she ever thought she'd lived before this very moment.

From this day forth, she just knew, with the supreme confidence of youth, the life before her would be filled with nights such as this and days of unending excitement, sailing the seas at Julien's side.

He stirred, nuzzling her neck and planting gentle kisses on her brow and lips. Then she murmured into his ear the words that sealed her fate, laid out her destiny.

"Julien, I love you."

# Chapter 10

London
1813

By the time Maureen arose and made her way downstairs, shaking off the unsettling dreams of Julien, she found the Johnstons' little morning room transformed into a bower of spring roses and lilies.

Lady Mary's prediction of Maureen's social success hadn't been off the mark. The cards and notes had begun arriving early, and the steady stream of footmen and messengers had continued ever since, her beaming "godmother" announced.

Along with the invitations came flowers and boxes of confections from dandies and swains who hadn't even been at Almack's. All it had taken were a few words around White's that Julien D'Artiers had uncovered a new sensation, and the fortune hunters and romantics followed like sheep.

Stationed at her desk, Lady Mary was going through the arduous task of opening and sorting the mountain of invitations, but from the smile on the woman's face, it hardly looked as if she found the task anything but a delight.

"There you are, my dear. Come look! Didn't I tell you?" Lady Mary sighed.

Before Maureen could respond, Lucy, the housemaid, came bustling into the parlor, an armload of flowers balanced on one hip, while teetering in her hand was a tray loaded with envelopes and cards.

"I'll never be getting the dusting done, milady, with all this racket. Why, that bell is driving me mad." Lucy dumped the flowers in Maureen's arms and the notes in front of her mistress. "And don't even think about seeing a shine on the silver before next Thursday."

"Do your best, Lucy. These are trying times for all of us," Lady Mary told her.

Maureen looked around for a place to put the flowers but discovered there wasn't an open spot to be had, what with all the other bouquets and prettily wrapped boxes. So she perched herself on the corner of the sofa next to Lady Mary's desk and sniffed at the sweet-scented blossoms.

The fresh, innocent fragrance of the violets did nothing to dispel her dour mood. She had a promise to keep this morning.

Even after a restless night of tossing and turning, she told herself it was no more than what anyone else would go through—it wasn't every day she sent a man to his death.

But in the early-morning hours, when she'd finally

drifted off to sleep, she dreamed of the last time she'd seen Julien, the last moment she'd heard his voice betray her, betray her father, and when she awakened it had been with a certain, clear vision of what needed to be done.

Lady Mary held out an open box of confections to her. "They are from a shop my father used to visit. He would bring us a box every time he came home from London. I haven't had them in years. Try the ones with the almonds on top."

Maureen settled her flowers on the floor at her feet and took one of the offered sweets. She'd never seen such a fancy-looking confection before. And once she'd popped it in her mouth, she understood Lady Mary's rapturous expression.

The almond paste and sugar flowed over her tongue like rich silk. How could anything taste so tantalizingly?

"What do you think of your success now?" Lady Mary asked, taking one for herself and settling the box in her lap.

"All of this is for me?" Her gaze moved over the flowers, gloves, books, and tokens littering the room. Perhaps she would let Julien live to see nightfall. At least until she had a chance to enjoy her newfound treasures.

*And your crew,* her conscience screamed. *What are they enjoying?*

She should be ashamed of herself, and she was, heartily so. But as she looked over her bounty, she wondered if perhaps the Lord Admiral would let her keep some of her gifts.

At least the sweet ones. There were, after all, five more such boxes awaiting her.

"Yes, all of it but this box of confections," Lady Mary said, patting the box in her lap. "The Earl of Hawksbury sent them to me." Lady Mary offered her another one, which Maureen eagerly accepted. "The Marquess of Trahern's heir, from what I gather, as well as Mr. D'Artiers's nephew. The ingenuous lad addressed them to me instead of to you, hoping to curry my favor in allowing him the honor of the first dance with you at his aunt's ball."

Maureen had only been half-listening to the lady until Julien's name came up. "This earl is related to Mr. D'Artiers?"

"Why, yes," Lady Mary said, as if Julien's relations were common knowledge.

Since he had never mentioned family, Maureen had always thought . . . well, she wasn't too sure what she'd thought. But she'd never imagined him having family, least of all ones with fancy titles.

"And this Mr. D'Artiers has other family here in London?"

Lady Mary smiled. "Ah, so this is how it is. You were so uninterested in the man last night, but now I see you were just playing coy."

"I am not playing coy," Maureen protested. "I'm just surprised such a rake as Mr. D'Artiers has family— at least, ones who claim a connection. Especially given what you told me about him last night."

Lady Mary nodded, though she looked unconvinced at Maureen's explanation. "If you must know, my good friend, Lady Dearsley, is his aunt. And his connections don't stop there. His eldest sister is the Marchioness of Trahern, while his other sister is married to Viscount Weston." The lady sat back, her pen still poised in her hand. "If you really want to know, your Mr. D'Artiers isn't the first member of that family to be embroiled in scandal. Why, even Lady Dearsley, bless her heart, has had her fair share of peccadilloes. She was a Ramsey before she married Lord Dearsley." The lady pursed her lips, as if having Ramsey blood allowed one any number of transgressions. "Oh, that family is quite mischievous, but don't think they aren't completely respectable, mind you."

Julien with a respectable family?

It seemed impossible. Now she'd have to add tearful, well-heeled mourners to her hanging scenario. Worse yet, with such influential relations behind him, he might well escape hanging altogether.

No wonder he'd walked out of Almack's with such supreme confidence.

"You'll meet all of Mr. D'Artiers's family at his sister's ball. The Viscountess kindly sent an invitation this morning." Lady Mary held up the gold-edged vellum. "Probably at the request of her nephew, Lord Hawksbury. That wily boy very likely means to out-court his uncle! Oh, how delicious to have the two of *them* vying for your attentions tomorrow night."

"Tomorrow night?" Maureen asked. By then she planned on being hell-bent for the West Indies and as far from England as the *Retribution*'s sails could get her.

"Why, yes. Every one at Almack's was talking about it last night," Lady Mary told her. "And now we have our invitations as well."

Maureen regarded the lady's littered desk. "It looks like the Viscountess isn't the only one hosting a ball."

"My dear, we've been invited to every social gathering. Balls, soirees, even a house party. I've been sorting through these invitations the better part of this morning. I think it is best if we accept only the most exclusive events through the end of the month." She turned and patted a select pile of vellum and the whitest of stationery. "Now, be a dear and begin opening and reading to me this latest batch Lucy brought in." She handed the collection of cards to Maureen and settled back into composing her replies.

"My lady," Maureen said, glancing up from the stack in her hands, "my work here could easily be completed by tomorrow."

"Nonsense," Lady Mary said with a dismissive wave of her hand. "It could take you most of the Season to find that devil de Ryes. Don't you think?"

Maureen wished she could tell the hopeful lady it would, but her work was already done.

Yet Lady Mary, while exacting in her demands, had shown her nothing but kindness. Almost as if she *were* a treasured goddaughter, not the wayward criminal the Lord Admiral liked to remind them all she truly was.

There hadn't been a day in the last month when Lady Mary hadn't risen at the first hint of dawn to start their lessons or go over fashion plates and magazines she'd borrowed from Lady Dearsley. Hours and hours of lessons and patient corrections, all to ensure that Maureen's arrival into London society was nothing short of brilliant.

The transformation hadn't taken place only with Maureen. From the light in the lady's eyes and the glow on her cheeks, it was obvious her renewed place in society—as fleeting as it might be—was a better tonic than any trip to the Brighton shore or waters at Bath.

What harm was there to let the lady live her dreams just a few hours longer? Maureen reasoned. At least until she could get a note to the Lord Admiral.

So Maureen set to work opening the invitations and discussing the merits of each one with Lady Mary. The acceptance pile had grown some, but it nowhere near matched the rejected engagements.

While Lady Mary composed an epistle of regrets to a Lady Osborne, Maureen looked at the next missive. Instead of being addressed to Lady Mary, as most of them were, this one was addressed to *Madame de Ryes*.

The cheeky devil, she thought, knowing only too well whom it was from.

Inside, the note read simply, *I have proof. Hatchards at three this afternoon.*

There was no signature, but it held one other clue.

The pressed petals from a long-dead flower. Withered and brown, the blossom, found only in the West Indies, still held a faint hint of its exotic scent.

She crushed the flower in her fist, unwilling to consider where it had come from.

Such flowers had decorated the nosegay Julien had given her to carry at their wedding—flowers she'd left behind in his cabin when she'd fled his bed and his life the very next morning.

**How dare he think I would fall prey to such false**

sentiments, she fumed. As if he'd kept this token as some heartfelt memory of her.

*But what if he did?* a small voice whispered, one calling out from the last vestiges of her innocence. *What if he still loves you?*

"Lady Mary," she said. "I think I would like to compose a response to this one myself." Armed with a pen and paper, she addressed the note.

But not in response to Julien, rather to the Lord Admiral.

*I have reason to believe our friend will be at Hatchards this afternoon. Meet me there at half past three.*

# Chapter 11

Maureen stepped through the doorway of Hatchards precisely at three o'clock. Right behind her bustled Lady Mary. Maureen didn't need to look back to know the lady's face was alert and alive, reflecting the activity within the busy shop.

It had taken only the smallest of lies to get the lady to agree to the outing. When Maureen casually suggested that she'd heard from the circles at Almack's that Hatchards was *the* place to be seen, then Lady Mary declared they needed to visit the illustrious bookshop without further delay.

"It is not as if, my dear girl," the lady announced, once they were in the carriage, "anyone would mistake *you* for a bluestocking."

Lady Mary had the right of that, Maureen concluded, looking down at the dress Lucy and Lady Mary had chosen for her. With all the dainty blue ribbons and white lace, starting from the top of her bonnet and ending at the delicately edged hem of her gown, she looked like one of Aunt Pettigrew's prized porcelain shepherdesses come to life rather than a woman used to climbing rigging and wearing tarred pants.

Truth be told, she looked like a bleedin' bluebell.

Maureen brushed aside the annoying ribbons falling from her bonnet. Eh, gads, how did women stand all this frippery and fuss?

Worst of all, in all the commotion of preparation and consultations just to get Lady Mary this far, there had been no time to stow her knife.

I might as well be naked, she thought, trying to recall the last time she'd gone anywhere without her knife. A sharp poke in the ribs from Lady Mary's parasol brought her attention back to the present, and when she looked up, her companion was holding up the edge of her own gown.

"You're stalking," the lady whispered. "Tiny steps, like a lady." She demonstrated, her own delicately shod feet taking the prim steps she'd shown Maureen time and time again that all ladies used in private and public.

So Maureen gathered up every vestige of femininity she possessed and minced her way into the bookshop, ready to do battle.

But her progress was halted in the middle of the room when she realized she and Lady Mary were the only women in the shop. And right now she was drawing more attention than the books or the warm lingering scent of freshly brewed coffee.

The other customers, gentlemen and businessmen,

made no attempts at hiding their interest in the latest arrival.

They are probably wondering where I lost my sheep, she thought, bemoaning her fate and wondering why she hadn't protested Lady Mary's choice of gowns a little more vigorously.

Gads, she must look horribly foolish.

Then Maureen really noticed the long approving looks slanted her way, saw how the gentlemen openly perused her from head to toe.

She realized, only too quickly, that she was the sheep rather than the shepherdess, and she'd just strolled into a den of well-dressed wolves.

Why, these *gentlemen* were giving her the same kind of looks that used to land drunken sailors in rough taverns a hard right hook and a few missing teeth for their trouble. But since no one said anything rude, just looked, Maureen realized she would have to live with the indignity of the situation.

Especially without her knife at hand.

She continued on, mincing and smiling demurely to her appreciative audience. If this was what it meant to be a lady, trussed up in ribbons and paraded before a pack of slathering wolves, then she'd take a hurricane any day of the week.

A clerk came forward, his glasses steamed with sweat and his leather apron dark where he'd obviously wiped his damp hands. "May I help you, ladies?"

Lady Mary shook her head. "We are just browsing."

He persisted anyway. "Might I suggest a wonderful new story we have in? Such a diverting pleasure, especially for our more discerning and quality customers," he said to Lady Mary, and without drawing a breath he turned to Maureen. "And may I suggest a delightful and improving tale for the young lady?"

"Oh, how kind you are," Lady Mary said, obviously warming to the young man and his thoughtful suggestions, for she was quickly off with the solicitous clerk, preening at being recognized once again as a member of the class to which she'd been born. She all but forgot Maureen as she went over to study the recommended volumes in a nearby section.

Not that Maureen minded the lady's absence from her side. She was too busy scanning the shop for de Ryes to have to divert Lady Mary herself. The ubiquitous little clerk had done that for her quite nicely.

After a quick check of the shop, she found, much to her disgust, there was no sign of the blackguard, at least none that she could see about the front of the shop. When she was about to instigate a hard search, her sharp gaze fell on the small, neatly lettered sign above a shelf in the back that read NAVAL HISTORIES.

It struck her that perhaps Julien's proof lay there, and he'd sent her here to Hatchards with the express purpose of having her discover the truth about her father for herself.

She wouldn't put it past the coward to leave his dirty work to someone else. Not that she believed him for a minute, but, anxious to prove him a liar yet again, she headed straight for that section.

An elderly man with white whiskers took offense to her arrival in this clearly masculine realm. He glared at her as if to drive her away, but Maureen ignored him, and soon he left her alone with muttered words about "indelicate snips not knowing their places."

She smiled to herself before turning to let the titles wash over her, most of them with familiar names and places and words. After scanning three shelves, one title finally stood out.

*The Registry and Recent History of His Majesty's Most Honorable Navy, Published 1780.*

Surely, if her father had served in the British Navy, as Julien claimed, he would be listed in this book. For the entire story to be true, her father would have had to be in the Navy before he met her mother, which had been two years after this book was published.

As if any of Julien's ranting held any hint of the truth. Still, she leafed through the dull book, the pages holding a faint damp, musty scent.

Names of ships and captains, some familiar and some unknown, drew her attention away from her surroundings, until she'd all but forgotten she was supposed to be a lady looking through the pages of some edifying piece of literature, not a manly volume. Then, toward the middle of the book, she found pages listing all the active ships in the various theaters, their commission dates, and their commanders.

For some reason she stopped, as if willing herself not to take the next step.

What if it were true? What if her father had sailed in the British navy? Did it really matter so much?

"Drat, Julien," she cursed. The scoundrel still had the power to twist her in the wind. His outrageous lies had lit a curiosity inside her. And yet, what if everything she knew about her father turned out to be fiction rather than fact?

She told herself she was continuing only to prove that Julien was the liar. To add another nail to his already far too long delayed coffin.

Slowly, she ran her finger down the list, certain she wouldn't find the evidence he'd so confidently boasted of, until she came to a standstill at an entry that left her shocked and stunned.

Capaneous, *Third Rate; Commissioned, June 1779; Commander, Ethan, Lord Hawthorne.*

She read it again, taking in each word slowly, running her fingers over the printed letters as if to verify that the ink and typesetting were truly real.

*Ethan, Lord Hawthorne?*

She shook her head at the name. Her father? It couldn't be. Her father had never said anything about having a title, let alone being an English nobleman. She tried to tell herself the similar names were a coincidence, a convenient one that Julien was using to turn her world upside down.

Yet in a blinding flash she knew this Lord Hawthorne was her father. As much as she wanted to deny it.

It explained too much, too many things she'd never questioned and probably should have.

The countless times her father had seemed to innately guess the movements of naval vessels they'd wanted to avoid. His lack of an Irish accent, which he'd explained away by saying he'd spent his early years working on the docks in Liverpool, where the other lads had beat the lilt of his homeland out of his speech. The hours he'd spent arguing philosophy with the Jesuit priest he'd kidnapped and hauled aboard their ship to give her a well-rounded education. This in spite of his own command of mathematics, literature, and languages, even Latin and Greek, all of which seemed well beyond what one would expect a poor, humble Irishman to possess.

There were times when she'd thought her father had only brought the poor Jesuit aboard so he would have someone to talk to, not, as he claimed, to educate her.

And then there was the ring she'd found in his sea chest when she'd been just a wee girl. He'd been angry when he discovered her playing with it and had startled her by snatching the piece of jewelry away from her grasp. Only now did she look back and realize the ring had been the focus of his ire, as if the strange animals entwined in the heavy gold, not her misbehavior, had taunted him into his rage.

Her father had been a titled lord. And for some reason he had lost it all, left it all behind, perhaps even as Julien had hinted, through some naval scandal.

So preoccupied was she in her reeling speculations that she barely heard the insistent voice at her elbow.

"Miss, miss," a voice said. "I do say, miss, I hardly think that is what you are looking for." Before she could stop him, the nosy clerk took the book from her hands. "Really, miss, this is hardly the section for a lady. Besides, we are receiving complaints. Now, why don't you let me find something more suited for you and something your companion would approve of?"

Maureen found herself reaching for her knife, more incensed at his superior attitude than she had been at the leering loafers in the front of the store.

When her fingers stalled over the lace at her hips, she remembered she was unarmed. Eyeing the clerk, she almost laughed.

As if she needed a knife to unman this barnacle.

"Give me back my book, you little flea," she demanded, her fingers pinching the fleshy part of the man's arm just above his elbow.

The clerk's eyes bulged, then watered. He'd all but risen up to his tiptoes trying to escape her grasp, but it was no use.

He might as well have fought the tide.

Still, Maureen had to give him credit. He continued to hold the book away from her.

"You're hurting me. . . ." he managed to squeak.

"Give it back, you maggot-ridden little biscuit, or you'll feel the pain of—"

"Tsk, tsk, tsk," a rich deep voice whispered into her ear. "Do you plan on dismembering him right here in Piccadilly?"

She froze.

*De Ryes.*

Fine time for him to make his entrance.

Glancing over her shoulder, she found him standing right behind her, close enough so she looked right up into the wry gaze of his green eyes.

Blast him if he wasn't laughing at her.

"Release him, Maureen," he said quietly, moving to

block them from the sight of the other patrons. "Do it before you actually succeed in pulling his arm out of the socket, or worse, someone sees you manhandling this poor fellow and it becomes an *on dit* that will put Lady Mary in vapors for a week."

"Not until he returns my book."

Julien held out his hand, and the clerk shoved the volume into his open palm.

Maureen felt cheated but released the fellow anyway, though not before giving him one last twist to remember her by. As she watched him scurry away, she felt some satisfaction in knowing that would be the last time he snatched a book away from a lady.

Julien turned the volume over and examined it. "I see you found my proof. Do you believe me now?"

She shook her head. "That book proves nothing that matters to me. So my father was in the Navy. That was over thirty years ago. It doesn't change the fact that you murdered him."

In the instant she said the words, she saw it again, the flash of something across Julien's face.

Anger. Denial. Or even, perhaps, guilt.

Guilt?

The Captain de Ryes she knew would never have felt guilt over a man's death. Not when it had assured him his fortune and future.

A fortune he so obviously wore now, what with his silver-tipped cane, perfectly cut coat and breeches, and the rich sheen of his Hessians.

She seized the book from him and reshelved it, closing its terrible truth away from prying eyes. "My father had a past that he chose not to share. So does every other man at sea, at least the ones who take to his profession." She glanced over him once again, the perfect Corinthian, hardly a man anyone would suspect was the nefarious privateer Captain de Ryes. "Including you."

She turned to leave the seclusion of the stacks, for surely it was close to the time that she'd instructed the Lord Admiral to arrive.

Julien wasn't about to let her go just yet. The bell above the door announced the entrance of another group of customers, this time a pair of ladies. He caught his impossible wife by her arm and hauled her deeper into the store.

Far from the curious glances of other patrons, far from her oblivious guardian.

"Maureen Hawthorne de Ryes, I've never thought you a fool, but you are trying my patience and my convictions." He gathered her into his arms, one hand clamped over her mouth to keep her from crying out. He had no illusions that once he grabbed her she wouldn't fight him like a wildcat, no matter the place or the possibility of scandal.

And fight him she did.

He held on with all his might, avoiding the well-aimed thrust of her knee and the sharp kick directed at his shins. When she finally settled down, he eased up a bit, but only a little.

He knew better than to ever turn his back on his wife. He had the scar to prove it.

Now with each jab of her toe, each wrench of her arm, it was as if those eight years were swept aside and he was being given a second chance—an opportunity to succeed where he had failed her so miserably before.

God, he'd loved her then. Loved her with all his heart. From the first moment he'd seen her, high in the rigging of the *Forgotten Lady*. Like some windswept sprite, her dark hair fluttering in the breeze, her feminine figure unmistakable even in the rough sailor's clothing. And when he'd stepped foot on the deck of her father's ship and taken one look at the heart-stopping blue of her eyes, he knew right there and then she would always be the only woman for him.

He'd been too young to see the consequences of his actions, too sure of himself not to believe that he could make everything work. All he'd known then was that he'd never be able to live without her, no matter what the fates thrust upon them.

She'd tempted him and infected him beyond reason and rational thought with her passion and fire.

And damn the fates, she still did.

But this time he wouldn't let her go. Not without a fight. Not until she understood why he'd done what he had to her father.

That she hadn't been the only one betrayed that night.

Then he'd make her understand the one most important thing: He'd never stopped loving her.

Never would, if he was honest with himself.

"Dammit, Reenie, stand down. Are you so blind that you can't see the gale coming up over your prow? Your life isn't worth a fiddler's funds if you don't listen to me. And listen to me you will."

She responded by biting his hand.

Sucking in a deep breath against the sharp pain, he released her immediately, shaking his stinging palm. "You little fool. Do you think seeing me hang will gain you and your crew their release?"

She stepped back, her expression wary. "I don't know what you are talking about."

"Your crew. You were arrested for smuggling off Sheerness a month ago. Your ship was towed to London, while you, my dear wife, and your crew were tried before a closed Admiralty court."

If she hadn't wanted to listen to him before, she appeared to be doing so now.

"How would you know?"

"I know. More than you would like to think. You could say knowing is my business."

"So what has this to do with saving your neck?"

"If I hang, there will be no one to protect you from what will surely follow."

She laughed, a hollow little sound, scoffing at her need for his safekeeping.

But dammit, she did need him, if only she would listen.

"If my information is correct—and it always is—you were promised your life and the life of your crew in exchange for my head. You were also promised the return of your ship. Once I hang, you sail away without a record." He paused for a moment. "Feel free to correct me at any time. I'd hate to think my informant was cheating me."

She grudgingly nodded. "You've gotten your money's worth."

"I have to admit it is a remarkable deal—especially the return of your ship."

She swiped at the ridiculous lace falling from her bonnet. "It's not like you haven't caused quite a few headaches around the Admiralty," she whispered back at him. "They say you've tripled the prices of goods and insurance rates, what with all the ships you've taken in the last year. The merchants want your hide and are willing to take the Lord Admiral's in exchange if he doesn't stop you soon."

He didn't miss the slight bit of respect in her voice. One pirate to another.

"I've taken my fair share," he acknowledged. "But back to you. You saved your neck and those of your men by bargaining with the devil. You obviously inherited your father's gift for persuasion."

"I've made deals with more scurvy louts than his lordship. And it was fair easy to bargain with him considering I held you as the prize."

It was his turn to laugh. "Don't fool yourself. Few would have received such generous terms. But then again, you are your father's daughter."

She glanced up at him, her lashes narrowed over her wary blue eyes. "What is that supposed to mean?"

"That this deal you've struck goes beyond the Admiralty's problems with lost ships and cargoes. It goes to the heart of the Lord Admiral's career. And you are the key."

"If you are going to start telling me this nonsense about court-martials and conspiracies by the Admiralty against my father, I won't listen," she told him. "These

Banbury tales of yours have nothing to do with my agreement with the Lord Admiral. And I certainly trust him more than I will ever trust the likes of you." Her hands went to her hips, her stance all sailor. "It's going to take a hell of a lot more than one line in some dusty old book to change my mind."

"Then you trust him with your life?" Julien asked, his arms crossed over his chest. "That he will honor your bargain?"

Her chin tipped up, her azure gaze flint-hard. "Implicitly."

He wanted to smile, now that he had her boxed into a corner, but he saw no joy in dashing her convictions.

Despite his reluctance he pulled out of his jacket pocket a folded broadsheet—an auction announcement he'd snagged from the board at Lloyd's this morning—and handed it to her. "Read on, Reenie. Read what your honorable friend has planned for you, and tell me if you still trust him."

He should have known better than to give it to her in public, for the sight of the first line widened her eyes, then sent a flush of fury across her face.

Not that he blamed her for one second. He'd felt the same anger when he'd spotted the advertisement this morning after his usual coffee and information-gathering session at the shipping mecca of London.

NAVAL AUCTION. THE SCHOONER *RETRIBUTION* . . .

"Why that—" she began, until he clapped his hand over her mouth. He was glad he'd moved as fast as he had, for the next moment the bell over the door jangled loudly, announcing the newest customer's arrival.

Julien wasn't at all surprised to see Maureen's mentor and partner slithering into the shop—Peter Cottwell, the Lord Admiral.

Studying his opponent through the stacks, Julien also spied a half score of loungers outside, burly minions come to assist the Lord Admiral in his brilliant capture of the infamous pirate.

"Time for a decision, Reenie," Julien told her, nodding to the broadsheet in her shaking grasp. "Do you still trust him? Or do you want to gamble further with your life and the lives of your men?"

He watched the play of emotions on her face but wasn't all that convinced she was going to see the right of it—that she couldn't trust that bastard Cottwell.

He had considered she would do this—call the Lord Admiral down on his head—when he sent her his note. That was why he'd left a horse tied up behind the shop, in addition to his carriage out front. Though fleeing was not his preferred plan, unfortunately it appeared to be the only choice she'd left him.

"Well, what will it be?" he asked again.

Her mouth set in a stubborn line. It was obvious she'd made her choice.

Damn her hide. He still had at least a week's worth of business in London, and now he'd be lucky to make the coast with his life.

Even as he went to make his flight, a soft feminine voice purred through the stacks. "Mr. D'Artiers, is that you?"

He recognized it immediately and realized he may have just found a miracle, a better escape route than the one he'd planned.

Miss Eustacia Cottwell.

Well, it seemed the fates were still on his side. Could the Lord Admiral have known his daughter was going to be here as well? More than likely not.

This could work out better than he'd ever hoped.

He plucked the broadsheet out of Maureen's hand and hastily stuffed it in his jacket. Against his better judgment, he turned his back to his defiant wife and turned on the charm for which he had become famous in London's elegant circles.

"Miss Cottwell! I have to say your arrival here is the most delightful surprise of my day."

The arrogant chit didn't giggle or feign a blush at his praise, only raised her chin a little higher as if his tribute was her due. She was her father's daughter, every arrogant inch of her. She held out her hand, and he took it, drawing it slowly to his lips.

"Whatever are you doing here?" he asked. "And looking as if you should be strolling the paths in the park catching the envious eye of everyone there."

Eustacia ran a hand over her stylish skirt before raising it to pat her pert and perfectly matched bonnet, drawing more attention to her best asset, her shimmering blond hair. "My cousin has an affection for novels. I find them most dull, but she must be indulged every fortnight or so, or else she becomes insufferable."

He smiled fondly at her. "And how kind you are to allow her such pleasures, when it is obviously not to your taste. Why, you should be be out where people can enjoy the sight of you, where you can be adored as you should be."

Eustacia sighed. "That is exactly what I told her, but the silly woman just isn't appreciative of the sacrifices I make for her comforts. Still, Papa says one must make allowances for our lesser relations."

Behind him, the nudge of an elbow in his ribs sent him faltering forward. Better her elbow than her ever-present knife, he thought, smiling gamely at a curious Eustacia.

"Is there someone behind you?" she asked.

He leaned over and said loud enough for Maureen to hear, "Some unfortunate bluestocking."

Eustacia nodded in understanding. "I believe she wants out."

"Just clumsy. I've heard tell that type never leaves Hatchards." He shook his head at such a sorry state. "Poor dears. Their own version of Almack's."

At this, the woman behind him held no further interest for the very high-brow and socially minded Miss Cottwell.

The narrow stacks had the advantage of allowing his body to block Maureen from Eustacia's view while also trapping her behind him.

He hoped she heard every word and was seething with outrage.

And maybe even a little jealousy.

"Now, we were discussing your sacrifices, were we not?" Julien crossed his arms over his chest. "I should think such kindness and unselfish regard for others should not go unrewarded," he told the girl before him. "Perhaps a trip for ices, if I may be so bold to presume that you would be interested in such an outing."

The sly smile curved slowly along Eustacia's rosebud lips. It wasn't that the girl wasn't pretty. She was in her own way outright stunning, but her cunning nature and predatory ways took away from what would have allowed another woman to shine like an angel.

Loud enough for Maureen to hear, he added, "It isn't often one finds a lady with such refined manners in one so divinely *young*."

The comparison about refined manners and age gained him a fist hammered into his back, this time below the rib cage, sending a shock wave of pain into his abdomen.

That was his Maureen. She knew where to hit and how to make it hurt.

He gasped for air before an open-mouthed Miss Cottwell, who was now regarding the bluestocking behind him with something akin to horror. Before his wife could take her next damaging blow, one that would leave Gentleman Jim reeling in his boxing ring, his second rescue of the day arrived.

"Maureen, Maureen, where are you?" came Lady Mary's call.

"Right here, my lady," she called out from behind him in a voice flowing like warm honey.

Eustacia's eyes widened, and she tipped her head to gain a peek around his shoulder. "*Who* is that horrible creature?"

"I haven't the faintest idea," he said. He turned and

allowed Maureen right of way out of the stacks. She pushed past him and Eustacia, her bonnet askew and her face glowering like a Nor'easter. Julien thought the Lord Admiral's daughter was going to swoon to be found in such unkempt company.

He, too, felt the sting of Maureen's antics. Her first step trod directly on his foot.

Julien grinned, aching toes aside. Maureen had the face of an outraged spouse.

Good, he thought, jealousy may work to my advantage.

"Oh, my mistake," he said, winking at the Lord Admiral's daughter. "I do know this young lady. Miss Cottwell, may I present Miss . . . Miss . . ." He paused as if her name had escaped him, letting it appear that Maureen wasn't as important as the illustrious Miss Cottwell.

"Miss Fenwick," Maureen filled in for him.

"Fenwick?"

"Yes, Miss Fenwick," she repeated firmly.

"Well, Miss Cottwell, may I present our blue-stocking, Miss Fenwick."

The two women eyed each other like warring cats, each sizing the other up. He could tell from the pinched look on Maureen's face, she didn't like what she saw.

Good, this was working out better than he hoped.

"Oh, there you are, Maureen," Lady Mary said, as she arrived from the front of the shop. "Whatever are you doing back here?" Then the lady's gaze rose to Julien and he saw the light of recognition in her eyes, as well as something else—maternal pride. "Oh, I see the attraction. And it isn't these dull books." The lady smiled slyly at Julien.

"Lady Mary, I presume," he said, bowing low over her hand.

"Oh, yes," the lady tittered as if she were once again a fresh-faced schoolgirl. The lady glanced over at Eustacia. "Oh, Miss Cottwell! I didn't see you there at all. Have you met my goddaughter, Miss Fenwick?"

"Yes," Eustacia said with a little sniff. "Mr. D'Artiers was just affording me the pleasure," she continued in a sugary tone that didn't fool anyone into thinking the experience had been in any way enjoyable.

Maureen made a rather rude noise in the back of her throat, which led all eyes to turn on her.

"The dust," she said sweetly. "It seems to have caught in my throat."

Julien wondered if that was all that was stuck there. "Then you and Lady Mary should join Miss Cottwell and me for ices. They have a rather soothing effect on one's *throat*."

Better an ice than a rope stretching it, he thought.

Maureen glowered at him. Clearly there was nothing that was going to soothe her temper—except maybe a hanging.

Just then the Lord Admiral stepped forward. His gaze passed over Lady Mary and Maureen and fell directly on his daughter. "Eustacia, what the devil are you doing here?"

"Oh, Papa, it is dreadful." Eustacia sighed, sidling up to her parent and wrapping her hand around his elbow. "Cousin Priscilla insisted she must have a new novel. And she demanded I come along, when I really should be shopping for ribbons for my gown for Lady Trahern's masquerade." The girl sighed, the effect of which was to tell all that the day had been a trying ordeal for her. "But as fortune would have it, I discovered Mr. D'Artiers here and he's invited us out for ices. Do say you'll join us."

"D'Artiers," the Lord Admiral acknowledged with a smile and a regal bow. "Always good to see you. Especially in the company of my daughter."

"My lord," Julien offered in return, matching the man's movements. He knew the wily old man considered him a fine catch for his daughter. Though it was well known the Lord Admiral wanted a title for her, Julien's family connections and rumored wealth more than made up for his lack of an earldom or other lofty background. Besides, it was common knowledge that the Lord Admiral's own barony would pass to his only child, Eustacia. "It is my greatest pleasure to spend time with your delightful daughter."

Maureen made that noise again. And Julien swore this time she was really choking.

"I assume, my lord," Julien said, "you know Lady Mary and her goddaughter, Miss Fenwick?"

"Yes, I've had the pleasure." Like his daughter, his tone belied his words.

The Lord Admiral turned his attention to Lady Mary. "And you, my lady. How is it you are out on this fine day? I thought you were staying closer to home these days."

"My dear goddaughter, my lord," the lady said. "She suggested we come. She thought it may be advantageous for her improvement."

The man's eyebrows rose slightly, as if he considered the notion impossible.

"My lord," Julien said, drawing the man's attention away from Maureen. "I had just invited Lady Mary and her goddaughter to join your daughter and me for ices. Will you be joining us as well?"

The man looked caught, for surely he didn't want his darling daughter associating with the likes of Maureen Hawthorne, but at the same time a match-minded father could hardly disparage Julien's offer.

So, just as Julien guessed, the man came up with a compromise.

"Allow me to escort Lady Mary and Miss Fenwick to your carriage, while you help Eustacia find her cousin. As for the rest of the outing, I fear Admiralty business will keep me detained for the remainder of the afternoon." With that said, he cast a significant glance over at Maureen.

Julien nodded and held his arm out to Eustacia. The girl made quite a show of taking it and, with her nose high in the air, paraded past Maureen.

Glancing back, Julien raised his hand to his jacket and patted his coat pocket.

Maureen acknowledged the gesture by turning a radiant smile on the Lord Admiral.

Now all Julian could do was wait and see. In the next few moments he would discover just how much his wife wanted to see him hang.

Or if she would trust him one more time.

Whether he liked it or not, he felt his throat constrict, as if she were already tightening the noose. He coughed slightly, and Eustacia glanced up at him.

"The dust," he told her. "Really quite annoying."

# Chapter 12

Lucky for Julien, he'd found safety behind Miss Cott-well's skirt. For if they'd been alone, Maureen would have knocked the smug look on his face right into the gutter.

It was all she could do not to call out his true iden-tity as they'd assembled for their outing to Gunther's. Right up to the last moment, when the Lord Admiral drove off in the opposite direction, she battled with her convictions to see Julien receive the justice he so rightly deserved.

But, the contents of the broadsheet Julien had shown her rocked her beliefs about the Lord Admiral's veracity.

A clear and clever forgery, she tried to tell herself. Julien's way of tricking her into trusting him.

Why, it couldn't be true. The *Retribution* being sold right out from under her?

The Lord Admiral had given her his word that the return of her ship was part of their deal.

*His word.*

In the end it had been the Lord Admiral's words that convinced her to hold her tongue.

Once they'd gone outside Hatchards, he'd sent Lady Mary ahead to Julien's carriage, where everyone else stood patiently waiting.

He drew her aside and out of sight of the other party. His hand caught her by the elbow and twisted it painfully. "What are you doing anywhere near my daughter?" His face turned an ugly shade of purple.

The vehemence and anger behind his question took her aback. What should he care if she was anywhere near his daughter? "I didn't know she would be here," she said, breaking his grip and rubbing at the aching joint. "Even if I did, what does it matter? I came here for another purpose. Remember?"

He glared down the long beak of his nose at her. "How dare you take that tone with me. You would do well to remember your place. I hold your life in my hands, and I will not tolerate such base-born insolence. You would do well, *Miss Fenwick,* to remember your place and just how temporary it is."

His odd, seething rage did more than alarm her, it frightened her, because it was obvious that he hated her.

And not because she was a smuggler or an impostor.

There was more to it.

But what? She'd offered him the means to save his career, and yet his every word, his every look and nuance since he'd entered Hatchards and found her in the company of his daughter screamed that he detested her with a vehemence born of years of malice.

Not that she cared what the Lord Admiral thought of her. But this type of irrational hatred could lead a man to do anything, even break his word, of that she was sure.

Suddenly, trusting him didn't seem such a good idea.

And she'd learned to listen when that little voice—the one like a soft banshee wail—called to her. She hadn't survived all these years dealing with smugglers and thieves by ignoring these whispers of caution.

So when the Lord Admiral demanded to know where de Ryes was, she did the only thing she could.

She lied.

Again.

And it galled her more than she cared to admit.

"So if you were here to capture de Ryes, where is he?" the Lord Admiral demanded for a second time.

"He didn't show," she told him. "His note said he would be here, and he hasn't arrived." Then, as luck would have it, she spied the Lord Admiral's hired help. "And who would blame the man, with half of Bow Street lounging about, just waiting to nab him? You've scared him off with that obvious lot of yours."

"I'll have you know they are the finest men for such a job," he blustered.

"If they are, then why are they out in the open like that? Why, I can see nearly ten of them from here! Ten men to capture de Ryes?" She shook her head. "Loan me a pistol and a good dirk, pay me what you just wasted on this bunch, and I'll bring him in on my own."

About this time, Julien wandered over. "My good man, you'll start tongues wagging if you spend too much time in the company of a charming young lady. Especially one as fetching as Miss Fenwick." Julien winked at the Lord Admiral. "I know the problem all too well."

Maureen almost laughed, for the Lord Admiral looked about to choke on the inference that he was delaying Maureen for his own courting.

"It is hardly like that, sir. Miss Fenwick's father and I served together. I was just offering my condolences once again."

"My apologies," Julien said, with a tip of his hat. "I can see from your expression, you have Miss Fenwick's best interests at heart." He held out his arm to Maureen. "But if you'll excuse us, I have promised your daughter and this young lady an outing."

"Remember what we discussed, Miss Fenwick," the Lord Admiral said, his tone anything but the protective regard one might expect from a family friend.

She tipped her head, as if in shy reverence to his wisdom. "I'll hold it close to my heart, my lord."

As they stepped away from the man, Julien whispered, "What was that all about?" His voice held a dangerous edge.

"I was gaining you another day of life."

"I appreciate it," the rogue said with a wry laugh. "But I'll need more than a day if I am to help you."

*Help you.* His words crept over her with the same intimacy she felt when she'd folded her hand into the crook of his arm and as he'd pulled her close so they walked with their bodies nearly touching.

She smiled, for they were coming closer to Lady Mary and the others. "I don't want your help."

"You need it. I'm all that stands between you and your friend back there." Julien paused. "And if you haven't noticed, he doesn't like you overly much."

"That's the first bit of truth I think I've ever heard you say," she muttered. "I find it odd that the man despises me so. He barely knows me."

"You're a living reminder of your father. A man doesn't like looking at his past."

"Doesn't seem to bother you," she shot back.

"Oh, it does."

There it was, that hint of regrets and guilt. They tore at her, teased her into believing he meant it.

And he wasn't finished. "But that's where the Lord Admiral and I are different. My feelings for you are quite the opposite of his. Always will be."

He made his remarkable declaration as they gained the open door to his carriage, leaving her unable to respond. He smiled at her, but this time without the intimacy that had tinged his voice just moments before. In a bat of an eye, he was once again the well-mannered, discreet Corinthian as he handed her up and then gave his driver directions.

He sat himself down next to her, opposite Miss Cottwell.

"My apologies, ladies. It seems Miss Fenwick and his lordship were discussing lofty matters of a naval nature." He shuddered with an unholy horror, at which

Miss Cottwell sniffed, as if to be caught so would be her utmost nightmare.

Had the man no shame?

Maureen didn't know whether to be outraged or stunned at his amazing transformation. She'd just saved his neck from the hangman once again, and now the witless ass celebrated his deliverance by insulting her!

She hadn't forgotten his performance or his words back in Hatchards, and now it appeared she was in for a second act.

Bluestocking indeed! And clumsy as well. Oh, if only she had her knife . . .

Miss Cottwell seemed delighted by his observations. "Why, Mr. D'Artiers, it is no wonder you are invited everywhere," the perfect miss said. "Why, I believe you to be the wittiest man in London."

"And you, my dear lady," Julien replied, "are the most discerning and elegant one I've discovered this Season."

Miss Cottwell's companion, her elderly spinster cousin, Miss Priscilla Welton, smiled in agreement.

The ride to Gunther's continued in this manner, until Maureen considered throwing herself under the wheels of the next passing conveyance.

Worst of all, it appeared Julien was Miss Cottwell's perfect match, for he met her inane chatter with his own wry, boring comments.

Obviously, his taste in women had changed. For there had been a time when he'd claimed such a perfect London miss would bore him to no end.

She remembered the nights of rousing conversations

onboard the *Forgotten Lady.* Hours had passed like minutes while she and Julien and her father traded stories and lies about the sea. Now, that had been interesting!

But this chatter—why, it was like listening to a flock of magpies.

They entered Gunther's and were provided an excellent table. Very soon she found herself stiffly ensconced in the corner seat, while Julien and Miss Cottwell held court.

She might have gone stoically on with her ice if it hadn't been for what Julien did next.

She looked up from her bowl of lemon ice and found him studying her.

"Are you enjoying your ice, Miss Fenwick?" he asked, as if he'd just noticed her presence at the table.

"Not as much as you obviously are," she replied, drawing sideways glances at her apparent lack of manners from both Lady Mary and Miss Welton. She smiled sweetly and turned her attention back to her melting treat.

"And you, Miss Cottwell," he said, once again turning his back to Maureen. "Are you enjoying your ice?"

"Why, of course, Mr. D'Artiers. I do so love ices. How kind it was of you to invite me."

Lady Mary and Miss Welton nodded their approval at this perfect response. Moments later Maureen felt Lady Mary's foot prodding her under the table.

When she glanced up at her guardian, she had no doubts about the meaning behind Lady Mary's expression.

*You could learn a thing or two from Miss Cottwell.*

Learn how to be a simpering, spoiled chit, Maureen fumed, cooling her anger with a mouthful of lemon ice. She'd like to see Miss Cottwell sail through a September hurricane off the Carolina coast.

"Miss Fenwick, where is it that you are from?" Miss Cottwell asked.

Maureen looked up at Lady Mary. *Bloody hell, she couldn't remember where they had decided she was from.*

"Portsmouth," Maureen said quickly.

"Devon," Lady Mary said at the same time.

Miss Cottwell cocked an elegant eyebrow. "Which is it?"

Lady Mary frowned at Maureen's lapse in their agreed tale.

Not undone yet, Maureen cleared up her mistake. "Lady Mary is correct. I am from Devon. But I spent most of my time in Portsmouth. At least when my father was home from sea."

The girl nodded. "What school did you attend?"

This was something they hadn't discussed, and Maureen wasn't too sure what to say. The truth seemed the only way out. "I never went to school. I was tutored at home."

What would Miss Cottwell say if she knew her tutors had been a rough mix of sailors and dockside whores, along with a defrocked Jesuit priest?

"Ah," the girl said. "I didn't think so." She directed the rest of her opinion toward Julien. "Finishing school has a way of giving a young lady a special polish that helps her stand out in good society, raising her above others."

Maureen wasn't too sure what came over her. She knew she should politely accede to Miss Cottwell's opinion, but she didn't like the idea of letting the smug little witch have the last say.

"I disagree," she said, drawing shocked looks from nearly everyone at the table. "My father was afraid of the company one finds in those schools. It was his belief that the polish that you think so highly of, Miss Cottwell, gives a young lady a false sense of pride and superiority that men find off-putting. Would you say that was your experience?" She turned her attention back to her ice, reveling in the red flush of anger sweeping over Miss Cottwell's normally icy features.

Why the poor girl looks exactly like her father when she loses her temper, Maureen thought. I suppose it would be in bad form to point that out.

This time she kept her opinion to herself, for Lady Mary looked about to have a fit of apoplexy.

"You have to excuse my goddaughter, Miss Cottwell," Lady Mary said in a rush. "Her education has been rather unorthodox, and her father was a man of unusual ideas."

"Obviously," Miss Cottwell sniffed. "Yet I believe it is breeding, not education, that always makes a lady acceptable. My mother was a Welton. Of Welton Hall." The girl made this pronouncement as if being connected to the Weltons was nothing short of a blessing from the King. Miss Cottwell glanced down her pert nose at Maureen, as if challenging her to best such an illustrious family connection.

Maureen wasn't sure why she said the next thing, but it just came out. "I've always heard that the Weltons had a touch of madness in their lines." She tipped her head and studied Miss Cottwell as if she were a likely candidate for this family curse. The girl's eyes looked about to pop out with sheer horror at such an inference. This time Maureen sniffed, "Perhaps it skipped a generation in your case."

The comment hit better than a twenty-four pounder fired at close range.

"Oh, oh, I can assure you, Miss Fenwick," Miss Welton sputtered, "those rumors are highly exaggerated." The horrified lady, realizing she may have just confirmed what Maureen said, turned her next comment to Julien. "There has never been anything remotely unusual about the Welton lines. I assure you, sir. No, never."

"I think it is Miss Fenwick who is highly unusual," Miss Cottwell pronounced, as if calling for a social moratorium on the inappropriate interloper in their midst. "What say you, Mr. D'Artiers, do you find Miss Fenwick unusual?"

"Yes," he said, "I do, indeed, find her highly unusual."

His tone implied that he didn't mind Maureen's eccentricities in the least, but his actions told another story.

He placed his hand over Miss Cottwell's and gave it a slight squeeze, as if to comfort the poor girl in her distress.

Maureen stopped mid-spoon and stared at her husband holding another woman's hand.

*Her husband.*

Well, he wasn't really. Well, perhaps he was, but that

didn't matter. Maureen tamped down the green-eyed rebellion rising in her heart. Even she knew that a gentleman didn't make such a public display of affection if he wasn't about to make an announcement!

Julien and Miss Cottwell?

How'd she'd love to stand up and announce to the elegant crowd that she was the very much alive and legal Mrs. D'Artiers.

Now, there was a little *on dit* to set Miss Cottwell's elegant composure into a tittering rage. Not that Maureen wanted for one moment to claim the likes of Julien D'Artiers as her long-lost spouse, but it would be fun just to wipe the conceited and victorious look off Miss Cottwell's face.

As if the two of them were locked in some battle for Julien's affections.

Maureen shook her head and tried to tell herself that she couldn't care less what Julien did with the rest of his life. As short as she hoped it would be.

He could make a fool of himself with any woman he chose. It didn't matter to her one jot what he did. Or with whom.

But still, did he have to single out Miss Cottwell for all the curious in Gunther's to witness his declaration? The very daughter of the man he claimed was out to kill her?

Hypocrite, she fumed under her breath, even as she discerned the first whispers rising above the din.

"The rake has finally fallen!"

"And for Miss Cottwell."

Why, not a half hour earlier he'd been whispering in *her* ear that he loved her.

Well, he hadn't said *love*, but it was what he obviously had meant. The man was utterly heartless and despicable. She wondered what other nonsense he'd say to her to keep his precious neck from being stretched.

With the growing attentions of the other patrons, Julien had released Miss Cottwell's hand. The young woman took control of the conversation at the table by discussing her costume for the Trahern masquerade and her search for the elusive but perfect ribbons to match.

Maureen's head spun, not only from the inane chatter but her own reaction to seeing Julien turn his attention to another woman. She stared down at her dish, her delicate ice now melted into an undistinguishable soup.

Still it galled her. Never mind that he'd let go of the silly chit's hand; he still gazed over at the blonde as if she were the only woman in the room.

Once he'd looked at her like that.

She stirred her dish until her spoon clattered out of her hand and landed on the floor.

Miss Welton gave a disapproving cluck of her tongue, while Lady Mary turned a delicate shade of pink mortification.

Well, he *had* looked at her like that, she wanted to tell them. But then, she had been the only woman around. For at least twenty leagues.

She pushed her dish away, and to her great relief Lady Mary announced that they had to depart. Only too quickly, her guardian hustled her from the shop, lecturing her on each and every social gaffe she'd made since they'd joined Mr. D'Artiers's lovely outing.

Listening with half a care, Maureen stared out the window of the carriage into the busy London street. The carts and horses and carriages whirled past, blurring into a riptide of color and motion.

Suddenly, the London streets faded before her cynical gaze and she was back on that faraway cay under a moonless, star-encrusted sky.

Julien laying reverent kisses on her naked body. His hands worshiping her, touching her, bringing her such aching passion. Her own wanton response.

She did everything she could to shake the images from her mind, but try as she might, she couldn't ignore the past.

A time when Julien had claimed there was only one woman he loved.

A time when he'd declared himself for her. For her alone.

For what she thought would last for a lifetime.

Instead of going out that night, Lady Mary announced at the supper table that they would be staying home for the evening.

When William protested, saying the Lord Admiral had an assignment for Maureen to complete, Lady Mary waved her hand at him.

"We mustn't have her about too much. Last night was a triumph, and tonight everyone will be looking for her. If she is missing, speculations will run rampant. It will make everyone all that much more eager to see her."

"If you say so, Mary," William said, glancing across the table at Maureen.

Maureen was of the same mind as the Captain. She wanted to be done with this business—most of all she didn't want the Lord Admiral questioning her commitment. "What about Miss Cottwell? Won't she take advantage of my disappearance to spread her stories of my 'unusual qualities'?"

Lady Mary sighed. "I highly doubt Miss Cottwell is going to be spreading any rumors about that discussion." She paused for a moment, her soupspoon in midair. "But how did you know about the Weltons and their . . . well, how can I put it . . . infirmities?"

"You mean about the madness?" Maureen stared at the lady. Oh, her comment had been better aimed than she'd originally thought. "It's true?"

Lady Mary nodded.

"I didn't know. I just said it to put that simpering puss in her place."

"Oh, Maureen! You can't say such things. Especially if they may be true, as it was in this case. It is a sorry story, but no one ever mentions it, at least not in public."

Maureen didn't miss the slight smile at the corners of Lady Mary's otherwise disapproving countenance. "If you don't mind me saying, that does explain a thing or two about Miss Cottwell."

The Captain began to laugh, the likes of which Maureen had never expected from the usually gruff man. She happily joined in, while Lady Mary looked torn between a mild giggle and the need to reprimand the unruly behavior.

"I hardly think it was a ladylike thing to do, Maureen," Lady Mary scolded, enough to settle the

Captain down and to get Maureen to cover her mouth with her napkin. "Especially in front of Mr. D'Artiers. I am sure Miss Cottwell thought you did it to cut her out of his affections."

"Didn't appear to me," Maureen muttered, "that he looked all that put out to discover his dear Miss Cottwell isn't all she appears to be. I'd say they were a pair of bedlamites if ever I saw 'em. He can have her and all her ladylike ways."

She hadn't meant to sound so defensive or so riled, but she had, and now both Captain William and Lady Mary stared at her as if in wonderment at this outburst.

"It's just that . . ." Maureen's protest faltered.

"Just what?" Lady Mary asked.

Maureen sighed. "Miss Cottwell obviously was right about the breeding and all. I suppose the truth of it just stuck in my craw and I let it get the better of me. I'm not a lady. I never will be. I'm just a rough sailor, and I proved that today. I'm sorry, Lady Mary. I won't do it again." She rose from the table and excused herself. "If we aren't going out tonight, I think I will go upstairs and rest. Good night."

As Lady Mary watched the downhearted young woman leave the room, tears welled up in her eyes.

At first she'd been shocked at the task the Lord Admiral had dropped into her lap, but now, a month later, she had all but forgotten Maureen's past and the reason she was in London. If she were to tell the truth, she'd grown immensely fond of having a goddaughter, even a pretend one.

The girl filled a spot in her life that had been empty

for too long, and it broke her heart to think that Maureen thought herself unworthy of being called a lady.

It wasn't true, and perhaps it was time someone told her.

She got up to follow her, but William caught her by the arm, as she passed his seat at the head of the table.

"Where are you going, Mary, my girl?"

"Why, after that poor child." She looked down at her husband, lips pursed. "She needs to be told."

At this William's eyes grew wide. "Why, you've gone as balmy as one of those Weltons. Tell her what?"

"Tell her she is a lady."

William rose and steered her back to her chair. "Sit down, Mary. Think about what you are saying."

"She's Ethan Hawthorne's daughter. She's a lady in her own right; why, she's even a—" Lady Mary haltered her speech as her husband's bushy eyebrows rose in alarm.

"We vowed a long time ago we wouldn't mention that name in this house," he told her sternly. "I'll have you keep that word, Mary. We have no proof she's Ethan Hawthorne's daughter, just her word on the matter."

"William, you may be many things, but you are not blind! The girl is the image of Ethan—those eyes. Why, I would have recognized them anywhere. And that hair; her grandmother had the same coloring. You know as well as I do who she is. And she has a better bloodline than a hundred Eustacia Cottwell's and more right to the life than that—"

Again, William halted her with a stiff shake of his

head. "No more, Mary. I won't hear it in this house. You may have the right of it, but we can't do anything about it. Not now, not ever." He paused and reached down to squeeze her hand. The chill in his fingers told her that she should fear the truth as much as he did.

"William," Lady Mary whispered. "Do you think when Peter is done with her that he'll do as he's promised? That he'll let her go?" She paused before she voiced the suspicions that up until now she'd been afraid to say aloud. "Will he let her live?"

"Of course, Mary. Why wouldn't he?"

He didn't sound all that convinced.

"If she knew, if she was told the truth—"

His grip on her hand tightened to where it was almost painful. Just as quickly he let it go, and in his haste to hide his alarm, he wiped his brow. "You wouldn't do that poor girl any good to tell her your fanciful tales. What could she do? Ethan couldn't stop the inevitable, and I doubt his daughter has any better chance. Allow her to do what she needs to do, and then let her sail away. 'Tis best for her and best for us."

But Lady Mary wasn't so convinced. Perhaps Maureen Hawthorne, armed with the truth, could do what Ethan Hawthorne had failed to do so many years ago.

For Maureen had one thing Ethan Hawthorne hadn't: her mother's fire. And that, Lady Mary suspected, might finally turn the tide on the Lord Admiral's unholy hold on the past.

For all of them.

# Chapter 13

Long before the first light of dawn, Maureen slipped downstairs and purloined the rest of her belongings from the Captain's sea chest. In her old clothes she felt comfortable for the first time in weeks, reveling in the freedom of her canvas breeches and loose shirt. Hiding her hair beneath a watch cap, she slipped out her attic-bedroom window, shimmied down the drainpipe, and carefully eluded the Lord Admiral's guards posted around the Johnston house.

As if his drunken lot could keep me contained, she thought as she made her way through the shadowy side street. Getting out of the Johnston house, she decided, was easier than climbing down from the crow's nest on a summer's day.

Through the long hours of the night, she'd come to the conclusion that there was only one way to settle her indecision. Discover the truth herself. If the *Retribution* was indeed for sale, then someone around the London pool would surely know of it.

Now all she had to do was find her way out of the maze of Cheapside to the docks.

As luck would have it, Maureen ran into a fishwife on her way to pick up her wares at the first corner.

The toothless old woman, after listening to her young companion explain that "he" was an apprentice running away from a brutal master so he could serve his King and country at sea, had no qualms about showing the lad the way to the docks.

Especially when Maureen offered to carry the woman's basket for her.

So with the bent-backed crone leading the way, Maureen made her way to the river.

Even before they came upon the Thames, the scent of the river—thick and foul with the refuse of the city—filled her nostrils. Maureen inhaled deeply, if only to catch for a moment the sweet, rich scent of the sea, filled with salt and life and movement, trapped as it was within the stew of the river.

Gulls and seabirds, who'd followed the ships inland, added their cries to the wee hours of dawn, beckoning her closer.

"There you go, my boy," the lady cackled, clapping Maureen hard on the back, as they came to the docks. "Take care now, and bring back a huge prize for your good friend Mag, eh?" The woman reclaimed her basket, slinging it over her bent shoulder, and then hobbled down to the left toward the fishing boats.

Maureen scanned the familiar sight of ships and sails and riggings, in the complicated web of the London pool. She wandered for close to an hour before she spied her ship, the *Retribution*, moored between two frigates. At the sight of her once-proud ship, its rigging loose and limp, the poorly stowed sails flapping raggedly in the breeze, she bit back the anger rising in her chest.

The Lord Admiral had promised that her ship and crew would be well taken care of, but this! Why, the *Retribution* looked more like a fishing scow than the bonny vessel Maureen loved.

She had wandered as close to it as she could, when she was accosted by two sailors. Navy, from the looks of them, she surmised quickly, trying to sidestep their approach.

"Have a mind to go to sea, lad?" the first one asked, a black patch over one eye, a striped cap pulled down low over his greasy pigtail. "I'm Sollie, and I could help you find a might' fine berth aboard me ship here."

She shook her head.

"Tell him, Ferg," Sollie said to his equally foul companion. "Tell him how he won't do better than to sail with us as mates."

All she needed was to be tossed onto the nearest outbound ship. Not that she wouldn't be put off at the nearest port when her true sex was discovered, but it might take time to find someone she could trust to tell.

She'd heard enough tales from her men—several of whom had served with the Navy after being pressed from other ships—to know what the scurvy lot who ruled the below-deck world of a Navy ship would do with a woman.

"What say ye?" Ferg asked, spitting a long stream of spittle into the river. "You want to go to sea?"

Wiping her nose with the sleeve of her jacket, she lowered her voice and replied, "Can't say that I do. I'm here for me master. He wanted to know what is' happening with that ship." She jerked her thumb out toward the *Retribution*.

"Tell your master it is set to go on the block next week."

So it was true. Her ship was being sold. Why that lying, thieving bastard of a Lord Admiral, she thought.

"Why is it being auctioned?" she finally managed to ask.

"Prize money," Sollie told her, puffing out his chest as if the act of catching the ship had been entirely his doing. "Your master interested in buying her?"

She didn't trust herself to open her mouth and speak, lest the words come spitting out in anger. Instead, she nodded her head.

"Well you tell 'em we took her just off Sheerness. A smuggler's ship, right handy for all kinds of crossings. Not much to look at, but in good shape, all things considered."

She didn't like the way he said that. As if there was something wrong with the *Retribution*. Why, it was the finest ship this pig would ever have the privilege of viewing from the wharf, for he'd never be welcome to serve on her.

"What things?" she asked.

The two men exchanged glances.

"Now you've spilled it, Sollie," Ferg said, jabbing his companion in the ribs. "Might as well go ahead and tell the lad."

Sollie leaned over, pointing his dirty finger under

her nose. The eye without the patch watered, as if it wasn't much better than the one hidden. "Don't be spreading this around or think of telling your master, or I'll find you and split you open like a mackerel and feed your guts to the rats."

She'd like to see the cocky bastard try. Wouldn't he be in for a surprise.

"You promise?" he repeated.

Maureen nodded.

"That ship was captained by a woman."

Maureen waved her hand at him. "Do you take me for a fool? A woman? What kind of crew would sail with a woman?"

"A crew headed for convoy duty." Sollie laughed.

"How's that?" she asked. "My master was told they were still aboard and willing to serve the next owner."

"Yer master should have looked a little closer at the auction notice. That there crew was convicted of smuggling, so they've all been sentenced to service in the Navy."

Service in the Navy? But the Lord Admiral had promised that her men would be released.

Another of Julien's assertions coming true.

Damn him, why did he have to be right?

"So there is no one aboard her?" she asked, looking out at her ship.

"Just the rats." Sollie laughed again.

"And the captain?" she asked, almost unwilling to hear her fate.

At this Ferg spoke up. "Gonna hang. Don't usually take to hanging a woman, but this one weren't natural, iffin you know what I mean. Thinking she could captain a ship and get away with smuggling right under the nose of the King's navy. Not natural, I tell you."

Maureen had stopped listening to his idiotic diatribe. But three words echoed and beat in her chest like the resounding clap of thunder on the horizon.

*Hang. Gonna hang.*

And who would stop it?

She didn't want to think of the one man she suspected could.

*Julien.*

No, it couldn't be true! She wasn't going to hang. She had a deal with the Lord Admiral. De Ryes in exchange for her life.

A deal her lofty friend obviously had no intention of keeping.

How had Julien known?

Having not paid attention to her companions, she suddenly found them on either side of her. They caught her by the elbows, their grips as sure as a reef knot.

"Unhand me," she told them, struggling to free herself.

"Now, why would we want to do that?" Sollie asked. "We're set to sail with the tide, and we are still short a few men. You look like a lively lad, well suited for a life at sea."

They began dragging her toward the gangplank.

"Let me go," she told them, twisting this way and that in a vain attempt to break their hold. "My master will be furious if I don't return."

"By the time he finds out, you'll be halfway to the Horn," Ferg told her.

The pair laughed and continued hauling her along.

"I don't think so, gentlemen," a deep male voice called out from behind them.

The command in the voice was unmistakable, so much so that her captors stopped immediately.

"Let the lad go."

The seafaring pair turned around in unison, carrying Maureen with them. There, a few feet away, stood de Ryes. He wore a plain jacket of navy superfine and buff trousers. A white shirt and a cravat tied simply finished off his plain, almost mercantile ensemble. Yet from the tilt of his hat to the sheen of his boots, there was no mistaking that this was a man of wealth, despite his rather nondescript fashion.

"Are you both deaf? Unhand that boy." He began taking off his gloves. He made each movement slow and deliberate, as if giving them time to consider their unlikely futures.

"And who might ye be, thinking ye can order the King's navy around? This here be Navy business. Be off with ye," Sollie told de Ryes, glancing over at his companion as if to see that he had the backing of his shipmate in this challenge.

Ferg had already released Maureen and had taken two steps backward toward the relative safety of their ship.

"If you must know," de Ryes said, his drawl taking on an annoyed tone, "I am that lad's *master*."

While she didn't like his emphasis on the word *master*, she couldn't help but be pleased to see him.

That in itself annoyed her even further.

"And if you must further know," Julien continued,

"I am here to see what is delaying the lad in obtaining the information I need before I purchase that ship." He paused and stared at the man.

Still the stubborn oaf refused to release her.

"We was just gonna give the lad a tour of our ship, like he requested, gov'nor. Didn't ye, lad?" The man's grip tightened until she thought he was going to twist her arm off.

"No," Maureen said defiantly. "You were trying to nab me."

"Tsk, tsk," de Ryes clucked. "That would have been unfortunate. I take it you sail with the frigate that brought in that vessel and will share in the prize money. Correct?"

The man nodded.

"Well, if you don't unhand my assistant this moment, not only will I not buy that prize, but I will tell every interested shipowner and investor at Lloyd's that she has rot from stem to stern. She'll sink into the river before your captain will find anyone willing to buy her."

"Let the brat go, Sollie," Ferg called out. "You'll be gutted if the captain finds out you lost us the prize money."

Sollie didn't appear too worried. "What if I don't?" he spat at de Ryes.

Maureen had never seen de Ryes lose his temper, so nothing prepared her for the ugly way his mouth twisted or the arrogant arch of his brow. He stalked down the quayside, eating up the distance between them with a menacing determination.

If Sollie hadn't still had her anchored to the planking, she would have taken a step or two backward like Ferg to get out of the way.

De Ryes stopped within inches of the man's foul-smelling breath. "Then I'll gut you myself, Sollie," he told him. And before the brawny sailor could react, Julien whipped out a knife and pressed it to the man's throat. "I doubt even the sea gulls will want what's left of you when I get done." He smiled, as if the prospect before him would offer no end of pleasure.

Sollie took one big gulp and finally released Maureen's arm. "Just havin' some fun, gov'nor. No need to get all cross with ol' Sollie. Just havin' some fun. Ain't that right, laddie?"

Maureen wasted no time. She whipped out her own knife and began fingering the edge. Glancing up at de Ryes, she added her opinion. "Gut him."

At this Sollie's one eye widened. Then the bulky man whirled around and fled, pushing his friend out of the way as they scrambled up the gangplank.

Julien moved to her side. "I think we should depart before Sollie finds himself some more reliable shipmates. The kind willing to defend him."

"I doubt that will ever happen." Maureen stowed her knife and turned in the direction opposite the one Julien had indicated, quickly moving down the quayside to where the mooring lines held the *Retribution*.

"Where do you think you are going?" he asked when he caught up with her.

"Onto my ship." She didn't know what she was going to do, but she wasn't about to let anyone sell her beautiful ship out from beneath her. She'd burn it to the waterline before she let that happen.

"With the Navy tied up on either side of you? And in daylight?" he asked, as she paced on either side of the iron bollards where the heavy ropes holding the *Retribution* against the tide were tied off.

Maureen paused. She hadn't really been listening to him; rather, she'd been gauging how best to board her ship with the least chance of detection, deciding whether to climb the lines or slip into the wretched water of the Thames and board her from the shadowed side.

De Ryes caught her arm and shook her. "Have you gone mad, Reenie? I can see the plans whirling about in that diabolical mind of yours. If you think you can retake your ship single-handedly, then I ought to let you do it. They'll hang you for sure, and then I can wash my hands of you for good."

"You'd like that, wouldn't you?" she shot back. "Especially considering how convenient it would be for you and your lovely Miss Cottwell."

Even as she said it, she regretted the peevish words, because they obviously delighted Julien.

"Do I detect a hint of jealousy?"

"No!"

He moved closer and whispered in her ear, "Careful, Reenie, one might think you an aggrieved spouse."

"Spouse indeed." She moved away from him, crossing her arms over her chest. "What would your Miss Cottwell think of you having a living, breathing wife?"

"*My* Miss Cottwell? I think you struck your head when you climbed down that drainpipe."

She whipped around. "How did you know that?

For that matter, how did you know where to send your note yesterday?"

"As I told you before, information is my business. As for your whereabouts, that was simple. I followed you home from Almack's. And I've had you watched ever since. Unlike the Lord Admiral, I pay my informants to stay awake." He paused, glancing up and down the quay. "Enough of this; I think it is time for us to depart."

Before she could protest any further, Julien caught her by the elbow and towed her along. As they passed the frigate, it appeared Sollie was licking his wounds by rallying his mates.

For now she didn't mind being pulled up the steps that led from the quayside to the busy London streets and out of Sollie's way.

It would hardly do her or her crew any good if she were caught around the docks, let alone trying to board the *Retribution*. The Lord Admiral would certainly view that as a breach of their agreement.

Hell, leaving the Johnstons' unescorted was a breach of their agreement.

Since yesterday's confrontation with the man, she had more than a sneaking suspicion the Lord Admiral would take great delight in seeing her hang right beside de Ryes.

"Come along," he told her. "My carriage isn't far, and I'll take you back to the Johnstons' before someone spots you in that outlandish outfit or, worse, someone spies me down here. I'd have a deuce of a time explaining what I was doing about the docks or even why I am up at this ungodly and unfashionable hour."

She didn't answer, because it would mean admitting that he was right again, so she followed him. Besides, a carriage would return her to Cheapside faster than her own two feet.

Once they were settled inside, Julien taking the seat opposite hers, he gave the directions to his driver through the opening in the roof, then drew the curtains to hide their identities.

Not long after they started out, Julien laughed.

"What is so funny?" she asked.

"I find it amusing that the Lord Admiral thought to stop you by posting only two guards. He's a bigger fool than I suspected. Obviously, he's never seen *you* climb rigging."

"T'wasn't all that much. The drainpipe is about the only thing on that house that isn't falling down," she told him, doing her best to ignore the tinge of wistful pride in his voice, as if he almost wished he'd been there to see her daring feat.

He leaned back in his seat, his long, muscled legs stuck out in front of him. Julien's carriage was a fine sight better than the hired hackney the Lord Admiral had lent Lady Mary. Her fingers ran over the richly upholstered leather; at the windows, velvet curtains shut out the world. An even more expensive conveyance than the open barouche he'd been driving yesterday.

Maureen had no doubts as to how he could afford such opulence. Captain de Ryes was rumored to be one of the best privateers on the American side. She'd heard Captain Johnston telling Lady Mary one evening that de Ryes had brought home nearly a million dollars in prizes in the first nine months of the war, all of them taken from along the coasts of England and Ireland. This season, the Captain had said, would net the American even more wealth.

So Julien's boast on the pier about buying the *Retribution* was probably true. He could buy her ship—and a fleet more like her. Before long he'd be able to buy the Admiralty, lock, stock, and barrel, with his rumored luck and skill at catching only the best prizes.

She looked up and found him studying her. Even in the dim light of the carriage, his eyes held an intensity that burned through her.

"Dammit, Reenie," he said, his voice strangely choked. "You don't know how good it is to see you. See you alive."

She glanced away. She couldn't look any longer into those familiar green eyes. The color of the sea after a stormy day.

Growing warm in the closed coach, she pulled off her cap, letting her hair tumble down.

Exactly how he liked it, she remembered only too late, hastily stuffing the cap back on her head.

"You look like you did the first time I saw you. High above the waves, the wind pulling stray tendrils from under your cap."

He crossed the space between them, his fingers catching one of those stray locks.

"I wanted you then. Just as much as I want you now." His fingers caught her chin and tipped it so she looked at him.

She'd heard the catch in his voice and didn't like what it did to her heart. His voice whispered of intimacy, a sense of connection, the tie between them.

One she feared, looking into his mesmerizing gaze, that she would never be able to break. Not until the day she died.

Her fingers knotted into fists at her side. She wasn't supposed to have any feelings when it came to this man.

None other than hate and revenge and anger.

But his declaration, like his arrival on the docks, had blindsided her heart. Breached the wall she'd built around her soul and kindled something she had no wish to see lit again.

Feelings for Julien.

She didn't say a word, mostly because she was afraid that her own voice might betray the truth.

He still made her breath catch. Left her heart fluttering. Made her long for his arms.

"Reenie," he whispered, drawing her closer. "Tell me you want the same things."

She shook her head, but he ignored her. He brought his lips down on hers, taking possession of them with the fervent, pent-up passion of a man dying of thirst.

*Stop him,* her mind screamed. *This is trickery.*

But that banshee cry, that lost part of her desire, was so much louder. It held back her reason, banished her common sense.

All the while his tongue teased her, enticing her to open up to him.

And she did.

He brushed her cap off her head, his fingers combing the tangled threads of hair until they streamed down her back in long coils.

For a moment he pulled back, both of them gasping for air. His lips found their way back to the nape of her neck, sending shivers down her spine. She arched toward him, and he pulled her tighter.

"I knew if you would just give me a chance, you'd forgive me," he whispered into her ear.

*Forgive?* It was as if she'd been dashed with a bucket of seawater from the North Atlantic.

She hadn't forgiven him! She'd only betrayed herself. Let her weakness for him overtake her.

Clawing her way out of his arms, she fled to the far side of the carriage, panting and cursing.

"What the devil?" he said, trying to follow her.

In a flash she whipped her dagger out of her boot and let it fill the space between them.

Julien stopped just before the point found its way into his chest. He backed into his seat. "What did I do?"

She knew she had to say something. She glanced up at him and saw the open desire in his eyes. It cut through her more surely than if he'd sliced out her heart.

Say something, she told herself. Tell him to go to hell. If she didn't say something, anything, she knew he'd try to cross the space between them again. That's exactly what his glance told her he wanted to do.

Suddenly, his fine, roomy carriage seemed more like the smallest of prison cells.

"Why hasn't someone blown you out of the water

and saved me the bother?" she finally managed to stutter. Even after she said the words, she regretted them.

Mostly because, for once, she didn't mean them.

He laughed, loud and hard. Better yet, he settled back in his seat and looked like he intended to stay on his side. "I suppose, I hoped you'd come back from the dead and that pleasure would be yours."

"If I had my ship, I'd—"

He held up his hand. "I know, you'd hunt me down, you'd see me fed to the nearest school of sharks, you'd run me through a thousand times before you'd finish me off. I know what you'd do, Reenie. I know only too well." It was his turn to glance away, part the curtains, and stare out into the London streets. "If I'd known you were alive, I would have probably given you the pleasure." He looked back at her, the resignation in his voice matching the weary lines around his eyes. "And if we both manage to get out of London alive . . . well, we'll see how you feel then."

"I'll get out," she told him, though at this point she wasn't too sure how she'd accomplish that. Before anything else she had to find her crew and see to their freedom. "And my feelings won't have changed. Make no mistake, I'll never forgive you."

"I suppose not," he said. It seemed as if he was going to say more, but he shook his head and looked away.

The silence between them was almost as uncomfortable as the memories of the kiss they'd just shared. "How did you know about my father?" she asked.

"He told me. When I was aboard the *Forgotten Lady*.

One night after you went to bed, he told me he'd been in the Royal Navy. That he'd been court-martialed."

"Why would he tell you?" Her question held an unspoken second part. *Why would he tell you, and not me?*

"I don't know."

"Did he tell you anything else?"

He shook his head. "Not much. Just that the Lord Admiral had been instrumental in bringing the charges and testifying against him. What I've been able to learn since is that your father was convicted and sentenced to life on a prison hulk. As far as the world is concerned, Ethan Hawthorne died there."

"But he didn't die there," Maureen said, more to herself.

Between them lay the obvious. Ethan Hawthorne had died later. Died by another's treachery.

An uneasy silence filled the carriage.

After some time he said, "I can help you. I'll find your men. And save your ship from the block as well."

Maureen felt it was akin to taking blood money to accept his help.

But she knew if anyone could locate her men, it was Julien. And he'd do it with the necessary speed. By the time she could gain access to that information, they'd be scattered to the four winds, trapped until their deaths in the British Navy.

She couldn't let that happen. They were her men. It was her fault they'd been taken off Sheerness, and she would do anything to see them safe.

Even bargain with the devil.

But the *Retribution*?

"You told me back there my ship couldn't be taken," she said. "How do you propose to steal it away from the Navy?"

"I don't intend to steal it. I intend to buy it."

"Buy my ship?" She nearly came out of her seat.

He shook his head at her. "Stubborn as ever. And what do you propose, to buy it back yourself? I'm sure the Lord Admiral will approve of that."

He had her there. She crossed her arms over her chest and told him, "You'll not buy my ship."

"You don't have any other choice. I won't let you lose the *Retribution*. I owe you that much." He paused for a moment. "She looks fast and trim. Good for smuggling. Probably even privateering."

"She gets me where I need to go," she said. Looking up, she caught him smiling at her, for there was no doubt he'd noted the pride in her voice. "Why should I trust you? Why do you want to do this for me?"

"You know why I want to do this for you."

"It won't change how I feel."

He nodded. Carefully, he drew back the curtain and gauged their progress. After he let the fabric slip back into place, he looked up at her.

"In the meantime, Reenie, do we have to spend every moment we have together locked in a battle over the past?"

"That's all you left me." Well, almost, she thought. There was more, but not anything she would share with him.

Never.

"Have you considered it was all I left myself as well?

That everything that died for you that day died for me as well?"

Maureen wished she could close her ears off to the regret in his voice, the gut-wrenching guilt.

As fast as she could, she closed her heart to the impossible.

He hadn't lost anything that day, she told herself. He'd gained everything he wanted. He'd made his name, started his fortune, all at her expense.

How dare he claim to have lost anything!

"Say what you will," she told him, matching his gaze with one she hoped showed only the iron in her will. "I'll nevertheless turn you in."

"I know. And I don't blame you. But I've still got some time to change your mind on that one as well."

"Not much. I can't keep the Lord Admiral at bay forever. And he's not a man to suffer fools gladly."

Julien nodded. "It will take me at least a week to find and free your men. I'll get them to a safe port on the coast, one I've used from time to time. By then I'll have your ship there as well."

"A week?" She shook her head. "You don't need a week. What have you to gain by that much time?"

"Your heart?"

It was her turn to laugh. "Mark my words, de Ryes. I'll give you a week. For once I have my ship and my crew, you'll be hanging from the front steps of the Admiralty, and you'll have no need of my heart."

# Chapter 14

Maureen found climbing back into her room as easy as it was climbing out—until she turned around from the windowsill and found a wide-eyed Lucy watching her.

The always-garrulous serving girl didn't stand gaping for long. "Miss Maureen, you could break your neck out there. Hasn't anyone shown you the back stairs? 'Tis a fine sight easier to sneak out from than down the drainpipe." With that the girl grinned.

"You won't tell on me, will you, Lucy?" Maureen asked, brushing her dirty hands over her rough trousers.

"Lol, Miss, if I was to tell on you, how would that make her ladyship feel?" Lucy put the bundle of laundry she held atop the bureau and started to put away Maureen's freshly cleaned unmentionables. The girl glanced over her shoulder. "She's happier since you arrived than she's been in years. She doesn't mind a bit iffin I don't get the silver polished or the ironing is behind. You've been a godsend to this house, that you have." She winked at Maureen from beneath the white lace of her mobcap and then started to leave.

Before she got to the door, she turned and said, "Himself, her ladyship, and *that man* are downstairs. Have been most of the morning. They've asked for you. I told them you were indisposed, but now her ladyship is insisting you come down. What should I tell her?"

Maureen didn't need to ask who the third party waiting for her in the salon might be—considering Lucy's tone, it could only be the Lord Admiral. "Tell them I'll be down presently."

Lucy bobbed her head.

"And, Lucy," Maureen said after the departing maid. "Thank you."

The girl shrugged her shoulders. "I'll be back in a few minutes to help you get into that day dress Lady Mary insisted you have. I think it is a fair sight better for company than what you're wearing now, if you'll pardon me saying it." Lucy closed the door behind her.

Maureen let out a sigh of relief and set to work getting cleaned up. She'd have a hard time explaining to her hosts and their guest why she smelled like the docks.

With Lucy's help she was brushed and dressed in no time, and as she came down the stairs, she heard the Lord Admiral's voice rising in agitation from Lady Mary's salon.

"Will, I tell you, this girl has to find de Ryes and find him fast."

Maureen's ears perked at the sound of desperation in the man's voice. It seemed he needed her as much as she needed him. She moved closer to the salon, careful not to give her presence away.

"Whatever is the hurry, my lord?" Captain Johnston was asking. "Mary's got the girl sailing every highblown event in town. She'll find this pirate, but it might take time."

"I don't have time."

At this Maureen moved right to the edge of the door. If she was going to believe Julien and trust him to help her, she needed another week, time the Lord Admiral obviously was not about to allow.

The lofty man cleared his throat and then lowered his voice, though Maureen could still hear his confession.

"This is highly confidential, William. I wouldn't tell you this if I didn't trust you. But you have to see the importance of finding this man, if it means you and Mary escort that chit to every soiree, musicale, and ball I've managed to secure invitations to. The *Bodiel* sails from Portsmouth the end of next week. It must be underway by then if it is to get across the Atlantic undetected."

"The *Bodiel*, eh?" Captain Johnston said. "Captain Frey has that command. Good man. But the *Bodiel* 'tis hardly a ship anyone would look twice at taking. Just a regular packet. What could be so important that she has to sail with so much secrecy?"

"She'll be carrying the officer's pay for the American blockades, as well as enough gold to pay all the naval suppliers in Halifax. There's been rumbling by the merchants there that they won't provision any more ships until they are paid. And paid in gold." The Lord Admiral snorted. "Impertinent devils, but they have to be kept mollified, or they may just up and join their Colonial cousins to the south of them."

Maureen stepped back from the doorway, the impact of this information staggering her imagination.

A payroll ship. A privateer's dream come true.

It was well known that the British Navy sent out packets nearly every day to all four corners of the world. The little vessels carried mostly administrative missives and mail, nothing to tempt a privateer or other ship. But occasionally, these nondescript, usually routine sailings also carried payroll. Gold enough to make the average privateer—and every man aboard with a stake in the prize—a wealthy man for life.

Not that most could catch them. Packets were deliberately stripped to carry minimal crew and arms, for they relied purely on their speed to outrun any pursuit, making them nearly impossible to catch on the open seas.

But coming out of a harbor—now, that was a different matter.

Maureen gulped. No wonder Julien wanted another week out of her. He must have heard rumors of a payroll being sent and was trying to find out from where and when it would sail.

It could be the only explanation for his determination to stay in London.

The gold the *Bodiel* would carry would likely tempt any man to flaunt his neck before the hangman. Even make him go as far as to trust a wife bent on revenge.

Do anything to convince her that he was trust-
worthy, offer her anything, including his treacherous
heart.

"Ah, Maureen, my dear girl," Lady Mary called
out. Lucy trailed behind her, bearing an overladen tea
tray. With the Lord Admiral's largesse, Lady Mary had
also seen to restocking her larders.

No more stale cakes in this house, Maureen had
heard her mutter more than once.

She turned from the door and forced a smile to her
face. "Yes, Lady Mary. I'm sorry I delayed you and
your guest. I was rather tired this morning."

"So Lucy told me," Lady Mary said, with a dismissive wave of her hand. At her ladyship's feet the ever-
present Baxter trotted along, his curly tale wavering
as he sniffed at Maureen's hem. His little flat nose
twitched in dismay as he backed away from her so
quickly, he nearly upset Lucy and her tea tray.

"Baxter!" Lady Mary scolded. "Whatever is wrong
with you?"

The dog sent an accusing glance at Maureen,
then turned back to his mistress, whimpering at her
reprimand.

Maureen wondered if the fussy little dog could
smell the stench of the Thames on her, though she'd
done her best to wash it away.

She smiled down at the traitorous little pug. At least
Baxter couldn't betray her.

"Now, where were we?" Lady Mary said, turning
her attention back to the matters at hand.

"My health?" Maureen prompted.

"Ah, yes, you poor girl. I thought turning in early

would be so relaxing for you, but I can see you barely slept a wink." She swept into the room. "Look who I found, Peter. Our dear Maureen. Quite fatigued this morning with all you are putting her through." The lady sent a significant glance at the Lord Admiral. Not waiting for the man's response, Lady Mary continued into the parlor, directing Lucy where to put the tea tray, as if the shabby room had a surplus of side tables.

Maureen followed and, after bidding her salutations to Captain Johnston and the Lord Admiral, settled onto a stool next to Lady Mary's chair—the only piece of furniture left unoccupied.

"Mary, my girl," Captain Johnston said, after his wife had finished serving the tea. "Peter needs you to put all your wits into this venture of his." After a nervous glance toward the Lord Admiral, he continued hastily. "I'm sure Miss Hawthorne would agree that it is in everyone's best interest to see this business concluded as quickly as possible, wouldn't you, lass?"

"Yes, sir," Maureen told him. "I want to see the last of London as soon as possible, and I am sure my crew is of the same sentiment." She turned to the Lord Admiral. "My crew is being well cared for, aren't they?"

The man had the audacity to look affronted. "Of course they are. I promised you myself they would be seen to, and they are awaiting your return in living conditions far better than those of many a good honest sailor in his King's navy."

She blew on her tea and looked up at the man as she asked, "Aboard the *Retribution*?"

"Why, of course," he said. "Where else would they be?"

She smiled. "I can't imagine. Though it will make it so much more convenient when I sail out to have my full crew at hand." She paused for a moment. "Would it be permissible for me to visit them? As their captain, mind you, I can't help but be protective of them. See to their welfare. I'm sure as one captain to another you'd agree."

Much to her chagrin, Lady Mary intervened before she was able to force the wily man's hand.

"Go down to the docks? Have you gone mad, Maureen?" she said with the same scolding tone she used on Baxter for his frequent indiscretions on the carpet. "Why, it is not only unseemly, but out of the question."

"Lady Mary, this really is up to the Lord Admiral," she told her.

Her guardian was not about to let that stop her. "Peter, I do protest. I will not have this girl mucking about the docks undoing all my hard work. Why, five minutes down there and she'll be as wild and unmanageable as she was when you brought her here. No, I won't stand for it."

The Lord Admiral nodded to the lady, only too willing to defer to her judgment in this matter. "If you say so, Mary. You know more about these things than an old sailor like myself would know." He turned to Maureen. "You'll be with your men soon enough. Just find de Ryes, and you'll get exactly what you've earned."

Maureen wondered if he meant her ship and crew or the smuggler's hanging she'd been sentenced to from the beginning.

"Mary, my girl, what have you got planned for Maureen tonight?" William asked, rejoining the conversation. "Like the Lord Admiral is saying, time is of the essence."

Maureen looked up at the ruddy-faced captain and not only saw misgivings behind his quickly hooded glance but also heard the reluctance in his voice.

He knows. He knows the Lord Admiral can't be trusted, she realized. And this wasn't the first time Captain Johnston had been caught by the Lord Admiral's net.

Nor does he know how to get out of it, she concluded. *No more than I.* She rubbed her bare arms, as if suddenly feeling the first draft of winter rush over them.

"Yes, Mary," the Lord Admiral said. "A speedy resolution to all this would be best for everyone."

Lady Mary's brows furrowed. Maureen knew the lady wanted nothing more than to see their charade continue for the rest of the Season, using the Lord Admiral's munificence to give her the social whirl she'd dreamed of for years. "I suppose we could add a few more appearances to our schedule, but I can't run the poor girl into the ground." She turned her worried gaze to the Lord Admiral. "She'll be no good to you, Peter, if she takes ill with too much night air or not enough rest."

As if to do her part, Maureen brought her hand to her mouth and coughed delicately.

Her ladyship beamed with appreciation.

"Just the same, Mary," the Lord Admiral said, his mouth set in a straight, hard line, "she's no good to me if she can't find this man. I need him found and found immediately. I'll do my best to secure invitations for both of you to Lady Weston's ball tonight. If he's going to be anywhere, this would be the evening for him to surface. Everyone with any connections will be there."

"Don't go to the trouble," Lady Mary said. She raised her nose in the air. "The Viscountess sent over invitations yesterday. She was quite apologetic that she hadn't sent them earlier."

The Lord Admiral looked as if he didn't quite believe her but wasn't about to lower himself to an argument. "I surmise, given the bills that have been arriving at my house daily, that she has an adequate gown in which to attend?"

The lady sighed, then reached down to scratch Baxter's head. "I believe we can find something that won't embarrass her standing with the *ton*, though I am still trying to find just the right costume for the Trahern masquerade."

"Well, never mind costumes for something she won't be attending. I have a feeling tonight will be the end of Captain de Ryes." He turned to Maureen. "An end we both look forward to, wouldn't you agree?"

She nodded, unwilling to speak.

For in truth, she wasn't so sure anymore.

Arriving at Lady Weston's ball that evening, Maureen wondered what the Lord Admiral was thinking sending her to this party—a crush so thick she would have been surprised to find anyone, let alone a notorious privateer within the press of bodies.

Even worse was her introduction to Lord and Lady

Weston, Julien's sister and brother-in-law. Rather than looking down her aristocratic nose at the less socially connected Lady Mary and her unknown goddaughter, the vivacious Lady Weston went out of her way to welcome them, especially when Lady Dearsley arrived and made quite a fuss about Lady Mary's return to society.

At her aunt's behest Lady Weston sought them out after the receiving line was finished and introduced them to her friends and family.

Maureen found herself charmed by Julien's sister, much to her chagrin. It was terribly difficult to continue plotting a man's demise when his sister was so kind. It was even harder to believe that he'd turned out so blackhearted with such a genuine and generous sister.

And the aloof and disarmingly beautiful Lady Trahern, whom Maureen had heard so much of from Lady Mary on the carriage ride over, was just as pleasant, telling Lady Mary that she was thrilled they would be attending her masquerade.

Maureen had kept as much as she could to the background during all this, unwilling to become any more familiar with Julien's relatives than she had to.

They were, in some strange sense, her family as well, and she didn't like the idea of accepting their warmth and hospitality any more than she felt a right to the motherly affection Lady Mary showered over her.

"Lady Mary," Lady Weston was saying, "have you met my nephew, the Earl of Hawksbury? He's a rascal and a terrible rake, but I still adore him."

Maureen didn't pay much attention to this introduction, taking only the slightest glance at the nephew in question.

The young man hardly looked the reprobate his aunt described, though he was dressed like the other young bucks circling the room, in the latest state of fashion.

"Lady Mary," he said, "please forgive my lady aunt. My mother says I inherited my talent for finding trouble from my Aunt Lily, and my aunt considers that a great compliment."

With that he took Lady Mary's hand and brought it to his lips, though his gaze moved over the lady's shoulder and sought out Maureen.

Maureen was startled to find herself staring into a pair of moss green eyes exactly like Julien's. From the chestnut hair to the tanned features, the resemblance between the two was startling.

For a moment the man's youthful features took her back to the decks of the *Forgotten Lady*, to the first time she'd leaned over the rail and seen Julien's handsome face close up.

Her eyes obviously reflected her shock, for the young Earl grinned at her. "This wide-eyed lady must be your enchanting goddaughter I have heard so much about, Lady Mary." He turned to his aunt. "I'm afraid she sees the similarities between me and Uncle Julien." Stepping forward, he took Maureen's hand. "Fear not, I haven't my uncle's reputation or reprobate ways. You are safe with me, dear lady."

She doubted that, considering the friendly way he

held her hand and the way he lingered over her fingers before finally relenting to let her hand go.

"We've met your uncle," said Lady Mary. "Such a handsome man, and so kind. I hardly see what all the fuss is about. He seemed perfectly amiable to me, though Maureen gave him quite a set down."

This drew an exchange of looks between nephew and aunt that Maureen couldn't quite interpret. Obviously, it wasn't every day a young lady of the *ton* rang a peal over the esteemed head of Julien D'Artiers.

"Then if my uncle is the cause of your discomfort, I must insist on escorting you two ladies about the room," the Earl said. He grinned at Maureen. "Especially given your obvious dislike of him, Miss Fenwick. For I know he is prowling about somewhere, and he would delight in causing a scene. Besides, I was promised Miss Fenwick's first dance, was I not, Lady Mary?"

"Of course! Why, of course you were!" Lady Mary fluttered her fan. "How ever did you know I loved sugared almonds?"

"Every lovely lady does," he told her, but again his gaze fell on Maureen.

She glanced sideways at the young man. She wondered how fast he'd retreat if he knew he was trying to charm his uncle's wife.

It was almost too humorous, too ironic.

Lady Mary, in the meantime, had conveniently disengaged herself from Maureen and the Earl and was happily chatting with Lady Dearsley on one side of the room, leaving Lord Hawksbury free to escort Maureen about the ballroom. While he entertained her with endless accounts of the other guests, she glanced again at his familiar features and let herself pretend for the moment that this was Julien and that this was the first time they were meeting.

If things had been different, this was how they might have met—in a ballroom with an innocent introduction. They would have danced and flirted and maybe even fallen in love without the disastrous consequences.

What was she thinking?

She was the daughter of a smuggler, and a smuggler herself. She wasn't a lady; she didn't belong here.

And yet . . . she remembered the line from the naval history.

*Ethan, Lord Hawthorne.*

If her father had been titled, as the book indicated, how different would her life have been if she'd been raised in England rather than at sea?

Ever since she'd learned of her father's secret past, there had been a litany of questions in the back of her mind.

Who was she? Did she have family beyond Aunt Pettigrew?

She might have. Looking about the room, any one of the multitudes could be her family.

As far as she'd been told, Aunt Pettigrew was the only one left in that line. Why, she didn't even know her mother's maiden name, only her first name, which she'd seen in her father's bible written in the column marking the family deaths.

*Ellen Hawthorne, died of fever, 21 September 1790.*

The puzzle of finding her father's lost place in society almost outweighed her desire to see his murder avenged, especially when she looked around at the young misses, most of whom were in their first Season and flushed with the prospect of falling in love.

Would she have ever fallen in love with someone like Julien?

She couldn't help but think she would have. She glanced at his nephew. Though the two men could be taken for brothers, there was also a difference.

The Earl of Hawksbury hadn't the wariness about him that Julien had always worn like a second coat. Vigilance brought on by living by the hard rules of the sea.

But then again, she told herself, this young member of Julien's family was an earl and heir to his father's titles. What would he know of the hardships of war or the problems of the world, raised as he probably was in a cradle of luxury and security?

She and Julien had too much in common; they understood each other—a connection she'd never grasped until now. Never wanted to believe.

As she looked up this time, her gaze crossed the room and fell on him.

*Julien.*

Across a room, across time, it seemed they were bound together, no matter how much she hated it, how much she wanted to disavow it, how much she wanted to change it.

His gaze met hers, and for a moment it was as if they were in another place, another time. Just the two of them, staring at each other across the narrow channel between their two ships.

The *Destiny* and the *Forgotten Lady*.

Together, yet separate.

If he acknowledged her it was so brief and so fleeting, she wondered if she'd imagined it. A flash of recognition, a need in his gaze she knew only too well, but when she looked again it was gone, his attention diverted by the lady at his side.

Because the room was so crowded, Maureen couldn't see who Julien's latest victim was.

"Ah, you see, Miss Fenwick," the Earl of Hawksbury was saying. "You have nothing to fear from my uncle. For he is quite occupied at the moment. And from what I hear, he will be for the rest of his life with yonder leg shackle."

"Whatever do you mean?" she asked, glancing back at Julien, but still unable to see his companion.

"Why, Miss Cottwell, of course. The betting book at White's is rife with speculations and wagers. It is said my uncle has finally fallen under Cupid's arrow."

*Miss Cottwell?*

Maureen looked again. The crowd parted, and she could see Julien bent attentively over the young lady's shoulder. Certainly, he was spending an inordinate amount of time with the girl, but Julien in love with the likes of that simpering, arrogant little snip?

Hardly.

"Given what I have heard about your uncle," Maureen said, "I doubt his affliction is serious and hardly as fatal as you seem to believe."

The Earl of Hawksbury laughed. "Would you care to wager, Miss Fenwick?" His tone implied something altogether different from a friendly exchange of coins.

"I haven't anything to bet," she told the impertinent young buck.

"Ah, but you do. Perhaps a kiss?"

Maureen nearly choked. A kiss? This boy was her nephew. "I don't think that is at all proper," she finally managed to say, doubting the young man would have made such an offer if he knew he was proposing it to his aunt.

"Then a ride in the park. I will bet you that my uncle will be engaged to Miss Cottwell before the stroke of midnight at my mother's masquerade next week."

"Engaged?"

"Yes, engaged. Do you agree to the wager?"

Julien, engaged? How could he? He was still married. Married to her. Had he forgotten the words he said aboard her father's ship eight years ago?

*'Til death do us part.*

How could he have forgotten? It wasn't every day a man said them with a cutlass nudging him in the back and a pistol aimed at his head.

But he'd said them, and said them quite willingly. Or at least she thought he had.

# Chapter 15

"Maureen Margaret Hawthorne, where the hell have you been, lass?"

Her father's voice bellowed across the deck, cutting through the still calm of the predawn with the ferocity of a cannon shot.

"Damn," she cursed under her breath, as Julien steadied the rowboat alongside the *Forgotten Lady*. They'd tarried too long on the beach, and now with the sun just starting to rise, they'd been spotted coming from shore.

Even as she caught the line to pull herself back aboard, she heard the unmistakable click of a gun being cocked.

"Give me one good reason, you rutting bastard, why I shouldn't blow your head off," her father hollered over the rail.

Maureen looked up to find him aiming a pistol straight at Julien.

"Papa!" she called out. "What are you thinking? Have you gone mad? Put that away; Julien has done nothing."

"*Julien,* is it now?" Her father's eyes narrowed. "I told you, lass, not to go over to his ship alone. I told him that as well. Ye both promised, but I see he couldn't honor his word, so I have no use for the man."

She stepped back in the boat and put herself in front of Julien. "You'll not shoot him, Papa. Not unless you want to shoot me first."

Julien pushed her down onto the seat and out of harm's way. "Sir, if you would let me explain. I didn't take your daughter to my ship, on that you have my word."

"Bah!" her father responded with a wave of the pistol.

For a moment the two men stared at each other, each weighing his opponent, but then the sun twinkled up and over the horizon, dropping a single ray of light on the beach where Julien and Maureen had spent the night.

Her father seemed to take this as a sign, for he looked from the beach back to Maureen and Julien. She could see he'd come to his own conclusions.

Unfortunately, they were entirely correct.

"Papa, I didn't break my promise. I love Julien. I always will. Please don't shoot him. If you do I'll never sail with you again."

The gun in his hand wavered, then fell to his side. "It looks like you won't be sailing with me anyway, lass.

For if you've gone and done what I think you've done, there's only one solution to this." The pistol raised again. "Captain de Ryes, I take it this is your rather unconventional way of requesting my daughter's hand in marriage?"

Maureen looked up and over her shoulder at Julien. For the merest of flashes, she saw something that sent a sudden chill whispering along the nape of her neck.

His eyes held a myriad of emotions. And none of them looked like love.

*Julien was hiding something.*

How had she never seen this before? And it went beyond her, she suspected, beyond even him.

Even as her questions and fears started to run faster than a full-moon tide, he looked down at her and smiled.

The light in his eyes bathed her in the same passion they'd just shared. She'd never had a man look at her like that, as if she were the only woman on the face of the earth.

Whatever uncertainties she'd fallen prey to melted away with just one glance from him.

He loved her. There was no doubt in that. Whatever his secrets, they meant naught, for Julien truly loved her.

"Well, Captain de Ryes," her father called down. "I would have an answer from you, and fast."

Julien's hand went to her shoulder. His fingers were warm, his grip sure and confident. "Aye, sir. I would be honored to take your daughter as my wife. With your permission, that is."

Her father nodded. "Then consider her dowry my

sponsorship into the Alliance. By noon the rest of the brethren should be here. We'll have your sworn oath and then your wedding." He paused. "But until then, you don't mind being my guest for the remainder of the day?"

Julien agreed, climbing aboard the *Forgotten Lady*, following Maureen's course up the side of the ship.

It was clear her father was still unwilling to trust Julien. At least not until he was safely wed to her. Maureen knew his misgivings would be only temporary, for eventually her father would see what a good man Julien was. She knew he would.

"Lass, can you have yerself ready before sundown?"

"Aye, Papa," she said. Turning to Julien, she told him, "I even have the dress."

As weddings went, it was by all accounts the most beautiful one Maureen had ever seen. Of course, it was the only one she'd ever seen, and in all likelihood every bride thought her wedding the best.

One of the captains in the brethren, Captain Smyth, had been a vicar of a fashionable London parish for five years before some scandal had driven him from England. Though his holy orders were in question, the man was more than pleased to perform the ceremony, assuring Maureen's anxious father it would be considered legal and binding by any court.

So with all the arrangements well in hand, the only thing left for Maureen was to get dressed.

She stood in her cabin for almost an hour, staring down at the dress Julien had given her.

How could she even think of wearing such an

elegant and daring gown? She'd look ridiculous. The white silk seemed to melt beneath her fingertips, and the seed pearls and gold embroidery were worth a small fortune.

What if she ripped it? Or snagged it on a beam?

But in the end she'd overcome her anxieties and carefully put it on. To her amazement the bodice fit perfectly over her unbound breasts, and the length of the skirt fell precisely to her toes as if it had been made for her by the best modiste in London. Simple in cut and design, the elegance of the gown was in its understated use of lace, embroidery, and pearls.

Even her wild dark hair seemed to cooperate on this special day, brushing into long coils that she tied up with the only ribbon she'd ever owned before Julien gave her one—an ivory piece of satin that had once been her mother's. She cut the blue one from Julien in half and used the two pieces to tie up her stockings.

Her father tapped on her door a few minutes after she'd finished her preparations. When she opened the door, he stared at her as if he were seeing his daughter for the first time.

"Reenie, lass," he said, a mist of tears rising in his blue eyes. "You're the image of your beautiful mother, God rest her soul. I don't know why I never saw it before."

She smiled at him, not sure what to say in the face of this unprecedented display of emotion. Especially now that she noticed he, too, had gone to great lengths with his appearance.

He wore his best coat, and his whiskers had been trimmed and combed.

"I've got something for you," he finally said, holding out his hand. "Your mother would have wanted you to wear these today. She wore them the day I married her. A gift from her Aunt Pettigrew."

Maureen took the small pouch he offered and opened it up. Inside was a pair of diamond earrings. Priceless, glittering gems set in gold. She held them for a moment and, for the first time, felt a connection to the mother she held no memories of—a warmth and feeling of love that this long-lost woman had given her daughter before a fever had separated them.

"Thank you," she said, wiping at the unfamiliar tears filling her eyes.

Her father wrapped her in a warm embrace and escorted her to the deck. It seemed every man from the *Destiny*, the *Forgotten Lady*, the *Avenger*, and the half dozen or so other ships in the Alliance that had joined them during the day hung from every yardarm, railing, or spare space their ship could afford.

The men cheered wildly at her appearance, their rowdy voices raised in wild "huzzahs" and whistles of appreciation.

To her surprise, garlands of flowers decorated the rails and mast, while the lines were filled with long streaming ribbons, fluttering happily in the light breeze.

"Your husband-to-be's doings," her father told her. "Sent his entire crew ashore to gather the blasted flowers and put them up. Even brought enough rum and food over to feed every man within fifty leagues. Never seen a man more intent on getting married."

Even then she could smell the scent of roasting pig wafting from the beach and the sweet scent of something heavenly rising from the direction of the galley.

She glanced up and saw Julien standing near the wheel, dressed in the clothes of a gentleman. A black jacket and buff breeches transformed him into a London dandy. The white shirt gleamed in the afternoon sun.

Beside him stood his ship's surgeon, Roger Hawley, the only cloud in this otherwise brilliant day. The dour-faced man had come over for dinner with Julien on several occasions and, even today, glared from his place as best man as if the entire proceedings were complete and utter folly.

Another of Julien's crew stepped forward and shyly handed her a bouquet of island blossoms.

"From the Cap'n. With his compliments, ma'am."

She brought the flowers to her nose and inhaled deeply, swearing never to forget their exotic Caribbean scent.

"I think he'll do right by you, Reenie, if this is any indication of how much he cares for you."

"I love him, Papa."

Her father held her hand for a moment and looked into her eyes. "I know you do, lass. And that's what scares me."

Before she could ask her father what he meant, he escorted her across the deck to the sounds of a pipe and drum. Soon she found herself holding Julien's hand before Captain Smyth.

She glanced back at her father and saw he had retrieved his pistol, while his good friend, Captain Jacobsen, held a cutlass. Both were pointed in the direction of the groom.

Julien glanced back and laughed. "I'll do this with or without your help, sir."

"My help it is," her father said with a loud laugh, at which all the crews joined in.

They made their vows as only it seemed they should. The sun shone down on them, while beneath their feet the *Forgotten Lady* danced and swayed to the gentle rhythm of the water.

With steady assurance, Julien professed in a deep, steady voice his commitment to love her, honor her, and keep her always. If she had any doubts before, she set them aside, happy in the confidence that the man who was becoming her husband loved her with all his heart.

She added her own vow, and before long she found herself pronounced Mrs. Julien de Ryes.

With that, her husband took her in his arms and kissed her soundly to the wild rejoicing of their audience.

She was his, now and forever.

Maureen wondered if every bride was this happy on her wedding day.

Before long the celebration started, with the food and rum and ale passing freely among the crews. For the officers and captains, Julien had produced several bottles of fine wine. The party continued well into the evening, and as the sun started to set, Julien glanced over at her and smiled.

She knew exactly what he wanted—the same thing she did—to be alone.

"Come, let's steal away from all this," he whispered in her ear.

She nodded happily. As they sneaked over to the railing, she saw a lone rowboat rounding the point of the bay and disappearing from sight.

"I wonder where that boat is going?" she said aloud.

Julien looked up, and for an instant she swore she saw his eyes fill with the same indecision that she had seen earlier. But he quickly masked his expression, and before she could ask anything further, he caught her in a kiss.

"Just one of the lads. Probably going to a neighboring island, hoping to find a treasure equal to what I've discovered here."

She blushed and said no more as they climbed down to the rowboat awaiting them and headed toward their new destiny.

She thought it strange that Julien sent her to his cabin on her own, but he said he wanted to check over his ship before he joined her.

And then he leaned over and whispered in her ear, "Unlatch the rear window and wait for me."

Entering his cabin, she almost laughed at her earlier speculations as to the decor of his pirate den. It was neither the Turkish harem she'd imagined nor the stark world of a puritanical American.

Instead, it held a warm, welcoming ambience. From the rich wood paneling to the worn oak table where she laid her wedding bouquet to the wide, deep berth she would soon be sharing with him.

She looked over at the bed and smiled. Scattered over the green coverlet were more flowers.

The back of the cabin, which took up most of the ship's stern, was dominated by long, wide windows.

Heeding his request, she unlatched them and threw them open.

Outside, darkness had settled over the West Indies cay. From the beach and the nearby ships, music still played, the wild, unbidden cadence rising and falling over the gentle waters, calling to her.

Truth be told, Maureen felt that the night before had been their wedding night, but tonight . . . there was something different in the air.

A hint of mystery, a wish for the future.

The soft scents of the ocean and the palm-covered cay floated inward. Maureen stepped back and closed her eyes, letting the magic of the night and the magic of what was to come wash over her soul.

She wanted to never forget this night. Ever.

"Julien, I love you," she whispered into the breeze.

When she opened her eyes, she found her new husband swinging in from a rope through the open windows.

He grinned as he landed right in front of her. "Ah, a bride calling for her groom."

He'd removed his coat and now wore only his breeches and white shirt. He'd tied a red sash around his waist, where an ornate dagger was tucked. His feet were bare, and his hair was still tied back in a queue—like a pirate of old.

"What are you doing?" she asked, stifling a giggle. Why, she never giggled, but tonight even that seemed possible.

"I swore more than one oath today, my lady. I am now a member of the Alliance, fully sanctioned to carry out the duties of a pirate." He waggled his eyebrows at her. "My first act as a buccaneer was to follow a rumor I'd heard."

"And what, pray tell," she asked, "was this rumor?"

He raised up one finger. "Aha. I'm glad you asked. I heard tell that the most beautiful woman was married here today, and I thought to come and steal her away." He caught her in his arms, tugging her close. "Could it be I've found her, or I have come across some lost Spanish treasure?"

It was Maureen's turn to grin. She was more than willing to play along with his game. It was made of pure magic.

"Oh, sir pirate," she exclaimed in mock horror. "I will not have you risk your life just to please me. My groom is a jealous, fierce man. Why, he'll kill you if he finds you here. Any moment he'll come through yonder portal," she said, pointing to the cabin door, "and then our time together will be lost."

He let go of her and crossed the room. With a wide flourish he latched the entryway and then pulled a nearby chest in front of it. "I'd say we have our privacy now, milady. Unless you prefer to await your groom?"

She shook her head. She didn't want to have to wait any longer.

"So I thought," he said. "Now, you mentioned something about pleasure? You are in luck." His gaze drifted over her with a slow, easy familiarity. "I have traveled every sea in search of that elusive mystery, and everywhere I went I was told to seek a woman with hair as dark as the midnight sky and with eyes that sparkle like sapphires. And she would hold all the secrets of my heart."

"And have you found her?" she whispered.

"Oh, yes." He tipped his head and studied her for a moment. When he spoke, his voice was edged with a soft, gentle touch. "I didn't realize until today that I've spent my life looking for you." He plucked the dagger out of his belt and tossed it aside. "Come to me, my beautiful bride. Tonight we start a lifetime of nights together."

Captured by his command and the sensual promise of his gaze, she moved wordlessly into his embrace.

Their lips met in a searing kiss. His arms wound around her, pulling her against him. Last night's gentle claiming was nothing in comparison to the wild heat burning between them now.

His teeth nipped at her lips, his tongue tasting her. She sighed and opened herself to him. They continued to kiss, until he pulled back and looked into her eyes.

She gazed up at him, and without breaking eye contact she reached up and plucked free the ribbon holding her hair. The long curls fell down around her shoulders. "Is this what you sought?" She said with a saucy smile, throwing her hair back, arching and stretching like a cat.

Julien seemed mesmerized by her movements. She stepped back and eased up the hem of her gown. Up over her stockings, up over her stomach, up over her unbound breasts and over her head. She tossed the dress aside and stood before him.

She reached out and caught his hand, guiding it to her breast. "Or was it this that you sought?"

His hand stroked her naked flesh, teasing her. She moved closer to him so his fingers could cup her, so he could taste her. His mouth dipped to the hard nipple, his tongue washing over the pebbled surface.

She sighed, a soft, throaty moan coming forth.

He pulled her closer, one hand around her waist. With a swift move he swept her up into his arms, carried her to the berth, and gently laid her down amongst the petals.

She inhaled deeply, breathing in the wild, sweet scent surrounding her. This magic would be forever, she thought.

In front of the berth, Julien quickly divested himself of his shirt and breeches. He joined her in their bed, cradling her in his arms.

"Maureen, my love. Whatever the future holds, know this: I love you. I'll love you always."

"I love you too," she whispered back.

Again they kissed, sealing their pledge, which seemed more sacred than the ones they'd repeated just a few hours earlier. And as they continued to kiss, he entered her, slow and tentatively. As her hips rocked to meet his movements, the heat between them grew, until it exploded in a fevered pitch.

They held on to each other, languishing in the afterglow, touching each other with a lazy reverence.

Several times during the night they made love. Each one with the same enchanted claiming.

Just before dawn she sighed and glanced over his shoulder and out the window, where night still held sway over the sun. From the cadence of the *Destiny*, it seemed as if they were moving.

"Have we gone adrift?" she said, sitting up.

He pulled her back down and into his arms. "I know I have." He laughed, as he began to make love to her again.

Maureen fell back into his arms, only too willing to believe her husband. And why shouldn't she? He loved her and she trusted him, trusted him with her life, with her heart.

But looking back, she should have said something, should have realized that his quick, witty answers about the lone sailor in the rowboat or why the *Destiny* felt as if it had gone adrift were nothing more than lies.

Just like everything about Captain Julien de Ryes.

# Chapter 16

"Miss Fenwick, are you feeling ill?" Lord Hawksbury asked.

Maureen looked up, still distracted by the sight of Julien hovering over Miss Cottwell. "Uh, yes—I mean, no. I am quite fine, thank you."

She glanced one last time in Julien's direction, then turned her back to him. "What were you saying about a wager?"

At this the young man's features lit up. "A ride in the park. If my uncle proposes to Miss Cottwell before the midnight unmasking at my mother's masquerade."

"And if he doesn't?" she asked.

"Name your price."

"Your fastest horse."

The Earl turned a faint shade of scarlet. "My fastest horse? But that would hardly be . . ."

Cocking an eyebrow at him, Maureen challenged his earlier offer to name her price.

The young man, honor- and duty-bound from the top of his head to the tips of his toes, nodded in reluctant agreement to her outrageous request.

She meant to win this wager. She may well need a fast horse to get out of London if her growing suspicions about Julien were correct.

He certainly couldn't announce his engagement to Miss Cottwell with his living and breathing wife standing nearby to add her happy returns to the couple.

There was only one way Julien could take another wife.

Remove the first one.

And Maureen had no intention of giving him that chance.

She found herself watching Julien all night, despite the numerous invitations to dance, offers for punch, and other gentlemanly favors and distractions. Try as she might, she couldn't stop seeking him out.

The very thought of him with Miss Cottwell made her furious.

Jealous, even.

Just as he'd accused her of being.

*What have I come to?* she chastised herself. Jealous of Julien with another woman.

From the rumors she'd heard, he'd had a long string of mistresses, everything from demimondaine, actresses, and dancers to widows, wives, and even some young ladies, tempted from their privileged lives to utter ruin at his skillful hands.

The monstrous cad, she thought. The worst of it was that she had to count herself among the many fallen temptations in Julien D'Artiers's less than straight path.

Yet Julien's nephew was right about one thing, she thought. Julien was paying too much attention to Miss Cottwell. But marriage?

Maureen closed her eyes and took a deep breath.

It was supposed to have been so easy. Point him out to the Lord Admiral, see him hang, and sail away.

But something was changing inside her. Years of hate were falling away and leaving something else, something she feared would never allow her to see her vow completed.

Instead, she'd betrayed her father by letting Julien live. As much as he had betrayed Ethan Hawthorne by murdering him.

Not long after midnight, he appeared suddenly at her side. Without a word he took her hand and led her to the dance floor.

She didn't protest.

His touch, as it had in the carriage, reignited the desire she'd once felt for him. Her body was more than willing to break the faith and revel in the passion that brought them together in the past.

The warmth of his fingers penetrated her gloved hand. And as they trailed a slow, blazing path up her forearm, she shivered when he came to the brief bareness between her gloves and short-sleeved gown, his touch bringing back the memories she'd been re-playing all evening long—their recent kiss in the carriage and now, as he held her so intimately, their wedding night.

His touch, his kiss, the feel of his naked skin over hers—it clouded her senses, left her missing the first step of the dance as the music began.

"What is it, Reenie?" he whispered. "What has you over a barrel tonight?"

They moved down the column of couples past Miss Cottwell, who appeared to be dancing with Julien's nephew.

He must have seen her glance in the girl's direction. "Eustacia?" He laughed. "I don't care how you may deny it, you're jealous of her."

"I would hardly say *jealous*," she told him. "Why she's young enough to be your—"

"Wife?" he teased. "I always fancied a young wife, not one of these long-in-the-tooth spinsters who seem to be so popular this Season."

She deliberately trod on his foot as she passed him. "So it seems you will have your wish. I understand congratulations are in order. The room is rife with gossip that you are about to announce your betrothal to that witless child." She paused for a moment, for the steps had left them facing each other. "I find that an interesting notion, but with only one problem."

"And that would be?" he asked, his eyes wide with innocence.

"You already have a wife."

"Yes, but she won't claim me."

Maureen clamped her mouth shut.

Nor will I ever, she wanted to tell him.

If only she could say it. And mean it. "I'm just surprised you think the two of you suit," she managed to venture.

He nodded, as if considering her advice seriously. But the light behind his green eyes told her he was enjoying her discomfort enormously. "And what type of woman would you choose for me?"

"One who understands who you truly are."

"Touché," he said. "But I must argue in Miss Cottwell's defense that she has some amazing attributes that other women don't possess."

Maureen glanced over at the other girl. The angelic blond hair, the clear complexion, the perfect manners. But she hardly had the spark to match the fire Julien could kindle in a woman. "She is pretty," she conceded.

"I suppose so, but I fancy something different about her, something she has that no other lady in the room possesses."

What could the Lord Admiral's daughter have that all the other misses in the room didn't have? From Maureen's vantage point the girl had everything. Position, wealth, breeding, family connections.

*Family connections.*

Maureen stopped herself. Eustacia was the daughter of the Lord Admiral.

*The Lord Admiral.*

That was the key. And while the Lord Admiral might want to see Captain de Ryes rot in hell, he obviously viewed Julien D'Artiers in an entirely different light.

A light that went on in Maureen's head.

She glanced up at Julien. "If you married Eustacia, the Lord Admiral could hardly denounce you as de Ryes. Why, he'd look the worst fool for marrying you to his daughter and letting you have free rein in his home."

"Someone cynical might say that, *if* I intended to marry the chit."

"And you don't?"

"What do you think?" he asked, raising his gaze to meet hers.

There she saw it—the passion, need, and desire she recognized so well.

The same look he'd used to entice her back into his arms in the carriage just hours before.

As he looked at her, Maureen could almost feel his touch, as if he wanted her to know what he would be doing to her this night if only she would utter the words.

She tore her gaze away.

It was a dangerous course Julien was navigating, and she knew the reason why. By being close to Eustacia, he could move into the Lord Admiral's circle of confidence. From there he could more easily obtain the information about the payroll ship.

But in the meantime, if the Lord Admiral found out who he was, he might not denounce Julien outright, but that didn't mean the ruthless man wouldn't remove the problem of Captain de Ryes by other means. . . .

The same method he obviously planned to use on her.

"What is it, Reenie?" Julien whispered in her ear as he crossed behind her in the dance. "There is more to this than just Eustacia."

She glanced over at him. She had the capacity to help him. To stop him from continuing this dangerous masquerade. All she had to do was tell him about the *Bodiel*. Tell him everything she'd overheard about the payroll ship.

But that would mean she cared about his welfare. Wanted him to live. Wanted him.

"I am supposed to turn you in." She nodded slightly toward the Lord Admiral. "It seems he is in quite a state to see you hang."

"You and he have much in common," he joked.

Maureen didn't feel much like laughing.

*Tell him,* a voice inside her called out. *Tell him and see him gone from London. You could both flee. Tonight. And be done with this place.*

That would mean she trusted him, and she couldn't. Not until he came through on his promise to see her men and ship freed.

Instead, she asked, "How are your plans coming for my men?"

"Good," he said. "If you would like I could come over tonight and tell you what I have planned." His scorching gaze indicated his plans for the evening had nothing to do with her missing crew.

This time she did laugh. "I can just see Lady Mary allowing you in at that hour. Especially with that light in your eye."

The music was ending, as was their dance. He bowed over her hand, but before they parted he leaned over and whispered in her ear, "Lady Mary need never know. Leave your window unlatched. I'll come to you by moonlight."

Maureen was thankful that Lord Hawksbury came to claim her next dance so quickly. If he hadn't caught her by the elbow, her knees surely would have buckled beneath her.

*Leave your window unlatched.*

This wasn't the first time Julien had whispered similar words to her. And she feared tonight would be no different. For as surely as she had the first time, she'd unlatch the window and let him back into her life.

It took Maureen another hour and a half to convince Lady Mary to make their good-byes and leave the Weston ball. She had hoped to slip away without having to face the Lord Admiral, but as her luck would have it, he was waiting for them outside.

"*Miss Fenwick,*" he said. "A word with you before you depart."

Lady Mary smiled bravely at Maureen, as if she wanted to protest the late hour to the man but didn't dare cross him. Instead, she allowed the recently hired footman to hand her into her rented carriage. The lady knew only too well that all her newfound luxury was due to the Lord Admiral's open purse strings.

The Lord Admiral took Maureen by the elbow and led her to his carriage. Maureen balked at getting in.

"What is this?" he asked. "Get in. I won't have my business bandied about the streets."

She didn't trust the man anymore, and she wasn't going to get into his carriage and allow him to spirit her off to who knew where. The streets around them were empty, for nearly all the guests were still dancing the evening away.

Crossing her arms over her chest, she stood her gound and remained on the curb's edge. "What is it that you want?"

Like most bullies and thieves, he backed down when challenged. At least this time. "Where is de Ryes?"

"I'd like to know the same thing, my lord," she said. "I've been trussed up and danced about for nothing. I'd like to be gone from London. But I can hardly be asked to point out a bloke who doesn't show, now, can I?"

The Lord Admiral looked up at the gaily lit windows of the Weston ballroom. "Well, he should have been here. Everyone who is anyone was here tonight."

"Not de Ryes. Perhaps his circles are higher than even your *lofty* status can afford." She'd said it before she thought, and his swift reaction came like a thunderbolt not even she expected.

He backhanded her across the face, hard and swift, with an anger and strength that told her only too clearly this man was dangerously close to the edge.

The blow sent her staggering against his carriage, but she didn't allow herself to fall.

Her hand went to her stinging cheek. "Don't cross me, my lord. I hold the key to everything you need. You and your Navy will never catch de Ryes at sea; he's too much a sailor for any of your lot to cross sails with. And without me you'll never find him on land."

The Lord Admiral's fist rose again, but it halted in midair as Lady Mary came flying out of her carriage.

"My lord! Have you lost your senses?" the lady cried as she rushed to Maureen's side. "How dare you hit her, my lord! It's unheard of!"

The Lord Admiral clenched and unclenched his fists, as if he were coiling for another strike, but Lady Mary's protests must have finally entered his conscience, for he tipped his head to her and then smoothed out his jacket.

But his words held all his pent-up anger. "If this creature were a lady, that would be the case. You seem to have forgotten, Lady Mary, I found her on her way to the hangman, and I can give her back to him at any time. You would also do well to remember that your husband's future depends on this creature's veracity. If she's played us false, everything you hold dear," he said, swinging his arm toward the carriage and footman, "will be lost. For all of us."

He turned swiftly on Maureen. "Mark my words, if you are lying to me, if you don't know de Ryes, you will regret ever crossing me."

"I know the man," she spat. "On that you can depend. But as I said, it is hard to find a man who doesn't want to be found."

"I don't care. I want him stopped now." There was no missing the finality of his words. "As it is, if you don't discover his identity before next week, I'll see you hang despite your claims."

With that he swept past them and reentered the Weston town house.

Maureen resisted the urge to fling her knife into his back. She doubted at this point even Lady Mary would protest such an unladylike demonstration.

She turned her attention to her kindly "god-mother." If she expected tears, she was surprised to find the lady looking equal daggers into the Lord Admiral's back.

"Why, that horrible man," Lady Mary said, wrapping her hand around Maureen's arm and hauling her back toward their carriage. "Are you hurt, my dear?" she asked once they were settled into the conveyance and on their way back to Cheapside.

Maureen shook her head. "My father always said I inherited his hardheaded ways. I suppose he gave me his thick skull as well. Besides, I've taken worse in the past. Far worse."

This didn't abate Lady Mary's anger with the Lord Admiral. "Why, I think I will have William lodge a complaint with the Admiralty. Such outlandish behavior is uncalled for."

Maureen reached over and patted the lady's hand. "Captain Johnston cannot cross his lordship, not if he hopes to ever get another commission." She leaned back in her seat. "Never fear, my lady. The esteemed Lord Admiral will regret the day he hit me."

This seemed to provoke Lady Mary even more. "Maureen, please don't do anything foolish. I won't see you abused any further, or worse . . ."

The lady obviously couldn't bring herself to say the final word—*hanged*.

She crossed the space between them and sat on the cushion next to Maureen. "The Captain and I have a high regard for you. In the past few weeks, you've come to mean more to us than I can say. Like family." She smiled and caught Maureen's hand in her soft one.

"Once you find this man, you don't have to return to the sea. You could stay with us. No one will ever question your position. As far as everyone would know, you'd remain my dear and beloved goddaughter."

Maureen didn't know what to say. Her eyes misted over. No one had looked out for her welfare like this since her father had died.

"Lady Mary, you know that is impossible. The Lord Admiral would never allow it, and as he said, I don't belong here."

"Bah!" the lady said. "What does Peter Cottwell know about the *ton*? As if he were born to his title and position. 'Twas his ambition and his ruthlessness that brought him to where he is. The man's a fraud."

Even as she said it, Lady Mary looked as if she regretted her heated outburst, for her mouth snapped shut and she looked away from Maureen.

"What do you mean, he's a fraud?" Could there possibly be a chink in the Lord Admiral's impenetrable armor?

Lady Mary's brow furrowed. "William would take away my pin money if he knew what I was telling you, but you need to see that crossing the Lord Admiral is dangerous. Others have tried and failed."

Like my father, Maureen thought, recalling Julien's warnings. "But how can he be a fraud? Surely his titles are his?"

The lady shook her head. "Hardly. He wasn't born to his position. Though he was a gentleman, he didn't have the connections necessary to rise as quickly as he wished. He was ruthless and ambitious, and it didn't bother him to see good men fall in his wake to get the promotions he wanted. Through a twist of fate. he inherited a barony from a cousin who died under mysterious circumstances."

"Certainly, this cousin's family had some say in the matter? Wasn't there an inquiry?"

Lady Mary shivered. "Hardly even a question asked. The other relatives, scattered as they were, didn't care to cross him any more than their cousin had." She looked out the window, as if she didn't dare look Maureen in the eyes as she said, "He will make good on his promise to see you hang if he thinks you haven't been honest with him. Don't cross him, Maureen. Find this de Ryes he wants so badly and hand him over. Then you'll be free of Peter Cottwell and his evil ways."

Maureen didn't think the lady sounded all that convinced that she would be free once de Ryes was caught.

But the warning was clear. Cross the Lord Admiral, and death would be her reward.

How could she tell the dear lady, she'd signed her own warrant the moment she'd laid eyes on Julien D'Artiers?

# Chapter 17

The first thing Maureen did when she entered her bedchamber was to unlatch her window. But not for the reasons Julien had offered; rather, she needed to warn him.

Tell him that the Lord Admiral had suddenly turned dangerous.

But as the hours passed, Julien did not arrive.

She paced about her narrow room and wondered if he truly intended to help her. And if he didn't, whom could she turn to?

Captain Johnston and Lady Mary? She paused at the foot of her bed. They were powerless against the Lord Admiral.

No, she needed connections. Powerful connections, like those Julien and his sisters could provide.

She glanced out her attic window at the rooftops of London. So many houses, so many people. Then it hit her: If her father had been a titled lord, surely there was family who remained, perhaps even members who might be willing to help her.

And there was only one person who could unlock those secrets.

Aunt Pettigrew.

She'd been planning to visit her aunt nearly a month ago, after she'd dropped her cargo off at Sheerness, but then fate had intervened and she'd been unable to go.

It had been nearly four months since she'd been out to visit her aunt, a long time even for Maureen. She'd done her best to schedule her shipments so she could visit the elderly woman periodically and check up on her welfare.

Now there was another reason to go, one she hadn't wanted to consider before today, but time was running short and she needed to get to Greenwich.

If the worst came to pass and she didn't escape the Lord Admiral's machinations, then she had best see to some final business at Aunt Pettigrew's.

The tide would be going out for another couple of hours, and she could catch a ride with a passing ferryman downriver to Greenwich, complete her business, then make the return trip on the incoming flow.

She left a quick note for Lady Mary, explaining that she would be back before sundown, and then went out the window. Despite Lucy's claims that the back stairs and coal door were a better way to elude the Lord Admiral's guards, Maureen felt more comfortable with what anyone else would consider a foolhardy climb.

Hopefully, this wouldn't be the last time she'd visit

the little house where she had lived for five years and that now harbored her future.

In more ways than one.

Julien had watched Maureen and her guardian leave the ball early and smiled to himself. In an hour or so he would make his farewells to his sister and follow his wife.

Much to his chagrin, he was waylaid by the Lord Admiral, who invited him to a late supper at White's. Julien, pressed as he was to discover the information he needed and wanting to appear the willing prospective bridegroom, had no other choice but to accept.

The dinner turned out to be a long, drawn-out affair, with the Lord Admiral doing most of the talking. The only information of any value that Julien gleaned from the big windbag had been pompous hints that he was about to bring the Admiralty its greatest victory to date.

Julien knew the man was more full of hope than truth. For if the tide of the American war didn't change soon, the people of London would be mobbing the Admiralty. Especially with the prices for imported goods skyrocketing and, in some cases, such as sugar, tripling.

The *Times* and other London papers had taken to printing scathing editorials and loathsome caricatures of the Admiralty's inability to stop the terrible losses being incurred by British merchantmen at the hands of American privateers, with the leader and key problem the notorious Captain de Ryes.

And unfortunately for the Admiralty, every day brought news of at least three more lost ships.

How was it, the British press wanted to know, that a group of bastards and upstarts with their fir ships could continue to outwit the mighty oak vessels of England? It hadn't helped that de Ryes had taken several merchantmen in the last month and a half, while another cheeky American privateer had sailed right into Dublin harbor and sunk a schooner.

Why, the very nerve! the press had cried. And if the Irish shores weren't safe, what the devil would the Americans try next?

For all the man's posturing stance and wild claims, Julien knew the Lord Admiral didn't want to find out.

But none of it seemed to bother the Lord Admiral tonight. He told Julien, in all confidence of course, that this naval war was about to change drastically. In a matter of days, the people of London would regard him with much the same favor that they still held for their dear, dead naval hero, Horatio Nelson.

It was nearly dawn before Julien was able to extract himself from the Lord Admiral's stuffy company, and despite the chance of being seen climbing into Maureen's window, he had to at least tell her why he hadn't been able to keep their assignation.

To his surprise he arrived at the Johnston house only to spy Maureen shimmying down the drainpipe, under the very nose of the Lord Admiral's guards.

With the skill born of years aboard ship, she clung to the building as if it were a second skin and descended to the street without making a noise.

Once she'd dropped to the cobbles below, she

moved as silently down the alley as a cat hunting a mouse.

Since he could hardly call out to stop her without being seen himself, he set out to follow her.

The little minx, he thought. She's probably coming to find me and give me a regular lashing for not showing up.

But Maureen didn't turn in the direction of his Mayfair address; rather, she slipped down the street heading toward the docks.

Where the hell was she going?

He trailed after her, curious to discover what his impetuous wife was up to. He assumed she was off on some harebrained venture to steal back her ship in the veiled light of early dawn, but at the docks, to his complete surprise, she hailed a passing ferryman and headed downstream, well past the *Retribution*.

There was nothing Julien could do but follow. It wasn't until he passed the Tower that it occurred to him where Maureen may be headed.

Her Aunt Pettigrew's in Greenwich.

But for what and why? The lady must be in her eighties by now and hardly seemed a likely ally against the Lord Admiral.

Since he'd come this far, he saw no point in turning back. Besides, he felt better watching Maureen's back, knowing she was safe.

So he followed her through the streets of the little village and down a lane to the edge of town, where a quaint stone house sat. The sun had now risen, and the bright morning light revealed a well-trimmed short hedge surrounding the small yard, while flowers bloomed from every available bit of earth. A stone walkway led from the gate at the lane's edge to the front door.

He smiled to himself as he heard Maureen's voice ring out in happy greeting as she bounded through the door.

Lounging back in an alley, he kept an eye on the house for about twenty minutes, when suddenly the door opened and someone came out.

Yet it wasn't Maureen who came stalking out the front of Aunt Pettigrew's house, but a young lad of no more than seven or eight.

The boy didn't look all that happy to leave the house and kept glancing over his shoulder as if he wanted to change his mind and return inside. He yanked his cap down lower over his head and kicked and scuffed his way to the gate. In his hand he held a turnover, which he proceeded to take vicious bites out of.

Julien looked at the lad closely.

A chill of premonition ran down his spine. There was something all too familiar about the lad.

As if he'd seen him before but couldn't quite place him.

Unable to help himself, he started down the lane to get a better look.

"Why, hello there," Julien said, stopping at the gate.

The boy regarded him warily from beneath his oversize cap. Neatly dressed, clean, and polished, the boy was hardly a servant or apprentice on an errand.

" 'Ello," he said back.

"That turnover looks mighty good," Julien commented, hoping to elicit more than a one-word response.

After the boy took another serious bite of his treat, he grinned, then turned a bit more talkative. "It is. Mrs. Landon made it."

"Mrs. Landon? She must be quite a cook."

"Oh, she's more than a cook," his newfound friend said, warming to his story. "She takes care of me and Aunt Pettigrew. She can be rather cross at times, but I don't mind. Not when she makes turnovers." He smiled up at Julien.

It was then he saw why the lad looked so familiar. He found himself staring into his own face when he was of the same age.

This close, Julien noticed the moss green eyes and the familiar reddish hue of the boy's hair that, with time, would darken to a deep chestnut.

A trait that ran deep in the D'Artiers line.

Julien's throat closed, and he found himself unable to speak.

It couldn't be. Maureen would have told him, wouldn't she?

He finally managed to choke out the only question that came to mind.

"What is your name, lad?"

The boy rose up proudly on his toes. "Ethan Hawthorne, sir."

"That's a fine name," Julien said, struggling to keep control of his emotions.

" 'Twas my grandfather's name," Ethan said in a rush, obviously happy to have an audience, and a male one at that. "Though I never met him. My mother says he was a brave man and a great sea captain as well. I mean to go to sea someday and be just as famous."

Or just as dead. Suddenly, he didn't want to see this boy grow up. He'd already missed so much. "You have a few years before that," Julien told him.

Ethan frowned. "You sound like my mother. Why, I'll be eight next February."

*Eight.* Julien didn't need to do the math. The lad had been born in February 1806. Nine months after . . .

Julien shook off the tidal wave of emotions threatening to swamp him.

Ethan Hawthorne was his son. His son. His and Maureen's.

How could she have kept this secret?

She'd had plenty of opportunities to tell him. He'd offered his life to help her regain her ship and crew, and she had still withheld the one thing he should be a part of—the life of his son.

"Would you like to see the model I made of my ship?" Ethan was asking. "I could go in and get it." Then the boy stopped and looked back at the house. "But you'll have to wait. I can't go in right now. My mother is talking with Aunt Pettigrew." He rolled his gaze skyward as if such woman stuff was beneath two men such as themselves.

"That's fine, Ethan. I promise to come back someday soon and you can show me your model, and if you want, we can go down to the docks and visit some ships so you can make another model."

Ethan grinned from ear to ear. "Really? You'd do that for me?"

Julien nodded, unable to say anything for fear he'd tell the lad the truth.

*There isn't anything I wouldn't do for you, son.*

He glanced up at the house. *But first I am going to deal with your mother.*

"Come now, Aunt Pettigrew, there must be someone left who can help me?" Maureen asked, pouring another cup of tea.

Aunt Pettigrew's sitting room was much as Maureen remembered from her years of living in the house. Bright and cheery, it was stuffed nearly to capacity with her aunt's treasures.

The small India chest with its many drawers and strange carvings that her father had given her aunt, the countless stitcheries that Aunt Pettigrew had worked over the years hanging from every available space, her precious porcelain knickknacks crowding every inch of the mantel. Lace curtains framed the two windows that looked out on the back garden, and a fireplace took up the rest of the other wall.

Aunt Pettigrew's ginger cat, a permanent fixture in the room, lolled in the morning sunshine pouring through the windows.

"Please try and think, Aunt Pettigrew. There must be someone!"

Her aunt's mouth set in a stubborn line. "I'm all there is left of your mother's family."

This was not the news Maureen wanted to hear. "But there must be someone on my father's side. With him dead, someone must have inherited his title."

For a second Aunt Pettigrew looked as if she were

on the verge of telling her what she wanted to hear, but then the lady's eyes got drowsy. "Your father's title?" She shook her head. "That's all gone, my dear. All of it. Reverted to the crown when he died."

"But he must have had family, or a house, or friends?"

Her hand fluttered to her wrinkled brow. "I don't remember, Maureen. It was a long time ago. At my age I'm lucky I can recall how to get home from Sunday services, let alone your father's family history. I don't think there is anyone there who can help you."

Maureen slumped back on the sofa.

"Is it so bad?" Aunt Pettigrew asked. "This business you are involved in?" The lady reached over and gently brushed the slight bruise on Maureen's cheek where the Lord Admiral had struck her the night before.

While Aunt Pettigrew knew full well what Maureen did to support them, she never referred to her smuggling activities other than as "this business."

"Not so bad, Auntie," Maureen told her, patting the woman's hand and smiling. "Nothing that should keep me away from you and Ethan for much longer."

"Ethan," Aunt Pettigrew said with a smile. "What a joy he is to my life, Maureen. He brightens my days."

"It is I who should be thanking you. You keep him in school and make sure he is safe. If he were with me, he would be in constant danger."

It wasn't until her son had been five that she realized why her father had left her marooned with Aunt Pettigrew. The sea was no place for a child. Not a bright, inquisitive boy like Ethan. And though Maureen missed him terribly when she was away, she knew he was better off living with Aunt Pettigrew. And at least she could visit every few months when she needed to lay low.

As if on cue Ethan came flying through the sitting-room door. "I met a man outside, and he wants to take me to the docks so we can visit ships!"

Maureen came out of her seat in a flash. Her own experience with the press gang recently told her how dangerous it was for a young boy to be about alone. "How many times have I told you not to go near the docks?"

"I wasn't going alone," Ethan said. "My friend is going to take me."

"And who might he be?" Maureen asked, not waiting for Ethan's answer but stalking outside and down the walk to give the stranger a piece of her mind about luring small boys down to the docks on false pretenses.

But outside, the lane was empty, except for a few stray chickens.

Ethan had followed close on her heels. "He's gone," he said, disappointment tinging his words as he looked past his mother, up and down the lane.

Maureen dropped to her knees and embraced her son tightly. "Ethan, you can't go down to the docks alone or with a stranger. You just can't."

*If I lost you, I would be lost,* she wanted to tell him.

He squirmed out of her grasp. "Mother, don't. Some of the other boys might see you."

"Of course," she said, rising from the ground. Her

son was growing up, and she wished for the days when he came running to her and threw himself into her open arms.

"Well, if I can't hug you, at least tell me how your lessons are going."

While Ethan launched into a long list of complaints about the additional studies the local reverend who tutored him had recently added, she looked at her son and saw him as if for the first time.

To her amazement she realized how much he looked like Julien. How had she never noticed it before? Probably because she hadn't wanted to see the amazing similarities.

But there was the way Julien walked, steady and sure, with a confidence born of generations of aristocrats. The flash of his green eyes as he told her about a recent visit to the Royal Observatory and how he'd been able to look through the telescope. And finally, his wide grin, so full of boyish charm.

Ethan had been *her* son for so long; now she realized he was as much Julien's as hers.

And if something happened to her, what would become of Ethan? Aunt Pettigrew couldn't live forever, and Ethan needed someone to see to his future.

If it came to it, she could only pray that Julien would offer his protection to his son. Beyond that there were Julien's sisters. Safe within the circle of the Weston and Trahern families, the Lord Admiral would never be able to harm the boy.

But until that day she couldn't let her son go.

She still had unfinished business with Ethan's father,

and she had to make sure that this time, if she were to trust Julien, it wouldn't end the way it had in the past.

Ethan's accounts were winding down, and Maureen smiled at her son. "What say you and I raid Mrs. Landon's turnovers again?"

The boy beat a speedy course up the path, with Maureen following close behind.

In her haste she didn't see the man slipping from between the buildings down the lane and heading quickly toward the docks.

# Chapter 18

For the next three days, Maureen didn't see hide nor hair of Julien.

As for her unscheduled trip to Greenwich, Lady Mary had been angry at Maureen's disappearance, but once she saw the faint bruise on Maureen's cheek, her outrage at the Lord Admiral's treatment outweighed any indignity over Maureen's unexplained outing.

However, the lady vowed that their social schedule must be maintained, and with the liberal use of an ointment and rice powder, Lady Mary was able to conceal the faint print of the Lord Admiral's fist on Maureen's face.

Throughout the social whirl, Maureen kept a strict vigil for Julien, but he was nowhere to be found. She could hardly ask as to his whereabouts without drawing attention to him, so she did what she would have done aboard ship.

She kept a steady watch.

Besides, he would have to appear at the Trahern masquerade, which was only a few days away. Of that she was sure.

Well, more like hopeful.

With the Lord Admiral's vow to see her hang growing closer to reality each day, she considered making a break for the coast and leaving England.

But then what would she do? There would still be a price on her head, and she could never see Ethan without endangering her son.

Even that option, as unlikely as it was, now appeared lost. The Lord Admiral, obviously sensing her unwillingness and possible flight, had doubled up his watch, making another escape from the Johnston house impossible.

He'd even added additional outriders to Lady Mary's carriage to ensure that Maureen didn't bolt from one of her social obligations.

Every night when they returned from their parties and balls, Maureen would take the steps to her attic room two at a time, hoping to find Julien there waiting for her, but all that ever greeted her was the empty chamber.

She hadn't given up hope that he would find a way to free her men and ship, but with each day she wondered if perhaps Julien D'Artiers's luck had finally run out.

And hers right along with it.

The night before Lady Trahern's masquerade, Maureen and Lady Mary arrived home early. Retiring to her room, Maureen unlatched her window, as she had done every night since the Weston ball, and slipped into her bed.

She didn't know what time it was when the shadowed figure crept through her window, but the creak in the floor brought her bolt upright, knife in hand.

He didn't say anything at first, just stood and stared at her. Clothed entirely in black, with the moon behind him, she couldn't see his features, but she knew it could be only one man.

*Julien.*

His tall figure towered at the foot of her bed, more a menace than the comfort she thought seeing him would be.

And when he spoke, a chill and anger rang from his voice like she'd never heard before, at least not from him.

"How long did you think you could keep your secret from me?"

Secret? she thought. What secret did she have from him? Then, as if on cue, a soft, haunting breeze whispered through the window, fluttering the meager curtains ever so softly. Gooseflesh broke out over her bare arms.

He took a step closer. "Tell me, Reenie, did you plan to ever tell me?"

She didn't say anything. What could she say? There was only one thing that would strike such a possessive, protective hard edge to his words.

"Ethan," she whispered. He'd discovered the truth about Ethan.

"Yes, dear wife. Our son. Ethan. I ask again, did you plan on ever telling me about him?"

Angry herself over his recent disappearance, she started to rise from the bed. She wore only her shift, so she yanked free one of the blankets from the bed and wrapped it around her before she faced him. "No. Not unless I had to."

"Unless you had to? What does that mean?"

"If . . . if all this didn't work," she shot back. "If in the end I went to the gallows. Then I planned to tell you. Or at least your family. Tell someone who could protect him."

He was quiet for too long. "And why wouldn't you have told me otherwise?"

She shook her head. "I didn't want to. Ethan is mine, Julien. He's all I have left in the world. I won't give him up."

"Did it ever occur to you that I would never ask you to?"

She glanced away.

When she didn't answer him, he continued. "I can't walk away from him. Not now that I know."

"Yes, you can. You walked away from me."

Silence filled the room again. He paced the few feet between the window and the door. "How was I to know you were alive? That you carried my child? I thought you were dead."

"And why did you think that?" she asked, sarcasm dripping from each word. "Could it be possible that it was a day of your own making that made you think me dead? A day you plotted and planned against my father?"

Obviously, he didn't like what he heard. He caught her in his arms and pulled her against his chest. "I made a mistake. Do you think there hasn't been a day since then that I haven't regretted it? That I haven't thought of you?" His fingers dug into her bare arms as if he'd never let her go. "That I haven't replayed that day in my mind a thousand times? That I haven't wished I could turn back time and change what happened?" He closed his eyes, and she watched his jaw tighten as if in pain, as if he were there once again.

"When I saw you . . ." His voice trailed off, then he abruptly set her aside. "But you lived. You and our son. Ethan." Julien took a deep breath. "Why didn't you send word? Once you found out. Once you knew. I would have come; I would have helped." His insistence was underlined by his anger for the years with Ethan she'd taken away from him.

"You'd helped enough at that point," she said. "And why should I have? I had no reason to trust you." It was her turn to pause. "I still don't."

She stepped past him to the single nightstand in the room. The darkness was unnerving her. His wrath seemed to fill the room, closing the tight space around her.

She lit a single taper, then turned around, wrapping the blanket tighter around her. The tiny yellow light illuminated the merest of circles, but it was enough for her to see him clearly.

His face seemed carved of stone, his fury pulling his mouth in a tight line, his hard-edged jaw set against her, and his eyes . . . she'd never seen a green so cold and impenetrable.

But the moment she stepped closer, his gaze flickered and his shoulders eased some of their bellicose stance. "What happened to your face?"

Her fingers went to the tender spot on her cheek. "Nothing. It was an accident. I slipped."

"You?" he scoffed. "You've never fallen in your life."

She turned from his searching gaze. "I'm not used to being ashore, that's all," she said over her shoulder. "I lost my bearings."

"You expect me to believe that, Reenie? Besides, I don't want any more lies between us." He stepped closer, his hand brushing hers aside while his fingers traced the edge of the bruise. "Who did this to you?"

She twisted away from his tender touch. "You know damned well who did it to me."

"Why didn't you send for me? Tell me about this?"

The concern in his voice edged at her own anger. "If you hadn't been gone for the last four days, I would have been able to tell you."

"So you thought I'd left you."

She shrugged, still unwilling to turn and face him. "Why wouldn't I? You promised to come to me, and you didn't. What was I to think? I have only the past to judge by."

He moved closer until he stood right behind her. His words whispered in her ear. "Never the past, Reenie. Haven't these last few days taught you that?"

She clamped her mouth shut, unwilling to tell him the truth: The past week had brought a change in her. One she didn't like. One she didn't want to trust.

"Perhaps," she finally conceded. "But what was I to

think? I've looked for you everywhere. I wanted to warn you—" She looked away.

"You wanted to warn me? Why is that, Reenie?"

"Not for the reasons you think," she said, annoyed at the way he kept twisting her words.

"Then why care about my welfare?"

She moved from him, putting the narrow bed between them, not so unlike the channel that had once separated the *Destiny* and the *Forgotten Lady*. "Your welfare is my welfare. You promised to see my men freed and get my ship back. I'm going to hold you to that, de Ryes. You owe me that much, if not a hell of a lot more."

"And what do you owe me for withholding my son from me for all these years?"

She laughed, a bitter, tight sound, even to her ears. "Ethan is mine. He has been from the moment you tossed me aside. Me and everything that was important to me." The ground beneath her felt more solid. If he thought to take her son away from her, he had another thing coming.

"I didn't toss you aside," he said, leaning across the narrow space. "If I recall correctly, you left of your own accord."

"Not before leaving you with a little memento," she shot back, fingering her knife.

He straightened and grinned at her. Then his hand went to the top button on his shirt. "Would you like to see the damage you wrought?" Slowly, he started to open his shirt, his grin changing to something else.

That smoldering look she remembered all to well.

Her legs started to quiver. Unwanted and unbidden, her memories rose up. She knew what she would see if he took his shirt off. The tanned, smooth planes of his chest, the thick, all too masculine muscles, the soft curls that ran from a triangle at the top of his chest down in a straight line to his—

Shaking her head, she turned away from him. "No, thank you. Since you lived, I obviously missed my mark. I was aiming for your heart." She glanced up at him, wishing her own wasn't hammering in her chest. She had to stop herself, stop him from believing that they had a future. Her words came out harsh and bitter. "I should have realized then that you didn't possess one."

He looked up at the ceiling. "How long are you going to continue punishing me for what happened that day, Reenie? Eight years? Eighty years? Forever?"

"And why shouldn't I?" she challenged, glad to be back to a subject where she could control her emotions. "You murdered my father. You took away everything. Did you think when I married you that I would go along with your plans? Or was that all part of your ruse? To pretend to love me to gain my father's trust and sponsorship?"

He shook his head. "No, Reenie. That wasn't what was supposed to happen. I never meant to fall in love with you. And I thought . . . I thought I could stop it all, or at least save your father and his ship. But I couldn't. I was so young and stupid. I thought I could stop even the fates. But it was too late, and only after I lost you did I realize how powerless a man is to stop destiny." He took her hand and looked directly in her eyes. "Can you tell me that you've never made a mistake in command? Never lost a man?"

She stared at him. "Not like that. I never betrayed anyone."

"What about yourself? Have you betrayed your own heart? Your own judgment?" he asked, stalking around the bed and closing in on her. "Why were you at Sheerness? Can you tell me that you were in control of your fate that night? It was folly to offload so large a cargo that near the shipping lanes. And well you knew it, or at least you should have."

"It wasn't like that at all." She backed up until she found herself imprisoned in a corner.

Cornered like she'd been at Sheerness.

"Then how was it?" he asked. "How could you have believed that you wouldn't be caught?"

He was right. Damn his rotten hide, he was right. She had risked everything that night. Her life, the lives of her crew, everything, all because she thought she could salvage what had become a costly mistake.

She closed her eyes, hoping to block out the memories.

"Tell me, Reenie," he said. "Did you make a mistake that night?"

She nodded. "A terrible one. I never should have taken that cargo. You're right, it was pure folly that found me there." She glanced back at him. "I haven't even youth to blame. I knew better."

He took her hand and led her to the bed, where she slumped down on the mattress. "What happened?"

She chewed at her upper lip. She hadn't spoken of

that night to anyone, and suddenly the need to tell her story bubbled forth.

"I took on a load of French brandy just south of Calais," she began, "and was about to depart when a merchant I'd never met asked me to ferry across a load of tea." She paused, the events and fateful memories flooding her senses. "I never take on cargo from someone I don't know or if I can't find someone to vouch for them. But this man was so insistent, and I had half a hold free. He claimed he was being pressed on all sides for gambling debts and if I would buy the tea, he'd let me have it at cost. He offered it so cheaply, all I could see were the profits. And then he told me of a 'merchant' in Sheerness who would pay ten times the going rate, since it was of such fine quality."

"So you took on the tea."

"Yes. It was too much money to pass up. Enough money to pay for Ethan to attend a boarding school, a good one, for the next year or two." She paused and looked up at him.

He sat down on the narrow bed beside her. "But you didn't feel right about it?"

She shook her head. "Every instinct told me to turn the man down. Something wasn't right. But there was that tea and an empty hold going to waste. I'd been crossing the Channel for several years without a mishap, and my men trusted me." Looking over at him, she suddenly saw that their situations weren't so different. "I thought if anything happened we could outrun it, or at the very least dump the load."

"But it didn't happen that way."

"No." She sighed. "The merchant's contact in

Sheerness wanted the tea brought in to shore all at once or else he wouldn't take it. He also wanted my crew to bring it in, claiming that his usual boys were busy elsewhere that night."

"Isn't that unusual?"

"Yes. But it was a moonless night. Dark as pitch. I figured we'd offload the tea and be gone before anyone saw us."

It should have worked that way, Maureen knew. She closed her eyes to the wretched memories—for when she and her men arrived at the beach, everything had gone terribly wrong.

*Suddenly, the darkness erupted into a hundred torches. Light illuminating their cover. Uniformed soldiers surging over the dunes, some on horseback and others on foot.*

*Shouts and orders to halt echoing across the beach. And then shots. So many shots.*

"Two of my men died there. On the beach. Shot down trying to get back to the *Retribution*. One of them only fifteen. He died in my arms, and after that I don't remember much. I was struck down, and when I awoke we were all in a cell." Her lips drew together. There had been many wounded men, men who sailed with her father. She'd tried her best to help them, encourage them, promise them she'd see them freed, but their eyes had told another story. Fed her guilt with the same foul taste as the bread and water they'd been offered by their guards.

Julien stretched his legs out in front of him. "So you made the deal with the Lord Admiral."

"Yes. At the time it was a perfect solution to two problems."

At this Julien grinned. "And now?"

"I was wrong, as wrong as I was to take that cargo. And again I've run out of time."

"Why is that?"

"Because if I don't turn you in by the stroke of midnight tomorrow, I'll hang in your place."

Julien shook his head. "You think I would let that happen?"

"It would give you Ethan."

"You said I haven't a heart. Reenie, I haven't one. I gave it to you years ago. You've held it all this time." He reached over and cradled her face in his hands. "Give it back to me with your trust, and I vow I will never break faith with you again. We can start over. We can put our mistakes in the past. I haven't been idle the last few days. I've found your men, and I plan on freeing them tomorrow night. And since you need a ship, I'll find a way to get back your *Retribution*. Then, if you want, we'll sail side by side, as we planned to all those years ago." He grinned, the pirate once again. "I've a prize in my sights that will satisfy even your greedy smuggler's desires."

"The payroll ship," she said aloud before she could stop herself.

This brought Julien to his feet. "How do you know about that?"

She looked up at him and knew she stood on a threshold. Perhaps she'd meant to tell him, knew it was time to tell him.

There was only one answer. One she gave with her heart.

"Because I overheard the Lord Admiral and Captain

Johnston talking." When his eyes grew wide with stunned disbelief, she continued. "The ship you want is the *Bodiel*, a packet bound for Halifax. It will be sailing alone out of Portsmouth at the end of the week."

Julien stared at her as if she couldn't possibly be telling the truth.

"Take the ship, Julien," she told him. "Ruin the Lord Admiral."

He knelt beside the bed, clasping her hands in his. "Aye, Reenie. I'll take it, but only with you at my side. We'll take it together." With that he brought her fingertips to his lips and kissed them, as if sealing his promise.

For a moment they stared at each other, their hands still bound together. His impassioned gaze told her he wanted much more than just a kiss. That he would erase the years between them this night and pledge a new beginning.

Maureen knew she was risking everything, allowing her heart to trust Julien again. But the risk seemed a small thing compared to her need for this man.

It seemed she couldn't escape her destiny.

# *Chapter 19*

Julien leaned forward and kissed his wife. His mouth covered the warmth of her lips; for the last eight years, all he'd had were haunting dreams of the only woman he could ever love.

*Maureen.*

Their kiss the other day in his carriage had been only a teasing glimpse into the past, and a hope for the future. But now, as she surrendered herself to him, offered him her trust, he wanted this night to go on forever.

For, as with his dreams, he feared waking and finding himself alone.

Her lips teased his, a soft sigh whispering his name. "Julien."

He reveled in the sound of it, and he pulled her closer. "I thought for so long that I'd lost you."

"I was lost," she told him. "Lost in anger and hatred and things that ate away at my soul."

"And now?"

She looked out the window. "I don't know. The past . . . how will I ever forget it?"

"You won't," he told her. "I haven't. I don't think I ever will." He drew her chin back so she looked directly at him. "Perhaps someday you'll see it in a different light. Your father's death was entirely my fault, but believe me, I tried everything I could to stop it. To save his life. If only . . ."

She pulled back and studied him, as if searching for more than just easy answers. "Was it like you said, did you try to stop it?"

He nodded, unwilling to say any more. How could he change her vision of the past? Words wouldn't do it, at least not from him. She was a stubborn woman, and her forgiveness would have to come from her heart, for her eyes would never see the past in any other light than what she'd witnessed in those few brief moments that had changed their lives irreparably.

"I'm so sorry, Reenie. Your father was a good man and a fine captain. His death was my fault. I truly never thought he'd die that day. I thought—"

"Sshh," she told him, pressing a finger to his lips. "I believe you. I have to. I can't live my life anymore with this emptiness." She paused for a moment, her eyes taking on a faraway gaze. "I just wish . . ."

He knew what she wished. That her father hadn't died. That they'd been able to live the life they'd only glimpsed in the few short hours they'd had together.

But there was nothing he could do to change the past. "From here on, Reenie, we chart a new course together. We'll explore it like an open sea. We'll share it with Ethan. Share it, Reenie. He's your son, first and foremost, but all I ask is for a chance to get to know him."

Maureen laid her head on his shoulder. "Ethan would like that. He needs a father. And family. He's never had anyone else but me and Aunt Pettigrew."

*Family!* He hadn't thought about that. How would he tell his family that he had not only a wife, but a seven-year-old son? He started to chuckle.

"What's so funny?" she asked.

"My sisters will have my hide when I bring you and Ethan home."

"I like them," Maureen told him. "They were kind to Lady Mary."

"My sisters?" He shuddered. "Sophia and Lily are the two worst busybodies who've ever stalked the face of the earth. They learned their lessons at the feet of a master, my Aunt Dearsley."

"Tell me more."

"Not now," he said. "We'll have plenty of time ahead of us to discuss my family. Wouldn't you rather talk about something else?" He nuzzled her neck. "I know for a fact that there is a fine tradition of leaving one's window open for your husband, and it isn't so he can chatter the night away about his harridan sisters."

"Ah, yes, the window," she said, her fingers brushing over his shoulders, her touch light and tantalizing. "I almost forgot. I did leave that open for you."

"And why was that, Reenie?"

"As I said before, because I wanted to warn you." Her voice carried the hint of a wishful dream. As she realized what she was admitting, she glanced away.

"And is that the only reason? Just to warn me?"

She shook her head softly. Turning toward him, she let the blanket she'd worn like a shield fall away, leaving her clad only in her shift.

In the candlelight, her soft, fair skin glowed. His fingers traced over her shoulders, tangling in the strands of dark silken hair that lay there in thick coils. He'd loved the feel of her hair from the first moment he'd touched it on the *Forgotten Lady*. Like silk. Thick and dark. So black, it held all the mysteries of a moonless night.

For a moment he just let it fall through his fingers, slowly moving each lock until he'd bared her shoulders.

Then he slowly eased the straps of her shift down, baring even more of her fair skin.

The sight and touch of her drew him closer. He nuzzled her neck, kissing and nibbling every inch, while his hands continued to ply through her long hair.

She arched, pressing herself closer. "Make me your wife again, Julien. Make me feel alive."

He kissed the hollow of her neck, the edge of her collarbone, and down to the tops of her rounded breasts. His hand at her hip, roamed upward, pushing the fabric along, tracing a path until it came to the rising peak of her nipple.

Brushing her slip up and over her head, he sighed as he saw her again, anew, for the first time in so long.

She was even more exquisite, the lush ripeness of her body having matured over the last eight years.

He kissed her, drawing her mouth to his, drowning

his needs in her soft sighs. Her lips teased his, opened to his, drew him closer.

"Julien," she whispered in a throaty moan, "I want so much more." She tugged at his shirt and pulled it over his head.

For a moment he paused, letting her touch him as he had touched her. She stroked his chest, ran her hands over his shoulders, as if reacquainting herself with every muscle, every line. Then he remembered, remembered the one thing he didn't want her to know, so he leaned forward and blew out the light, plunging them into darkness.

It would be so easy to prove to her how sincerely sorry he was about the past. To show her the proof of his claims. But that seemed too easy. He wanted her to come to him because she'd found the way on her own.

"When did you become so shy?" she teased, her hands on the waistband of his breeches.

"Hardly that with you as my wife," he said. "But the light may draw attention from the servants or the guards below."

She glanced at the door and the window. "I'd hate to be interrupted."

"My thoughts exactly," he told her, pulling her to her feet and allowing her to ease his breeches off. They stood together, with only their sense of touch, exploring each other's body anew.

Hips brushing together, her breasts softly leaning into his chest, her leg winding around his so her thigh edged against him.

Slowly, their eyes adjusted to the meager light

floating in from the window, until he could easily see the dusky passion in her eyes.

He kissed her again, this time deeper and with a rush of need. When he pulled back for air, he felt like a man deprived for years, insatiable in his need for her. He needed to kiss her everywhere, taste her, feel her.

With his hands cradling her breasts, he used his lips to tease and suckle first one, then the other nipple to a fevered peak. She arched and moaned under his touch, while her hands steadied herself on his shoulders.

He let one hand dip lower, slowly parting the curls below, stroking the heated place between her legs.

Maureen writhed under his touch, lost in the first waves of a passion she never thought she'd know again.

"Julien," she whispered over and over.

It was as if he'd never forgotten her body and how it answered to his touch.

Then he taught her something new. He knelt before her, his mouth closing over the spot where his fingers had been.

Before she realized exactly what he was going to do, his tongue teased open the feminine folds and then lapped at her with an intimacy so intense she found herself gasping.

She rose up on her tiptoes, her breath having stopped in her throat, her mouth gaping, her hands gripping the nightstand behind her to steady herself. "Oh, Julien, what is this?"

He looked up. "Steady now, Reenie. Let me love you."

As he began anew to kiss her so sweetly, her eyes

closed and she gave over to the delicious sensations. His mouth closed over her, suckling her, opening her further, drawing from her waves of desire. Her hips moved with him, dancing in cadence to his sensual call.

When she didn't think she could take the sweet torture of it any further, her release came, catching her unaware, shuddering through her body. It was all she could do not to call out, let free a siren's cry equal to the sensations he'd brought out in her.

Just as quickly, Julien held her in his arms, cradling her, laying her onto the bed, and holding her through the delicious aftermath.

She lay there, spent and dreamy.

"Did you like that, Reenie?" he asked, kissing her ear and running his fingers through her hair. "Did that make you feel alive?"

"Uh-huh," she managed to murmur.

He laughed softly, and for a time he held her in his arms and stroked her passion-heated skin.

Eventually she rolled toward him. "Why didn't you teach me that before?"

He smiled and shrugged. "You can't expect a man to give away all his tricks in one night, now, can you?"

"You have any more tricks you care to share?"

"Greedy girl," he said, kissing her deeply.

Her hands roamed over his back, recalling every muscle, every line, until she came to something she didn't remember: Her fingers traced a ragged scar, wide and deep, as if it had been burned into his flesh.

She strained to look over his shoulder. "What happened here?"

He pulled her away. " 'Tis nothing. I just got hit by a bit of falling timber last year during a fight. Really, it was nothing."

Before she could ask anything further, he was kissing her, reawakening her passions. However, this time she was determined that she wouldn't be alone in finding release.

He wasn't the only one with a trick or two to share.

. She kissed him back, hard and hungry. Her hand trailed down his chest until she found his manhood, aroused and waiting for her. Wetting her fingers with her mouth, she stroked the length with long, languid motions. Her toe traced a line up and down his leg, so her thigh rubbed against his. She wanted him to feel the same aching need that he'd unleashed in her.

Then she wanted him to be overcome by it, succumb to it. Let it take him over the edge.

A throaty growl issued from his throat, making her smile. She continued to stroke him while her lips sought his, teasing his tongue. It was definitely Julien's turn to writhe beneath her touch.

When she knew he was close, she let go of him and kissed him deeply. Then, catching him by surprise, she rolled on top of him, drawing the tip of his manhood inside her, moving over him with a slow rocking motion until he was encased within her.

She worked the rhythm of her movements like the cadence of waves on a beach. Fast and steady, then backing off and riding him with a slow, easy pace that kept him just at the brink.

His breathing became irregular, as if he couldn't find enough air in the room.

She knew how he felt, for even as she worked her own brand of magic on him, she found herself caught in the passionate web building between them.

His hips rose to meet hers, thrusting deeper into her, rubbing against her and drawing from her the same waves of longing. He wanted his release, and he was charting a course to take them both there together.

His thumb moved over the spot where their bodies joined and added an additional friction to her rising needs, and then he made one last thrust into her, deep and full of his pent-up need for her.

Like the crash of thunder, the ragged cry of a sea-bird, the release they both craved came over them. It pounded over their senses, leaving them staring into each other's eyes with a sense of awe and wonderment.

Julien's arms wrapped around her, drawing her down on his chest, so their bodies rocked together through the last vestiges of the storm.

Eventually, the stillness of the night surrounded them, cradling them in their own world. When they finally spoke, it was of their future, of Ethan, and of what they would do once the war ended.

It seemed to Maureen that in this night she'd redis-covered life, found a new beginning.

Renewed what had been lost for too long.

*Her heart. Her soul.*

"Ah, Reenie," Julien finally said. "Where the devil did you learn those tricks?"

She was almost too embarrassed to tell him.

He rolled on top of her, tickling her. "Don't tell me you've got a lover hidden in one of your smuggler's hideaways?"

Her mouth opened wide in outrage. "I certainly have not."

"Come on, tell the truth," he said, his fingers teasing her sides until she couldn't help but giggle.

"Stop, stop," she said. "I'll tell you."

He paused, poised over her. "So?"

"I'm a smuggler, and sometimes I don't always carry tea and sugar."

"I don't understand," he said.

"I make runs from France all the time. One time I got a load of books."

"Books?" he said, his eyebrows rising. "What type of books?"

"Books with pictures," she said, feeling a hot blush rise on her cheeks.

"What sort of pictures?"

"Pictures the likes of which I'd never seen." Or thought possible, she realized, until tonight.

He laughed softly. "I can well imagine. What did you do with them?"

"Sold them, of course. You wouldn't believe what they fetched. Better profits than brandy or silk."

"I can imagine," he said. "Did you keep a volume for yourself?"

She grinned. "No, but I have an amazing memory."

"Do tell," he teased.

And so she did.

# Chapter 20

The afternoon of the Trahern masquerade, Lady Mary was in a high state about their costumes. Since the Lord Admiral had all but cut off any more expenses associated with Maureen, the lady was forced to make do with what she could.

Maureen had told her not to fret so much over the costume, for it mattered little what she wore, considering the fact that after tonight she would be free of London and the Lord Admiral's demands.

Her night with Julien had set her free. Free of the past, free to live her future. She hadn't minded in the least when he'd crept out her window at the first light of dawn. She knew their night was just the beginning of a new life for both of them. One they would start in just a few hours.

And she couldn't wait.

But Lady Mary would hear none of her protests.

She stitched tirelessly, consulting Lucy and digging through trunks and clothes presses, stealing the bits of trim and fabric she needed to complete her designs.

With Maureen's dark hair, the lady had decided the perfect choice for her would be to attend as Cleopatra, a choice Maureen protested vehemently. Lady Mary continued blithely on her course and, with Lucy's help, completed the incredible costume about two hours before the ball began.

As the lady laid out the beautiful creation on the narrow attic bed, Maureen could only stare dumbstruck at the costume she was to wear.

A sheer white muslin would drape from her shoulders to the floor, leaving her arms entirely bare. The neckline plunged deeply, trimmed with a gold cord that looked suspiciously like it belonged on a naval uniform. An Egyptian-styled motif had been embroidered around the hemline.

For her hair, a gold coronet shaped like an asp had been fashioned from silk. The fabric shimmered as if it were truly a precious metal. An elaborate mask with paste jewels and peacock feathers completed the ensemble.

"How did you do this?" Maureen asked, since her own sewing skills were limited to repairing sails and an occasional ill-fitting patch for her trousers.

Lady Mary smiled. "I suppose the 'economies' of having William on half pay for so long have finally paid off. I've been redoing my gowns and William's uniforms for nearly thirty years. I suppose you could say I've picked up a thing or two."

A thing or two? The lady was being entirely too modest.

"I shouldn't wear this," Maureen said. "Even you've told me that a young lady's dress should never be daring. And this . . ." Maureen looked down at the costume again. "Why, I'll draw too much attention."

"This is exactly why you will wear it," Lady Mary snapped. "Maureen, this dress may well save your life. If you create a huge sensation tonight, the Lord Admiral wouldn't dare hang you. How will he explain your disappearance?" The lady looked back down at her creation. "He won't be able to. So he will have to leave you alone, especially if you gain the protection of someone. A man with the power to shelter you." The lady held up the dress before Maureen. "What you need to do tonight is find someone to propose marriage."

Maureen stared at her "godmother" as if the woman had finally fallen completely prey to her own fantasies.

"You want me to find a husband? In one night?" She hoped she didn't have to tell the lady that she already had one, and look at all the trouble he'd caused her! But another one? Hardly.

"It's been done before," Lady Mary said with the assurance of one who thought it quite likely. "Very successfully, mind you. And by young ladies with half your beauty."

"But it won't be—" Maureen started to say, but she stopped herself as she saw the disappointment lining the lady's mouth. She'd gone to so much work to help

Maureen in the only way she knew how; how could Maureen dash her dreams? Instead, she picked up the mask and looked at the delicate stitchwork around the edges.

It won't be necessary, she wanted to tell her. I'll be gone at midnight, and you won't have to worry about the Lord Admiral ever harming me again. But that would only distress her guardian even further, so the less said, Maureen reasoned, the better.

"Oh, you don't think it will be possible wearing the mask," Lady Mary finished. "That is why you will wear your hair unbound. No one will mistake you for anyone else." She smiled and shooed Lucy into action.

In no time Maureen found herself staring into the hallway mirror, unsure of who the mysterious lady in the reflection could be.

Surely, not her!

Lady Mary's promise of a transformation meant to captivate hadn't been a boast—Maureen barely recognized herself. If the Trahern masquerade was meant to be a night of illusion, then Lady Mary had completed the task admirably.

Maureen wondered what Julien would think of her disguise. This costume hardly fit his recommendation to wear something that she could slip away in unnoticed. The gold thread caught the light and one's eye with its flickering cast. The paste gems in the mask sparkled as if they had been dug from the ancient queen's tomb.

Even dressed as she had been of late in the current English fashions, she hadn't felt so . . . naked. She'd never seen herself as a woman before, not in the way she looked now. She wondered if the fabled temptress of the Nile had ever felt so wicked.

Oh, Julien would have a fit for her to be out in public dressed so. And that, she knew, would have its own rewards later.

She grinned to herself, thinking of their night together, of the vows they'd renewed, of their future.

The bell over the door jangled loudly, startling her out of her daydreams. She could hear Lady Mary and Lucy holding a loud discussion in the kitchen over the ironing, while the Captain seemed to have disappeared into his study. None of them seemed to notice the bell as it jangled a second time, so Maureen opened the door.

To her complete shock, there stood a disheveled and grief-stricken Mrs. Landon.

"Oh, Miss Maureen," the lady cried, "I found you." She rushed forward and crushed Maureen in her ample embrace. "I was so frightened, and I didn't know where else to go."

"Come inside, Mrs. Landon," Maureen told her, drawing the woman in from the front steps. The last thing she wanted was the Lord Admiral's guards to overhear anything the distressed lady might blurt out. She closed the door and led her to the small office Lady Mary kept off the front hallway.

"What has happened?" Maureen asked. "Is it my aunt? Ethan? Are they hurt? Sick?"

"Oh, if only it were so!" Mrs. Landon wailed as she collapsed into a chair. The lady dissolved into a deluge of tears, pulling her ever-present apron up to her face to cover her anguish.

"Mrs. Landon, what is it?" Maureen asked, kneeling before the woman and pulling away her apron. She looked directly into the housekeeper's watery eyes. "You must tell me, so I can help."

"Oh, there's no help to be had!" the lady cried.

"How is that?"

"They've taken away our dear boy."

Maureen's breath froze. "Ethan?"

The lady nodded.

"Was it a press gang?"

"No," Mrs. Landon said. "It couldn't be. They came to the house with a carriage, and before I knew what was happening they took . . ."

"They took Ethan," Maureen finished for her when it seemed the lady could not utter another word of it.

Mrs. Landon nodded, new tears welling up in her eyes.

"Did they harm Aunt Pettigrew?" Maureen couldn't imagine her aunt allowing anyone to take Ethan without putting up a fight. The lady might be in her eighties and like to play the infirm, but Maureen knew well enough that Aunt Pettigrew was still cast of iron.

"That's the puzzle, miss, and why I came to you," Mrs. Landon said. "They took your aunt as well."

With Lady Mary and Lucy still engaged in the kitchen, Maureen was able to sneak Mrs. Landon upstairs to her attic room. For the better part of the next half hour, Maureen carefully extracted the complete story from the distraught woman.

The housekeeper had been out doing some shopping in town. When she returned she noticed a black carriage parked in the lane. As she drew closer she saw three men coming out of the house. Two were dragging Aunt Pettigrew, while the third had a trussed-up Ethan slung over his shoulder like a bale of cotton.

Mrs. Landon had shrunk back into the alley and watched in horror as her employer and young charge were tossed into the carriage and driven away posthaste.

Maureen knew she had little time before Lady Mary would be calling her downstairs to depart for the Trahern masquerade. Instead of alerting anyone to the lady's untimely arrival, Maureen instructed Mrs. Landon to wait for her in the attic room.

Stalking down the stairs, Maureen knew she'd been deceived.

*Dammit, how could I have been so blind?* she cursed.

There was only one man who knew of Ethan's existence. Only one man who would have wanted her son.

*Julien.*

They'd agreed to leave Ethan at Aunt Pettigrew's for the time being. It would be safer for their son to be in England rather than sailing the seas with them. Julien had said he would set up an account for Aunt Pettigrew and send his solicitor instructions to see to the lad's future in case their plans went awry.

Lies, all of it lies, she realized. He'd never intended to see any of it through.

Instead, he'd betrayed her again with the same ease and charm as he had all those years ago. Before she reached the bottom of the steps, that fateful day, eight years past, replayed in her mind.

A painful reminder of lessons learned and lessons so easily forgotten.

# Chapter 21

Maureen awoke from her wedding night to the sound of thunder. She bolted upright in the strange bed, disoriented by her unfamiliar surroundings and the echoing retort of the brewing storm.

She turned over and found the space beside her empty. Her hand went to where Julien had been, but the sheets were cold, as if her languid memories of the night before were just a dream.

Again, a mighty thunderous clap boomed from the heavens, rocketing through the cabin, shaking the ship from stem to stern. But this time Maureen realized it wasn't thunder.

It was cannon.

They were under attack.

She leapt out of bed and to the door, ready to take

her place beside her husband, but she realized she was still naked. She ripped through the cabin, opening chests and drawers until she found a shirt and breeches, all the while listening to the growing battle outside.

As she looked for a weapon, her gaze glanced past the window. She stopped her frantic search and stood as if frozen in the middle of the mayhem of Julien's now thoroughly ransacked cabin.

Beneath her feet, the slope of the deck and the pitch of the floor told her that the *Destiny* was maneuvering to join the battle. But what stopped Maureen was the direction the ship was taking.

Out the great windows of the cabin, she saw her father's ship and his fellow Alliance members trapped in the cay's inlet. Yet the *Destiny* wasn't turning to aid them; it was turning to join the line of ships bottling up the mouth to the bay, blocking any escape for the Alliance ships.

Including the *Forgotten Lady*.

She pressed her nose to the glass and caught sight of several ships firing at the trapped pirates. Over each of these fluttered the Union Jack.

The British! There had been rumors of late of an organized hunt to stop the Alliance, but there had been such rumors for as long as she could remember.

Now it seemed the rumors were true, and they'd been betrayed.

Betrayed by her husband.

She looked at the offensive being mounted and spied three frigates and a ship of the line, at least a three-rater, she judged. While the Alliance had them outnumbered, their positions in the shallow water left them prey to the British, who could maneuver easily in the deeper waters of the channel.

And now the British could add the fleet *Destiny* to their number.

Then she remembered what she'd seen the night before—a lone sailor rowing out of the bay. Julien had joked that the man had been going to find his own true love, but she suspected now that the sailor had been sent to tell the British where to find the Alliance.

And later, when she'd thought the ship had come adrift, he'd distracted her, kept her from discovering the truth.

She flew to the door and tried to open it, only to find it locked. Infuriated, she searched the room again—this time for a weapon. There wasn't a pistol, dirk, or sword anywhere in the room that could be used to open the door.

It was almost as if Julien had planned everything, right down to the last detail.

Yanking open the last chest, she overturned it, spilling the contents of shirts and linens. Falling to the floor, she tossed the contents this way and that, hoping to find something he had missed. Then, when she was about to give up, she spied her salvation.

The dagger from Julien's pirate costume. He'd tossed it aside last night and hadn't noticed it this morning, hidden as it was under the table.

Her hand wrapped around the horn hilt, and for a moment she contemplated what to do.

There would be no opening the sturdy oak door with the wicked blade, of that she was sure, but there remained one avenue of escape.

The window.

The window her husband had climbed through to join her in their wedding bed.

If she had any sentiments about that evening before, they quickly evaporated. The room that had seemed her own piece of tempting heaven last night was now nothing more than a prison cell from which she could watch Julien's version of hell.

She went to the casement but found it, too, was locked, probably latched somehow from the outside. Frustrated but unwilling to admit defeat, Maureen picked up the empty chest and hurled it through the ornate glass.

It shattered the panes, opening the cabin to the acrid stench of gunpowder and flames. She slipped through the jagged opening and caught a rope hanging from the stern. With the dagger tucked in her belt, she climbed hand over hand up the rope through the smoke.

Once she made it over the railing, it took her a moment to get her bearings in the apparent chaos of the battle. But Maureen had been in battles before and immediately discerned the tight organization with which Julien's men worked.

*Now to find my traitorous husband,* she thought, the dagger clenched in her hand.

The cannon from the closest English ship exploded with a hail of fire, the shot flying through the air in precise order. She watched the deadly spray of iron balls broadside the *Forgotten Lady,* opening her to the sea and soon, destruction. The once proud and beautiful ship listed precariously to one side, while flames licked and grew near the waterline.

Near where they'd stowed the Portuguese munitions they'd taken.

"No," she muttered. If she didn't warn her father soon, their ship would explode.

Revenge could come later.

As she climbed up on the railing to dive into the waters below, a pair of hands caught her around the waist and snatched her back from the rail.

"Reenie," Julien shouted at her over the raging din around them. Just then a round of answering shot whistled toward them. He threw her to the deck, knocking the wind from her and sending her dagger clattering across the debris-strewn planks. He lay over her protectively, as a second round swept over them. "Watch yourself. We are about to come about."

"You bastard," she spat. "You murdering, lying bastard." She struggled against his grip, but he held her down, sheltering her from the falling debris showering down around them. "You told them. You told them where we were. The only reason you came to us was to find us. To betray us."

"No, it's not like that. I tried to warn your father, but it was too late. The tide turned; they couldn't get out."

She wouldn't hear his lies. Never again would she believe another word he said. She struggled anew to get him off her. "Let me go. I won't stay here."

He shook his head. "I won't let you go. There's still a chance . . . but I need your help."

"My help?" she said, incensed that he would even think she would help him betray her father. "The only help you'll get from me is to send you to hell."

"You don't understand," he said, shaking her. "I don't have time to explain; you have to trust me."

*Trust him?* She'd show him a measure of his own brand of trust.

Feigning despair, she let her head loll to one side, faking the tears and wails of a woman unable to stop the inevitable.

He fell for her deception, as she had believed in his, and relaxed his grip.

The instant he did, she drew up her knee and caught him hard in the groin.

He rolled away, groaning and swearing. She was on her feet before he could stop her. She drew back her foot and kicked him in the ribs. "Why, de Ryes? Why did you do this to us?" she said, kicking him over and over.

But her husband wasn't a man to give up. His hand snaked out and caught her foot, pulling her legs out from beneath her and sending her crashing to the deck.

The force of her fall stunned her for a moment. A sweet, metallic taste filled her mouth. She spat on the deck, only to find that it was blood.

Not far away she saw Captain Smyth's ship take the final pounding of cannon that reduced it to flames and shards. His men were either diving for safety or floating ashore, dead. The other Alliance ships were in the same condition, with only the *Avenger* and the *Forgotten Lady* still afloat and able to fight.

Then, before her eyes, the *Avenger*'s magazine exploded, the sound deafening. Even as the last echoing retort faded, the victorious cries from the British lines haunted her stunned ears.

Now the British had one remaining target to sink. And from the look of the *Forgotten Lady*, it would take only a few more rounds before she, too, would be at the bottom of the inlet, or lost in the wrathful fire like the *Avenger*.

She turned away from the slaughter before her. She'd never get off the *Destiny* in time to save her father. She could fight all she wanted, but in the end, she knew Julien had the advantage of size, strength, and the backing of his crew.

As she turned her head to see where he'd moved to, a glint of steel caught her eye.

Her dagger.

She might be alone in this final battle, but she was not unarmed. At least she could take Julien and a few of his men with her before she died.

She grabbed the dagger, a surge of renewed will coursing through her. Now it was Julien's turn to taste the bitter bile of betrayal.

For a moment he seemed to have forgotten her; there was a fire on the deck and he was shouting orders to have it put out. One of the masts was broken, and the shards and lines littered the deck.

She crept through the wreckage, her gaze never leaving his back. As she gained her vantage point, she raised her dagger to strike a mortal blow.

"Captain, behind ye," one of his men shouted as her arm arced down.

Julien stepped back as he spun around, so instead of cutting to his black heart, she sliced through his shirt and left a thin line of blood down his chest.

Before she could attack him again, a pistol retorted,

the bullet catching her in the shoulder. The dagger fell from her hand as the burning sting of hot lead ripped across her shoulder blade.

"Don't shoot," Julien shouted to his men. "Leave her be. She doesn't understand."

She staggered a step or two backward, stunned by the intense pain burning through her arm. Her blurry gaze caught sight of a man's face.

Julien's—his features a mixture of grief and concern.

Lies. All lies, she told herself, reaching for her fallen dagger, now holding it in her left hand. It wavered back and forth, as unsteady as her senses.

Julien moved closer to her, looming large and dangerous.

She was losing blood, for her shirt was soaked, and the effects were leaving her unsteady. She backed away from him until she found herself pinned to the railing.

Over her shoulder she spied her father's ship. It was still listing but hadn't exploded. Where the *Avenger* had been moored there was nothing but a burning shell.

She'd never stop Julien, but there was still time to join her father . . . even if it was in death.

Catching hold of a line, she swung herself up onto the railing.

"Reenie, no!" Julien cried out. "Don't jump. Please don't jump. Let me explain."

She teetered on the railing, dagger in one hand, the other clutching the rigging. She hoped he could see the hatred in her eyes.

Seething, searing hatred, as hot as the shot that had ripped open her flesh.

"Don't do this," he told her, as he slowly moved toward her. "Let me explain what is happening here."

She didn't need him to tell her what was happening; she could see well enough: The *Destiny* was moving between the two frigates to join them in the final destruction of the *Forgotten Lady*.

"Steady men," Julien called out. "Hold your fire until we can make it count."

*Make it count?*

There was nothing more she wanted to hear from him, nothing more she could do but hope his double-crossing soul found a special place in hell.

And very soon.

As he sprang forward to stop her, she dove into the churning water.

# Chapter 22

*The Trahern Masquerade*
*London*
*1813*

Maureen had no choice but to proceed with the night's events and go with Lady Mary to the Trahern masquerade ball—though the evening would hardly be what she and Julien had planned not twenty-four hours earlier.

Anger at his betrayal left her shaking with fury. He'd done it again.

No, she vowed to herself, not again. This time Julien would finally take his rightful place before the hangman and then in hell.

She entered the room, head held high, stalking past the footman as if she truly were the Queen of the Nile.

A hush of silence moved over the room like a wave rippling across a pond. All eyes turned to see the latest arrival, and Maureen was now more than willing to play the part.

The stilled voices quickly turned into a gaggle of excitement and speculations as to the real identity of Cleopatra.

Lady Mary had chosen to enter a few minutes behind Maureen. "It will add to the drama of the moment," the lady had told her in the carriage.

Maureen wondered if perhaps a little less drama would have been better, for immediately she was swamped with would-be beaux. She could hardly find the Lord Admiral, let alone finish her plans for Julien, hemmed in as she was by the eager young bloods of the *ton.*

If only the lying son of a bitch would show his face. Her hand brushed over her skirt where her dagger lay hidden. Then she could finish this the way she preferred.

Face to face.

Not that she expected him to appear tonight.

No, if her suspicions were correct, more than likely he'd taken Ethan and headed to the coast, where he kept the *Destiny* hidden. Why he'd taken Aunt Pettigrew was a complete mystery, but she wouldn't put it past him to harm a defenseless old woman just to carry out his own twisted plans.

What she needed now was to find the Lord Admiral so she could reveal Julien's true identity as well as his scheme for the *Bodiel.* Then she'd make her own escape and finish the plans he'd explained to her last night, which would enable her to free her crew before first light.

There was no reason to believe she couldn't do it alone. With any measure of luck, she'd be down the Thames on the *Retribution* before the Lord Admiral was aware of her duplicity.

And if the Royal Navy didn't beat her to the task, she'd find the *Destiny* and retrieve her son. Then she'd finish Julien D'Artiers in the only way fitting.

Let him wake up with sand in his ears. At the bottom of the Atlantic.

Through the melee, a man dressed as a pirate parted a path and caught her by the arm. "Beloved Queen," he said, with a low, courtly bow. "May I bask in your elegant shadow for a moment?"

Lord Hawksbury. Maureen would have recognized his voice anywhere. Maureen gave the man a regal nod of acceptance. Perhaps he knew where his uncle was.

Behind the man's black mask, his eyes glittered with the same green as Julien's. "Would it be beyond my humble station to ask the legendary temptress of the Nile for a dance?"

Again Maureen nodded. At least on the dance floor she would have a better survey of the room from which to spot the Lord Admiral or, at the very least, Eustacia.

The swarthy pirate took her arm and led her through the crowd to the dance floor. They took their places in the set, and the music began. All throughout the dance she searched the room for the tall, imposing figure of the Lord Admiral, but it wasn't until the very last strains that she spied him all the way across the room. He turned and looked in her direction, so she lifted up her mask to reveal her identity.

The man nodded at her and cocked a finger, as if to summon her to his side.

She all but forgot her partner, trying to discern the best way to negotiate the crowd between them.

The young Earl, it seemed, had other plans for her. He maneuvered her to the edge of the crowd, and then, before she could thank him for the dance and cross the room, he caught her by the arm and pulled her onto a balcony.

"My lord, let go—" she started to protest, turning from the locked door to Julien's overly attentive nephew.

But she found herself no longer facing the Earl of Hawksbury. Dressed in identical outfits, somehow uncle and nephew had switched places in the confusion after the dance.

*Julien.* He'd actually dared to come to her.

Of all the devilish, rotten arrogance, she thought.

"How was that for outmaneuvering the Lord Admiral?" he asked, his tone implying that nothing had changed between them.

She stared at him in disbelief.

What more could he want from her? He had the information on the payroll ship, as well as Ethan. Why had he come? To gloat? To mock her?

She didn't care. He'd underestimated her for the last time. As far as she was concerned, he was here to die.

"I thought we could slip away now, before that devil Cottwell spies you." He glanced over her shoulder, back into the room beyond. "What were you thinking, wearing that outlandish costume? Don't you remember what we agreed on—something you could climb in?" He shrugged and turned to consider the ledge beneath them, as well as the latticework that supported the climbing vines edging up the side of the stone house. "If you were anyone else, I'd fear you'd break your neck going down this ledge, but you know best what you can manage, and if you think you can in that gown, then . . ."

His words trailed off as he turned back to her.

In the time he'd spent blithely continuing as if they truly had a future together, she'd retrieved her dagger and now pressed it to his throat.

Beneath his pirate's mask his eyes narrowed. "What mischief is this, Reenie? We haven't time to waste."

"You haven't any time left, you double-dealing bastard," she said, rearing back with the knife.

Julien reacted without even thinking. He sidestepped her attack and caught her arm just above the fist. Using her momentum, he swung her around so now her own dagger rested against her neck.

Beneath the steel he could see her pulse fluttering wildly. Her eyes were just as untamed, feral almost, like those of a rabid animal, unseeing and uncaring for anything.

"Kill me, Julien," she spat out. "Kill me now. For I swear if you let me go, I will not stop until I see you take your last breath."

"What are you talking about?" he asked. "Reenie, tell me what is wrong."

"You know bloody well what is wrong! Did you think I wouldn't find out about Ethan? Or my aunt? How could you?" She glared up at him. "If you've harmed either of them, I'll not give you any measure of mercy."

"I can see that," he said, trying to make sense of her wild accusations. "Now, what is this of Ethan and your aunt? Has something happened to them?"

She made a rude noise in the back of her throat. "As if you don't know. I'll not listen to your lies anymore. Tell me they are safe, then finish me off, if that is what you mean to do."

"I'm not going to kill you, Reenie," he said, pulling back the knife and pushing her across the balcony, out of range and with enough distance between them that he could watch her every move. "Dammit, I love you. Or didn't last night prove anything?"

"It proved I'm a bigger fool than I was eight years ago." Her unbound hair fell about her shoulders in a wild disarray. For a moment he thought himself faced not with the noble leader of ancient Egypt, but of one of England's ancient warrior queens. As wild and untamed as the barbarians they'd led.

Something had obviously gone terribly wrong, something to do with Ethan and her aunt, and now she blamed him. He'd lost the trust he'd so carefully rebuilt between them, but he wasn't about to give up just yet.

He took a deep breath and held out the dagger, pointing the hilt toward her. "Take this. And then tell me what I have supposedly done."

She regarded him warily, then snatched the blade out of his hand. "While you may have been able to kidnap Ethan and my aunt, your henchmen didn't notice the housekeeper. She told me everything. How you stole my son away—"

He held up his hand to stave off any further accusations. "I kidnapped Ethan?"

"Yes. Don't try and deny it."

"Well, I will. I didn't do it. We agreed to keep Ethan here in England. If what you say is true, we have to find out who's stolen our son."

"I don't need to look any further than right here."

Julien ignored the dagger in her hand and stalked across the balcony. He caught her by the shoulders and gave her a good shake. "Listen to me, Reenie. I didn't do this. If it is true, we have to find Ethan and find him fast. Who could have done this? Who else knows about us? Knows about Ethan?"

"No one," she said, fighting off his grasp. She edged past him. "No one but you."

"Someone does. Someone who means to use him against us."

She swiped at the tendrils of dark hair falling over her face. "There is no *us*. Why do you persist in these falsehoods? I don't believe you any longer. You took my son, and I want him back."

She once again flashed her dagger dangerously between them.

"Why would I be here if I took Ethan? If I'd had any inclination to take my son, I certainly wouldn't be here—I'd be halfway to the coast by now."

He could see the questions fluttering behind her gaze, as if she, too, had asked herself the same things. But she was beyond making sense; her anger from the past clouding her judgment. Just then a movement over her shoulder caught his eye.

Someone was approaching the balcony, cutting a sharp course through the costumed crowd like a frigate under full sail.

*The Lord Admiral.*

Oh, perfect, Julien thought to himself. With Maureen going off half-cocked, he hadn't enough time to make her see the sense of his words before she'd have a noose around his neck, courtesy of Peter Cottwell.

There was only one thing to do, and it was his last choice. Flee. He'd have little chance of finding a way out of this tangle if he were locked up in an Admiralty cell.

Or, worse, swinging from a hangman's noose at Tyburn.

"Reenie, listen to me. Believe me. I didn't do this. Someone else did. We have to find Ethan and your aunt, but there isn't much time." He pushed aside the dagger and pulled her close. Without a second thought he kissed her, hard and thoroughly, hoping his passion would convince her of what his words seemed unable to do.

She fought him like a wildcat, and when she got away she wiped her mouth as if she'd just swallowed poison.

"I'm going to see your men free and the *Retribution* set adrift, just as I promised you. Then I am going to do my damnedest to find our son. If you come to your senses, meet me after midnight at Vauxhall Gardens. Down at the docks. I'll be there on my yacht."

The Lord Admiral was now steps from the balcony door, and his hawkish gaze locked with Julien's.

The two men stared at each other, and then the recognition flickered between them.

"De Ryes," the Lord Admiral mouthed, then he grabbed the door to the balcony, rattling the locked portal with all his strength.

His actions diverted Maureen, and she turned to aid the man in opening the door.

Julien saluted him over his wife's shoulder and then swung over the edge of the balcony. He dropped into the latticework and was down the two stories before the Lord Admiral could wrench the locked door open.

"I love you, Reenie," he called up to her as his feet hit the stone path below. From above she stared down at him, obviously furious at his escape. "Believe me. It is all you have left." And with that, he loped through the back garden and fled into the night.

"What took you so long?" Maureen asked, whirling around from the edge of the stonework to face the Lord Admiral. "He's gotten away!"

She threw her leg over the balcony, fully intending to follow the blackguard, but the Lord Admiral moved too fast.

He caught her by the arm and held her fast. "De Ryes? That was de Ryes?" he asked, his eyes glittering with excitement.

Shaking off his hold, she nodded. "Yes, Julien D'Artiers is your pirate. But if you haven't noticed, he is getting away."

She went to make her escape yet again, but the Lord Admiral grabbed her arm again.

"Where do you think you're going?"

"After him," she said, this time unsuccessful in her attempt to free herself.

"Hardly. This is no longer your concern."

"Like hell," she said. "I'll see him hang, and no one is going to stop me."

"Perhaps if you'd thought to tell me this sooner, he would be dead by now." The Lord Admiral studied her. "You knew. You've known since that night at Almack's who de Ryes was, yet you kept your mouth shut. It seems to me if you truly wanted your husband dead, you would have said something that night. Why, you've been in league with him this entire time."

Furious at this turn of events, she blurted out before she could stop herself, "I'm not in league with him. I've been trying to gain enough proof so that he won't slip away. He's too well-connected with the Traherns and the Westons not to find a way out of this. But you can stop him now, for he'll be at Vauxhall Gardens, near the docks, at midnight. He'll be carrying the proof with him, and nothing will stop you from seeing him hang, not even his high-blown relations."

Even as she made her confession, she realized her error.

The man's eyes glittered dangerously. "You're right about that, you little slut. I'll see de Ryes hang. And you right beside him."

"Me? I'll not hang. We have a deal," she shot back. "De Ryes for my life and the lives of my men."

"An honorable agreement you willfully voided

when you withheld evidence from His Majesty's Navy."

Julien's warnings about the Lord Admiral came back to haunt her.

*It won't prick his conscience to betray you any more than it did when he consigned your father to life on a prison hulk.*

Suddenly, the chill of the night invaded her very soul.

"Hardly," she shot back. "He's been threatening me this entire time. I didn't know what to do. He said he'd see my throat slit, that not even you could protect me."

She spotted a glint of metal lying on the floor. She reached down and plucked up her dagger, holding it gingerly as if she'd never touched such a dastardly weapon before. "As you can see he tried to finish me off this very night, but the coward fled when he saw you."

"Do you really think me a fool?" the Lord Admiral sneered. "I saw him kiss you. No, Maureen Hawthorne de Ryes, you'll hang on the morrow beside your husband. Hang as you rightly should. I'll remove all traces of you, as I did your father."

Just then Lord Hawksbury poked his head through the doorway. "Miss Fenwick, there you are. Our next dance is just about to begin, and I thought to steal you away before my wicked uncle convinced you otherwise."

Maureen swung her hand behind her back to conceal her dagger. There was no use in dragging Julien's nephew into this havey-cavey business.

The young man stepped outside and looked around. "Where is my uncle?"

But then again, she thought, perhaps he could be useful.

Maureen shrugged her shoulders. "Gone. The cad left me out here alone, and the door latched as he left. Thankfully, the Lord Admiral came to my rescue." She smiled coyly at the Earl, whose title and family connections surely outranked even the Lord Admiral's social standing.

"Yes, that's it," the Lord Admiral said, finally entering the conversation. "Poor Miss Fenwick is quite overtaken by her experience; I was just going to see her home." With that he took Maureen's arm and started to lead her away.

"My dear Lord Admiral," she said as sweetly as she could when all she wanted to do was drive her dagger into his back. "As I was saying, that is entirely unnecessary. I feel more than able to continue my evening. Besides, I would hate to disappoint Lord Hawksbury."

Lord Hawksbury immediately stepped up to the bait. "She looks well enough, sir. Kind of you to offer, but this task belongs to someone who has a vested interest in the lady's welfare."

Before the older man could protest, Lord Hawksbury took her hand and led her to the dance floor.

The Earl smiled as if nothing were amiss, but when they were well away from the Lord Admiral, separated by a half dozen or more dancing couples, he said in a voice edged with concern, "What happened to my uncle?"

"As I said, he left."

Lord Hawksbury frowned at her. "I've been watching the door ever since you two went out there, just as he asked me to. He never reentered the ballroom."

Maureen pursed her lips.

"I know more than you think," he said, as if he sensed the questions behind her mask. "Enough to get me hanged. I don't agree with my uncle's politics, but he's family. I'll not see his fool neck stretched, even if it does put me in a bit of a quandary from time to time."

"You know, my lord?" she whispered.

At this he grinned. "Stop that 'my lord' business. You should call me Charles, like a good aunt."

Her eyes must have reflected her shock.

"Oh, yes, I know all that as well. It was quite disappointing to find out that you were, shall we say, otherwise engaged, but I can't fault my uncle's taste in wives. Welcome to the family, Aunt Maureen." He whirled her across the floor, nodding every once in a while to a friend.

She shook her head, trying to make sense of this.

"What I don't understand is why you didn't go with him. He said you both would be leaving tonight. What happened, did that old goat catch up with you before you had a chance to get down the wall?"

"I didn't want to go."

"I can see why. I told Uncle Julien it was foolhardy to think a lady—even one with your illustrious background—could navigate that wall. But he swore you could climb it in your sleep."

"No, it wasn't the wall. I didn't want to go with him because he betrayed me."

"Uncle Julien?" Charles shook his head. "Never. He loves you. I know. I tried to convince him to let you stay here in London. But he wouldn't have it. Said you two had been apart too long."

"Well, he lied to you as well."

At this the young man took affront, his shoulders and eyebrows ruffling with the dishonor of hearing a family member being called a liar. "I don't believe you."

"He stole something of mine earlier today. Something I value more than life itself."

Charles shook his head and lowered his voice as he said, "I was with him today. The only thing we stole were ten barrels of rum and some fireworks. I hardly call such trifles betrayal of one's wife."

"Rum and fireworks?" she said. "I'm talking about my son. He kidnapped my son this afternoon."

"Today? I hardly think so. I was with him the entire day. He needed help and I provided it—Wait a minute, did you just say 'son'?"

She nodded. "Ethan. He's my son."

Charles shook his head. "And Julien's as well, am I to assume?"

"Yes."

He whistled low. "But you said he stole Ethan? Today?"

"Yes," she told him. "I have proof."

"I don't see how he could have. We left at first light this morning, and it took us most of the day to steal—" Charles lowered his voice even further. "To steal the rum and fireworks off a dock near Richmond." He grinned at her. "Never been a common thief before. Quite exciting, really, though my parents would have my head and Julien's if they knew what mischief we'd been about this afternoon."

Richmond? How could he have been in Greenwich

*and* Richmond? Even the tides wouldn't have worked for him.

Still, Maureen wasn't about to let Julien off so easily. "But his men, they were in Greenwich. Did you hear him say anything about Greenwich?"

Again Charles shook his head. "No, nothing. As for his men, he never lets his crew ashore in England. For their safety as well as his. In London he works alone. Oh, he has his contacts, but he only buys information from them. That was why I was so surprised when he asked for my help."

If what Charles was saying was true, then perhaps Julien hadn't taken Ethan.

But if he hadn't, then who had?

Her gaze fell on the Lord Admiral, standing at the entrance to the ballroom. The man was directing several well-dressed men, who despite their fancy clothing she recognized as the guards from Cheapside. The Lord Admiral then turned and pointed her out.

She glanced away and feigned indifference to his machinations.

Could it have been the Lord Admiral who took Ethan?

But how would he have known? At this point it didn't matter.

There was only one way to find out.

"Charles," she said. "What if you could help your uncle even further?"

Julien's nephew didn't hesitate. "What do you want me to do?"

# Chapter 23

Maureen knew she couldn't leave without saying something to Lady Mary. She owed her that much.

"Maureen, there you are," the lady exclaimed. Her gaze fell on Charles. "And in such fine company."

Maureen leaned forward and whispered into Lady Mary's ear. "Your plan worked. I'm off with the Earl. He's asked me to join his family." Maureen didn't feel overly bad about leading the lady on. It was, after all, nearly the truth.

Lady Mary's eyes grew wide. "Such happy news. Are you off to Scotland then?"

Maureen nodded, flinching at this outright lie.

"Oh, you must be careful which road you take. My sister eloped, and she and her husband were nearly caught by my father. The Lord Admiral will have all the posting inns watched. And if he captures you . . ."

Hoping to abate Lady Mary's obvious fears for her safety, Maureen decided to taint her story with a bit of the truth. "Lord Hawksbury keeps a yacht near Vaux-hall Gardens. We are off to it so as to elude the Lord Admiral. He'll not catch us."

Lady Mary's eyes shone with tears and gratitude as she unexpectedly took the Earl into her arms and hugged him. "You take care of my dear girl, my Lord. She'll make a fine wife."

Charles looked at Maureen, confusion covering his features.

Maureen just shrugged as if she weren't sure what the lady was talking about.

"Now go," Lady Mary said, shooing them away. "Here comes that horrid man, and I won't have you within his reach for another second."

Maureen kissed Lady Mary quickly on the cheek and followed Charles out a side door and then down a hallway. As Charles led her into a bedroom, Maureen cast a questioning glance in his direction.

"My mother would skin me alive if she knew what I was doing," Charles said, striding across the room and around the vast bed.

"I don't think your uncle would approve either."

He glanced back at her and then down at the bed. "I suppose this does look rather compromising, but we don't have any other choice." He paused for a moment.

From down the hall rattled the footsteps of half a score of men. The Lord Admiral's bellowing orders echoed right behind them.

"Find her! Find her now!"

"Do I have your vow that you will not reveal what you are about to see?" Charles asked.

Maureen glanced toward the closed door to the hallway and then back at him. From the sound of it, it was apparent the Lord Admiral was undertaking a rather unethical search of his hosts' house.

It wouldn't be but a minute before he arrived here.

"Yes," she said hastily, wondering what the devil Charles was up to.

"You vow on the honor of the D'Artiers?"

"Yes, Charles, I promise, I vow, I swear. But get on with it!"

He nodded and then turned to the tapestry hanging on the wall. He stepped behind it and then, moments later, poked his head out and gestured for her to follow.

"Grab that taper," he said, nodding to the unlit candle on the nightstand.

She snatched it up and followed him. What she found amazed her. Behind the tapestry the oak paneling gave way to a secret door. In moments they were inside a small chamber and the paneling moved silently back into place to fill the opening. Just then she heard the Lord Admiral burst into the bedroom.

Maureen didn't ask Charles why his parents—the very proper and stylish Lord and Lady Trahern—kept a secret passageway in their London town house.

So Julien wasn't the only one in the family with secrets.

After the Lord Admiral finished his search of the room and it had been silent for a few minutes longer, Charles struck a light and lit the candle. From there he led her down a steep, narrow stairway and then through a long, stone-lined passageway.

She had heard of such places but thought they hadn't

been used or built since Cromwell's time. And the Traherns' Mayfair home wasn't more than ten or twenty years old. If that wasn't odd enough, the passageway appeared clean and free of cobwebs or dust, evidence that it was oft-used.

They exited in the alley beyond the gardens, and Charles bid her to wait in the shadows.

He came back to the hidden entranceway, an ivy-covered doorway, about twenty minutes later with his phaeton and team.

Always the gentleman, he started to climb down to assist her, but Maureen waved him off and bounded up into the carriage without a second thought.

Charles let out a low whistle at this. "I suppose you are also going to hold me to our wager."

"Of course I am. A wager is a wager," she said, grinning at his crestfallen expression. "This team ought to suffice." She nodded to the matched blacks prancing in their traces.

"Not my best set!" he moaned.

"This will teach you a good lesson, *nephew,*" she said. "Never wager with a lady."

"Does Uncle Julien know about your mercenary ways?"

"Only too well," she said softly, realizing she'd let her pride and stubborn hold on the past cloud her judgment.

Julien had tried to tell her, tried to warn her, but she had refused to believe him. Even when her own common sense had told her he was probably right.

Now what had she done? Made a mistake more

grave than his eight years ago. She'd scorned him and betrayed him and put their son in even greater danger.

Perhaps there was still time to stop it, to erase their past and start over. Just as Julien had proposed.

Plucking off her mask, she yanked free one of the ties and set to work braiding her hair and binding it out of her way.

The truth whirled through her mind—Julien had been right all along. The Lord Admiral was her enemy, not him. And there was more to Cottwell's anger with her than just this de Ryes affair.

What had he said?

*I'll remove all traces of you, as I did your father.*

Why would he be so concerned about her?

Unlike her father, she didn't stand in the way of his being promoted in the Admiralty. Yet the man hated her, was almost afraid of her, as if she could turn back time and avenge the wrongs of the past with just her presence.

It all revolved around one question: Why had he betrayed her father to begin with? He'd risked far too much just to gain a promotion.

No, it went beyond what Julien had been able to uncover.

And if the Lord Admiral had Ethan, she could only assume her son's fate would be just as dire as the one Cottwell had planned for her. The vile, deranged man seemed bent on removing any trace of the Hawthorne lineage. Maybe that explained why he had her take another name while she was in London.

He hadn't wanted anyone to know who she was.

But why?

She shook her head. There must be someone who knew the answers, for the Lord Admiral couldn't have carried out such an elaborate court-martial and deception without witnesses, people who would vouch for his veracity over her father's word.

*Witnesses.*

People the Lord Admiral had coerced into helping him. People who would more than likely still fear the man's wrath.

Like Captain Johnston.

Why hadn't she thought of it before?

She considered her choice of actions. She glanced up at the sky to guess the hour, but the pall over London covered the stars and the moon from her. "What time is it?"

He pulled a timepiece from his jacket. "Quarter past ten. Are we for the docks, or do you have another plan?"

If Julien had stayed the course they'd set out originally, he would already by sailing up the Thames with the last vestiges of the tide.

Charles had pulled the horses to a stop in the middle of the intersection. "Which way, *Auntie*?"

She glared at his use of her familial title. Why, he made her sound like an old lady in her dotage. She'd teach him a thing or two about ladies before the night was through.

"Cheapside. I have unfinished business there."

Julien's plans went better than he expected. Earlier in the evening he'd had the barrels of rum delivered to the two naval ships moored on either side of the *Retribution*.

As he sailed his yacht past the dock, it was easy to see that the sailors aboard were taking full advantage of the free bounty, having quickly drunk themselves into a frenzied stupor rather than keeping a sharp watch on the smuggler's vessel they were supposed to be guarding.

Whores, courtesy of an anonymous patron of the Navy, danced on the decks, flashing white calves and parts even higher up, for the men still able to stand.

The officers were nowhere in sight, but that was to be expected. While the regular sailors were rarely, if ever, granted shore leave, the officers were free to come and go. Such a debauchery had probably driven the high and mighty from their cabins and into the city to find a more refined form of entertainment.

Higher priced rum and a better class of light-skirts, Julien thought cynically.

He glanced at his watch and saw the *Retribution*'s crew scurrying silently along the quayside like shadowy rats.

Right on time.

Freed just a few hours ago from a prison hulk not far away—through the same liberal use of rum and whores—the crew of the *Retribution* were only too happy to escape their inebriated guards.

The men now slipped one by one onto their ship, climbing up the mooring lines and readying their vessel. The tide would be with them for only a short time; then it would turn, and pursuit would be difficult if not impossible.

When everything seemed to be in order, Julien struck a match and lit the first of the Chinese rockets he and Charles had stolen earlier that afternoon.

It sailed straight and true into the sails of the first Navy ship, exploding in a hailstorm of blue and green sparks. He sent the second one and the third one into the ship that flanked the *Retribution's* port side.

He continued sending up the volleys of flame and fire until he was out of his stolen stash. Then he sat back for a moment and watched as the two drunken crews tried to stop the small fires glowing and flaring up in the tar and sails.

And in the ensuing chaos, no one paid any heed to the *Retribution* as she slipped her mooring lines and began drifting with the tide out to sea.

Reenie had her ship back.

Julien wondered, as he pulled hard on the rudder and set a new course, if she'd have him as well.

He knew only one way to find out.

Maureen bounded up the steps of the Johnston house. The Lord Admiral's guards were gone, probably having been ordered to seek her out, as well as to find Julien.

The house was strangely silent, the Captain nowhere in sight and Lucy probably having sought her bed after the exhausting day Lady Mary had put her through. Satisfied no one was about, she continued upstairs to her room.

There, much to her relief, Mrs. Landon was still waiting for her. The last thing she wanted was another innocent life in harm's way. It was bad enough Aunt Pettigrew had become embroiled in all this mess.

"Miss Maureen, you've come back." The lady rose from the chair in the corner. "I've been worried sick."

"You'll need to come with me," Maureen said over her shoulder to the woman, as she tried to shake herself free of her costume.

The housekeeper stepped forward and helped her get out of the elaborate gown, but when she saw what Maureen intended to put on instead, the lady clucked her tongue in displeasure at the breeches, shirt, and dark coat.

"You're going to find nothing but trouble wearing those rags, Miss Maureen."

"I'm counting on it," she told the woman, as she stowed her dagger in the top of her boot. She looked around the room to see if there was anything else she needed, but this was all she'd arrived with, and it seemed fitting it was all she would take with her.

But she needed something more. She needed answers.

"Come on, Mrs. Landon. I want you to meet your new employer."

They started down the stairs, only to be greeted by Captain Johnston. And in his hand he held a pistol.

Mrs. Landon let out a nervous shriek.

"She has nothing to do with any of this, Captain," Maureen told him. "Let her walk out of here."

The Captain shook his head.

"How much more innocent blood do you want on your hands?" she asked him. "Let her go."

He seemed to consider her words and then nodded to Mrs. Landon.

Maureen turned to her and said softly, "There is a

man in a phaeton outside. Go to him; tell him you are his new housekeeper. If I don't come out in five minutes, have him take you to his house and tell him he is to pay you twice what you made at my aunt's."

If Mrs. Landon found these instructions strange, one more glance at the pistol aimed in their general direction erased whatever questions or objections she seemed about to lodge.

The woman hurried down the remaining steps and sidestepped the Captain in a matter of seconds.

"Thank you," Maureen told him, moving slowly down the steps until she came to the last one. There she sat down and looked up at the man who might well hold the keys to her past and her future. "You know that I am Lord Ethan Hawthorne's daughter."

He flinched at the name, but after a moment he nodded.

"And you know why the Lord Admiral is so determined to see not just de Ryes hang, but me as well."

His hand wavered, and Maureen knew from the sight of his bloodshot eyes that he'd been drinking again.

Drinking to erase the past.

She decided to test her suspicions. "You testified at my father's court-martial. You know what all of this is about. Tell me, Captain Johnston, I'm not so wrong when I say there is more to this than just a court-martial based on false evidence, am I?"

He remained silent, unwilling to give her the facts she wanted.

Straightening up, she faced him. "How is it that

you've continued all these years, knowing what you did to my father?"

She took a step toward him. "That he was forced to take to piracy." And then another one, even closer. "Into a hard life that killed my mother." Another one. "That he was eventually hunted down and murdered because you drove him out of the world he belonged in."

She stopped as the muzzle of the pistol came to rest in the middle of her breastbone. She took hold of it and moved it over her heart. "You can pull the trigger now and give me a quicker death than the one you condemned my father to, or you can tell me the truth. Wash the blood off your hands." She looked up and stared hard into his watery gaze.

William's hand wavered, his finger shaking over the trigger, but then his shoulders slumped and he shook his head. "I can't kill you, lass. How could I?"

"That didn't stop you from what you did to my father. You might as well have pulled the trigger."

"It was because I had no backbone that I let the likes of Peter Cottwell chart my course, rather than standing up to him." He sighed and walked over to the steps, slumping down on the threadbare carpet covering them. He put his hands on either side of his head and sobbed.

Maureen crossed the entryway and sat down on the step beside him. "Tell me about my father."

It took some time for the Captain to find the words, but when he did, the entire sorry tale spilled forth.

"Your father was like a brother to me. Ethan kept

me safe when we were just lads starting out. We weren't much more than nine or ten, any of us— Ethan, me, Peter, and James Porter."

"Porter?" she said, wondering why the name sounded so familiar.

"You know Porter. The judge who tried your case."

Maureen had always thought it unusual that their case had been moved to an Admiralty court, but now she saw the Lord Admiral's hand in even that twist of fate.

"Ethan was the best of us, but Peter was the cunning one," William said, continuing his story. "Never seemed to matter much, cause we all rose through the ranks together. Helping each other out. I thought we'd always be friends, until . . ."

"Until?"

"Until about two years after we'd all made captain. We'd been in a squabble with the Dutch, and it turned out bad. The way Peter told the story, it made it look like your father had committed treason. At first I didn't believe him, but then he brought me evidence—other men who'd seen what Peter claimed—like a fool I went along with him. I didn't realize until then that Peter hated your father."

"But why? Why would the Lord Admiral hate my father so?"

"Because Ethan had a title, and Peter didn't."

"I never knew about the title until recently," Maureen told him. "Why should the Lord Admiral care if my father had a title?"

"Your father was a baron in his own right, and Peter

had nothing. It gave him a leg up on promotions and connections, or that's what Peter believed. Didn't matter to him that Ethan was a good captain, a fine leader, just that he was being earmarked for a promotion Peter wanted." The Captain closed his eyes for a moment, as if recollecting all those events. "And then there was your mother."

"My mother?" Maureen looked up in surprise. "What did she have to do with all this?"

"Ethan and Peter had been vying for her affections for over a year. By gad, we were all in love with Ellen. She was pretty as a picture. But any fool could see she loved your father to distraction. Peter had himself convinced it was the title she wanted, not the man, and that if he had a title or superior rank, she would forget Ethan."

Maureen bristled at this notion. "She didn't. They were married."

"Aye. They weren't just married, they eloped. Peter was beyond furious. He thought your father had disgraced her by carting her off to Scotland. It didn't help that her family agreed with Peter. They were a bunch of high sticklers; hadn't paid much heed to any of us courting Ellen, because they thought she would never take anything less than an earl as a husband. Her sister had eloped six months earlier—bad business, it was— and they just assumed your mother wouldn't be so foolish."

"In the meantime, Peter Cottwell set out to have his revenge."

"Yes, revenge." William paused, glancing down at the pistol in his hand. Hastily, he set it aside. "He falsified evidence, though I didn't know it at the time. From the looks of it, your father had let Peter and another captain go into a skirmish unaided. Treason, it was, and a hanging offense. He convinced Porter and me to join him in testifying against Ethan. To bring honor back to the Admiralty, he told us." He laughed bitterly. "Like a fool I went along with his plans." Captain Johnston turned his head, but Maureen could see the single tear glistening in his eye.

"Then what happened?" she prompted.

"There was a court-martial. I'll never forget your father's eyes on me as I testified. The accusations behind them nearly tore me apart." He looked over at her. "You've got his eyes, lass. Shook me right back nearly thirty years when I saw you that day in Porter's court." He looked away and then continued. "After I was done testifying and saw the disappointment in your father's eyes, I knew that Peter had been wrong all along. Oh, it wasn't anything definite, but Ethan's expression just told me—I was on the wrong side."

"But it was too late."

He nodded. "At least for your father's career. They sentenced him to life on a prison hulk. Again Peter was furious. He wanted your father dead."

"So he could marry my mother," Maureen whispered.

"Aye, that and other reasons. But I couldn't be part of it anymore. Your mother came to me and begged for my help. She was a bold lass, like you, full of spirit and fire. Afraid of nothing. She never believed Peter's lies. She stood steadfast by your father, no matter how damning the evidence."

Maureen glanced away. A lesson she might have taken to heart if only she'd known.

What had Julien said to her that fateful day on the *Destiny* as it appeared he was moving to join the British lines?

*There's still a chance . . . but I need your help.*

*Please don't jump. Let me explain.*

What if she had been more like her mother and trusted with her heart? What if she hadn't jumped and instead let Julien explain?

The Captain cleared his throat, bringing Maureen back to the present. "Aye, Ellen could be quite convincing when she put her mind to it."

"What did my mother want you to do?"

"She had a plan to get your father off that hulk and out of the country. It would mean that they would never be able to set foot on English soil again, but she didn't care. All she wanted was your father's freedom, so they could be together. And so I agreed to help. 'Twas the least I could do."

Maureen looked at the Captain with a new measure of respect. "And you succeeded."

"Yes. It was a bold plan, one your mother carefully plotted. Right down to the last detail. She knew Peter Cottwell would never rest until he had what he wanted most—your father's death. So she went as far as to bring along a body." William shuddered. "I never asked her where she got it. It was unthinkable—a lady like her, carting a body around, the dirt still clinging to it as if she'd dug it herself. She'd even found a poor bugger that was about your father's height and coloring."

The Captain shuddered. "After we got Ethan out, the guards began firing down on us as we made our way to shore. In the darkness and confusion, we set the poor stiff afloat."

"Wouldn't someone realize it wasn't my father?"

William cringed. "Have you ever seen a body after it's been in the water for a few days?"

She nodded. After the slaughter of the Alliance, the bodies had floated ashore for days.

"Well, then you know there isn't much left to identify. That poor fellow could have been the Prince of Wales for all the authorities could tell. Your mother had even gone so far as to shoot a few bullets into it to make it look like the fellow had died in the escape."

"And when they found the body, they assumed it was my father."

"Aye. He was declared dead. After that he and your mother slipped away, free to start their new life."

For a moment they both sat in silence, each considering this extraordinary tale.

Maureen gave the man's hand a gentle squeeze. "Thank you, Captain Johnston. Thank you for telling me the truth." She rose from the steps. "Now I know what I am up against."

"He'll stop you, lass. He'll not rest until he does."

"I know. But I have to face him. He's taken my son, and I can't leave without my child."

"Your son?" William shook his head. "The lad's in grave danger then."

"I know. But I have de Ryes on my side. And I'm off to join him. We'll get our son back and see to it that

Peter Cottwell never harms another Hawthorne for as long as he lives."

"But, lass, there's more. You need to know—"

She expected his protests and that he would try to stop her. Before he could utter another word, she snatched up his pistol and clouted him over the head. As he slumped forward she caught him and laid him gently down on the steps.

"Are you coming, Maureen?" Charles called from the street.

"Yes." Maureen looked down at the prone figure at her feet and hoped she could repair her life in better fashion than Captain Johnston had tried to do with his.

For the past, she now knew, was a traitorous mistress. One best forgiven and left behind.

# *Chapter 24*

Lady Mary had watched the Lord Admiral follow Maureen and Lord Hawksbury out of the ballroom and could only pray they would escape. And when they did, she knew full well, Peter Cottwell would be back to question her as to Maureen's whereabouts.

Instead of remaining at the Traherns', where he could easily find her, Lady Mary slipped out through the crush and waved down a hackney to take her home. William would protect her, or at least he'd know a place where they could hide until the Lord Admiral's wrath subsided.

As she entered the house, to her horror she found her husband slumped at the base of the stairs.

Could it be that the Lord Admiral had beaten her home?

"William, oh, William, what has that monster done to you?"

She cradled his head in her lap and began to cry over and over, "Oh, what has he done to you?"

After what seemed like forever, William stirred. He sat up slowly, blinking his eyes and rubbing his head.

"It wasn't Cottwell who hit me, Mary," he said sharply, "but that damnable niece of ours."

Lady Mary sat back and stared at her husband. "Our niece?"

"Yes, you heard me say it. Our niece."

She stared at her husband. "Maureen did this to you?"

"Aye, Maureen."

"Why would she hit you if you finally told her the truth? I can't see how knowing that Ellen was my sister would be cause for violence. I thought she would be happy to find out she is our niece."

Much to Mary's distress, he shook his head. "No, the lass still doesn't know. She didn't give me time. Not that I should have told her anyway; it will just put her in greater danger."

"How can knowing that we are her family put her in danger?"

"Because then she could unravel the rest of this sorry business."

Lady Mary hardly saw the sense of that. She rose to her feet and glared at her husband. "Well, where is she? I will tell her myself!"

"If I knew that, Mary girl, I wouldn't be lying here on the floor with a lump on my head the size of a goose egg." He tenderly touched the swollen flesh. "She packs a wallop, that one. She's got Ellen's spirit, all right, as well as her father's foolishness. Thinks she can stop Peter Cottwell." He shook his head sadly.

"Oh, no, William. You have to stop her. You have to tell her the truth. Then she'll see the sense of it."

William snorted. "If I tell her the truth, it will only drive her harder."

What a vexing muddle, Lady Mary thought. Why, none of what William told her made any sense. Maureen had left the ball to elope with Lord Hawksbury, not to go after the Lord Admiral.

"I thought the Earl would protect her," Lady Mary said aloud.

"What earl?" he asked.

"The Earl of Hawksbury."

"That young cub?"

"He's not so young," Lady Mary told him. "He's quite eligible. I think he will make a splendid husband for our niece."

"A husband?" William shook his head. "Mary girl, I would remind you that Maureen is already married. The girl has enough problems without adding another husband to the mix."

Lady Mary had quite forgotten that. Oh, how terrible for her to be still married to that wretched pirate when Lord Hawksbury seemed so interested in her welfare.

William rubbed his head again. "I don't know anything about this Lord Hawksbury you think she's run off with, for she claimed to be joining up with de Ryes."

"De Ryes? Why, he's a villain. See what we've driven her to with all our secrets." Lady Mary sat back down, tears rolling down her cheeks. Oh, this was a sorry, sorry mess. "But William, why would Maureen tell me she is eloping with Lord Hawksbury and tell you something entirely different?"

"Aye, it seems odd," William said, rubbing his head again. "Perhaps there is some connection between this Earl of Hawksbury and de Ryes. Has she shown any preference to any other man? Were any of them suspicious or capable of being de Ryes?"

Lady Mary considered all the swains who had flocked to Maureen's side, but only one stood out.

"Mr. D'Artiers," she whispered. Could it be?

"D'Artiers, eh? Is he connected to Lord Hawksbury?"

"Yes," Lady Mary said. "The Earl is his nephew."

William let out a low whistle. "Isn't that D'Artiers fellow supposed to be rich as Midas? And rather mysterious?"

She nodded, afraid of the truth that now seemed to stare them both in the face.

"Mary, I think we've found de Ryes."

"How can this be? She said she was eloping with the Earl. That they were going to Vauxhall Gardens to take his yacht to Scotland."

"If that isn't the finest tale I've ever heard. She may be going to Vauxhall Gardens for a yacht, but I doubt she is on her way to Scotland." He rose to his feet and looked around the base of the stairs.

"What are you doing?" she asked when he let out a frustrated sigh.

"Your niece is a thief."

"William! Ellen's daughter is no such thing."

His bushy eyebrows cocked with a wry humor that was hardly appropriate at a time like this. "Madame, she took my best pistol. Now I'll have to make do with those fancy dueling pieces your brother gave me." He strode down the hall toward his office.

Lady Mary followed him and caught his sleeve. "What are you planning on doing?"

"What I should have done years ago."

"Charles, you cannot come with me," Maureen told her honor-bound nephew as they pulled up alongside the fence at Vauxhall.

"I cannot let you enter that place unescorted. It would be unseemly and ungentlemanly of me."

Maureen gazed upward and wondered why she had to find the one relative of Julien's who had more honor than sense. "I have been alone in far worse places than this, let me assure you."

Charles looked unimpressed. His team pranced uneasily in their traces, and he steadied them with a firm hand.

"I think you should listen to his lordship, Miss Maureen," Mrs. Landon piped in. "I've 'eard terrible things about them gardens. A wicked place they can be."

"You see," he told her. "Even Mrs. Landon agrees with me." Charles started to get down out of the phaeton.

"Yes, certainly, Charles. By all means, come with me," Maureen said. "But then you would be leaving poor Mrs. Landon here unprotected."

Charles paused and then settled back into his seat.

He looked as if every noble intention he possessed was about to tear him in half.

Perhaps his honor would work to her advantage, she thought.

Maureen grinned at her poor nephew and hopped down from the carriage.

"And where do you think you are going?" he asked. "You are just as unescorted and unprotected as Mrs. Landon would be."

"Yes, but I doubt Mrs. Landon can do this," Maureen told him. She knelt quickly, snatched out the dagger concealed in her boot, and threw it at a nearby tree, striking it in the middle of a large knot.

Charles let out a low whistle. When he recovered from his awestruck shock, he continued to protest. "Still, Aunt Maureen, I cannot, by my honor, allow you—"

Maureen gave up on diplomacy. She pulled out Captain Johnston's pistol and fired it over the heads of the nervous blacks.

Charles's team took off as if the hounds of hell were at their hooves, and the last thing she heard of Charles was a rather loud, ungentlemanly curse about dishonorable relations.

She easily climbed over the fence and then made her way through the gardens until she found a secluded spot at the river's edge where she could wave down Julien before he came to the docks.

Hopefully, she wasn't too late.

Behind her the gardens were strangely quiet. A few stray couples wandered along, while others with more bold intentions took their wanton embraces into the shadowed alcoves. The only sounds were of murmured voices, false promises, and the deep, throaty gasps and moans of someone who'd found a different type of entertainment within the aptly named pleasure gardens of London.

She glanced at the river. The tide had changed, and she could see that the time-old battle of the Thames had begun—the push of the sea inward while the river strained to empty its way against the ocean currents. The water ebbed and flowed at her feet.

Down the banks from her, ferrymen traded quips and barbs as they waited for their next fares.

And to her growing chagrin, there was no sign of Julien.

For a moment Maureen thought she was too late. Either he'd given up on her or, worse, he'd been captured by the Lord Admiral.

Then through the dark mists of the night, she spotted a boat coming upstream. A small, sturdy sailing yacht, riding both the incoming tide and the slight breeze filling its sails, guided by a lone mariner.

She knew that only the best of sailors could navigate such a course, and for the first time all night she realized there might be hope.

"Julien," she whispered across the water. "Over here."

If he heard her, the only indication he gave was a slight course change that brought him well around the ferrymen and closer to her.

She stepped from her hiding place, only to hear a voice behind her say, "Good, guide him to us."

*The Lord Admiral.*

She started to turn around, but he barked a hard, quiet order.

"Stay still or your son dies." The order was followed by the unmistakable cock of a pistol's hammer.

Maureen froze. "Ethan? Is he safe?"

"For now," Cottwell said. "But I want de Ryes, and you're just the bait to draw him in here."

What could she do? If she called out a warning to Julien, Ethan would surely perish, but if she didn't, what hope was there for any of them?

"You must think yourselves quite ingenious to have freed your ship and crew." He laughed as if the loss mattered not.

Maureen rejoiced silently. Julien had succeeded, even without her help.

"I wouldn't celebrate quite yet," he told her. "I have sent messages to the coast and ordered a ship of the line to meet your men as they enter the Channel. If they are smart they will surrender, but if they choose to fight, well . . ." He paused. "Then they will die, as they should have."

Maureen wondered what the Lord Admiral would say when he found out that the *Retribution* wouldn't be alone. Sailing alongside the *Destiny*, the two vessels stood a good chance of besting the Admiral's ship.

And then they'd sail on and take the *Bodiel.*

She may not live to see it, but she still had faith that Julien would find a way to elude the British as he had so many times before.

Time seemed to slowly tick by as Julien sailed closer and closer to her position. She discarded one plan after another, wildly trying to think of a way to warn Julien and keep Ethan safe.

"Don't try anything foolish," the Lord Admiral hissed. "I have you surrounded, and my personal schooner is anchored just upstream with a squad of marines fresh from a recent encounter at sea with your husband. I'm sure they would be more than happy to cut him down now rather than wait for his hanging."

She swallowed and turned her head slightly back and forth. There in the shadows, up and down the banks, she could make out the shadowy figures of the Lord Admiral's hired brutes.

With every second that Julien drew closer, Maureen thought she would go crazy.

Julien had to get free. He had to save Ethan, since she had failed their son.

Please, Julien, hear me, she said silently. *Turn around. Leave me be.*

But again the fates turned against her. The wind freshened and brought Julien that much closer.

Her knees wavered and buckled as she saw the schooner coming into sight, the lines filled with sharp-shooters.

It seemed that after all these years the Lord Admiral had finally won.

Julien heard his name whispering across the waves like a siren's call.

Slowly, his gaze swept over the shoreline until he spied a sole figure standing alone in a secluded spot.

*Maureen. She'd changed her mind. Discovered the truth.*

He nearly cheered at the sight of her waiting for him.

Whatever her reasons for coming, he didn't care. They would find their way together, find their son, and then be gone from England to start a new life together.

But even as he drew closer, he could see the concern on her face, as if she feared his arrival as much as she welcomed it.

Something wasn't right, if her wild-eyed gaze was any indication.

He scanned the banks again, alert for danger, but he saw nothing. Still, he couldn't shake the notion that something was terribly wrong.

Then a single shot in the night drew his attention away from his wife. The pistol report echoed across the water, carrying its warning cry out to Julien. Suddenly, the banks exploded with gunfire, the shots sailing around him, chipping at the lacquered sides of his yacht.

He cursed roundly and dove to the bottom of his boat. The gunfire continued for another few moments, then subsided. Cautiously, he peered out over the railing.

Troops were everywhere, stumbling over themselves, revealing their positions. There was only one person who could have engineered this trap.

The Lord Admiral.

And then from behind Maureen stepped the man himself, his hand coming to rest possessively on her shoulder.

Maureen glanced up and over her shoulder at her partner.

How could she have done this? Betrayed him after everything he'd told her, the promises they'd made? Had her wild behavior and accusations about kidnapping Ethan at the masquerade been just that—an act to drive him into this snare?

Obviously, he'd truly underestimated her need for revenge. But if there was no hope for him and Maureen, he wouldn't let his son fall prey to her hatred.

He pulled the rudder hard and turned from the shore. The shots were whizzing past his head again, rifling his sails with holes, leaving them listless. Even more dangerous, they were putting holes in his craft.

Water poured in around his feet.

He was a sitting, sinking target.

Turning the boat once again, he put the port side toward the shore and slipped overboard on the other side. The chill and foul smell of the water hit him hard, but he ignored it. Taking a deep breath, he dove under, swimming hard out into the middle of the river. When he thought his lungs would burst from want of air, he surfaced quickly, took another breath, and dove into the murky depths anew.

He reached the other shore, choking and sputtering on the wretched water, and made for a spot where the shrubs were thick, so as to climb to shore unseen. To his frustration, the bank was too steep and covered in a slippery clay.

The freezing seawater, brought in with the tide, had left his muscles stiff and burning. Even his hands had seemed to give up, for his fingers refused to bend so he could take hold of the branches overhead. He'd slip into the water and drown if he didn't find a way up the steep slope.

Julien was struggling for the strength to save himself, trying to recall Ethan's face, Maureen's smile, anything to urge him forward, when a sturdy pair of hands caught his coat by the collar and tugged him onto the bank.

"There you are, Mr. D'Artiers. Thought you were a goner for sure when I saw you slip into the water. You've got gumption for certain. Ethan would have been proud to call you his son-in-law."

Julien spat out the last of the putrid water choking his throat and turned his face upward to his unknown savior. To his amazement he found himself staring into the watery gaze of Captain William Johnston.

# *Chapter 25*

Julien didn't know if he should be relieved by Captain Johnston's assurances that Maureen hadn't betrayed him—because it meant that her insistence on coming to his aid had left her an easy prey in the Lord Admiral's trap.

"You've got to help, sir," the Captain told him. "And I'm here to see that you do."

He didn't doubt that the Captain wanted to help Maureen and him, for he'd all but hauled Julien up the steep bank and assisted him into a waiting hackney. The Captain didn't waste any time in seeing them driven away from the Lord Admiral's snare to a less-than-reputable tavern at the docks, where the Captain seemed well known.

The barmaid found dry clothes for Julien, and it wasn't long before he was cleaned up and sitting before a fire with a mug of hot rum in his hands.

All the while the Captain told him the most remarkable tale. Parts of it Julien had guessed, but the rest . . . well, he thought perhaps Lady Mary's husband had fallen prey to a bad batch of gin.

Julien looked over the rim of his mug toward his newfound companion. "What you say is incredible, if not unbelievable."

The Captain nodded, taking a long draught from his own cup. "'Tis true. Every word of it. Shamed I am to admit that I had a hand in it, but if you'll accept my help, I'd be proud to serve beside you, Captain de Ryes."

Julien glanced up and saw, along with the man's serious offer, the twinkle in his eye.

"Oh, don't deny it. Me and my Mary figured it out. I don't mind none having a niece of mine married to you. Good captain, from what I hear, and honorable when it comes to prisoners and such. Though you don't see that printed about town. But I hear. And there's a lot of us old sailors who admire that in a man." William held out his hand. "Will you accept my help? One sailor to another?"

Julien took the offered hand and shook on it. "Does Maureen know any of this?"

"Not all of it. The little minx knocked me over the head afore I had the chance. I still don't know what good it will do her to know. The Lord Admiral will never let her live."

"She's my wife. He'll not harm her."

The Captain shrugged and then lowered his voice. "That may be true, my boy, but you're also a wanted man. He'll hang you as well. Won't bother him none."

Julien wasn't so sure. "I may not hold much power

in this country, but surely not even Peter Cottwell would risk the wrath of the Marquess of Trahern or Viscount Weston. Maureen is their sister-in-law, after all. They are, shall we say, well connected with the Foreign Office and held in high regard by the most powerful men in the House of Lords and Parliament, as well as by the Prince Regent." Julien stared into the flames. "He'll not dare cross them. Not if he wants to spend another day outside of hell."

The captain still looked skeptical, but he rose from his seat. "It matters not to Peter Cottwell. He's been the Lord Admiral so long, he thinks he's the law unto himself. If we are to save Maureen and that son of yours, we need to move quickly."

Julien nodded. "Do you have any idea where he would take them?"

"Aye," the Captain said, setting his mug down on the oak-planked table. "I've a hunch that coldhearted bastard will want Maureen to see everything she's a right to before he takes it away from her."

Maureen stood on the shore and watched with horror as the yacht sank, with no sign of Julien. If he'd been shot, coupled with the chill of the water, he'd never be able to make it to shore, and if he did, the Lord Admiral's guards would no doubt be waiting for him.

She turned her fury on the man behind her, whipping around, first knocking the pistol out of his hand, then balling up her fist and sending it crashing into his jaw.

The Lord Admiral staggered back at her unexpected attack. But he wasn't such an easy target for her

second swing. He blocked her fist in midair and twisted
her arm around her back with surprising agility and
strength for a man of his age.

"You ill-bred bitch," he seethed. "What other surprises do you have?" His free hand patted over her
jacket and sides until he found the pistol tucked in her
belt. He yanked it free and held it to her temple.
"You've just earned the privilege of seeing your son
die first. Then that interfering biddy of an aunt of
yours and, finally, your own well-deserved death."

A shout to his men brought two burly oafs lum-
bering forth. He ordered them to bind and gag Maureen, which they did with sure-handed efficiency.

She thought about fighting them but gave up that
notion. She knew the Lord Admiral would only delight in seeing her clouted and battered further.

Besides, if she was to be any help to Ethan and Aunt
Pettigrew, she needed to stay alert.

In short order she was slung over a shoulder and
hauled out of the gardens along a dimly lit side path.
Outside the fence she was dumped onto the floor of a
foul-smelling carriage. The guards climbed in and sat
on the rough benches above her, their feet resting on
her supine figure.

The ride turned out to be an endless ordeal of
being bounced along on rough roads at a quick pace.
They'd obviously left the city and had driven far
into the country. But where and for how long she
couldn't tell.

Every once in a while, Maureen swore she smelled
the unmistakable odor of the Thames, and even at
times a hint of the sea, but she couldn't be sure.

It may well be this lout's socks, she thought, looking up at the lounging wall of muscle over her, his feet resting on her stomach as if she were his personal ottoman.

Finally, she caught a hint of dawn, as spidery threads of light started to drift through the ragged curtains of the carriage. Not long after that the horses turned from their course and ambled up a winding drive. They drew to a halt, and the carriage doors swung open.

At first the shock of daylight blinded her, and she blinked and turned her head away from the painful sunshine. Her guards caught her roughly and shoved her headlong into the brilliance.

She landed on her feet and for a moment stood there, her cramped limbs burning at this sudden freedom. Slowly, she raised her head and studied her surroundings.

She didn't know what she expected, but it was hardly the bucolic splendor around her. Great oaks and willows graced a wide green lawn. Neatly tended beds of spring flowers bloomed in vibrant reds, yellows, and whites along the drive. Beyond the manicured grass lay freshly tilled fields, some of them bursting with the first verdant blush of spring, sturdy growth shooting up from the rich, black earth.

Out here in the freshness of the morning, a breeze ruffled over her, carrying with it a tang so sweet, so salty and familiar that when she strained her ears, she swore she heard the whispering hush of the sea close by.

Slowly, she turned and found herself staring at the most remarkable house she'd ever seen. She hardly knew anything about architecture, but she could tell the house was old, very old. It rose three stories above her, the stonework graced with ivy and flowering vines. On those stones that were exposed, elaborate carvings of grotesque creatures and villainous fiends peeked out, as if warning those who dared enter that they did so at their own peril.

There was something vaguely familiar about the animals and figures and their arrangements, as if she'd seen them before.

"In with you." Her guard prodded her toward the massive oak doors before them. She looked again at the carvings above her and made out letters tangled within the devil's menagerie of carvings. Just before she was shoved through the heavy doors, she made out the ancient script.

*Hawthorne Hall.*

She turned around and found the Lord Admiral following in her wake.

He smiled at her, the corners of his mouth barely rising from their usual menacing line. "Welcome home, Baroness Hawthorne," he said. "Enjoy your lofty status while you have it, for I don't intend for the likes of you to wear my title any longer than necessary."

Given what Captain Johnston had told Julien about the Lord Admiral, he knew he couldn't rescue Maureen without help, so Julien rode for Mayfair.

He found his brothers-in-law still up, holding court in the Marquess of Trahern's private office, toasting their own fortitude at having survived their wives' social events for the Season.

". . . I would rather take another trip to the Russian court in January," Giles Corliss, the Marquess of Trahern, was saying as Julien was ushered in, "than have to endure launching another daughter into this hellish Marriage Mart." He looked up. "Julien, there you are, you devil. Don't let Sophia see you. She's boiling mad you didn't show your face tonight. She was counting on you to cause a stir or some sort of scandal to ensure that her party was a complete success."

"I think I can do that tonight, even to Sophia's satisfaction," he told his brother-in-law.

From a corner Charles rose up from an oversize chair. "Uncle Julien, what the devil! Where's Maureen? I thought the two of you would be—" His mouth froze open, the words halted in his throat, all eyes now bearing down on him.

Especially his father's. Giles's intelligent, measured gaze moved from his son back to Julien.

"Maureen?" Webb Dryden, the Viscount Weston, asked from where he lounged in a chair near the fireplace. His legs were propped up on Giles's desk and he held a glass of whisky. "Now, this sounds interesting." A wide grin split his face. "I have a feeling Sophia is about to get her scandal and much more. Do tell, Julien. I want to hear all of it before she and Lily divide up your carcass over your latest *on dit.*"

Julien waited for a moment as the butler moved about the room refilling glasses and then left, closing the door behind him.

"Maureen is my wife."

Giles let out a low whistle, his gaze snapping over his son. "You knew about this?"

Charles nodded. "But where is she, Uncle Julien? She said she could find you at Vauxhall on her own."

Giles stared at his son as if he were seeing him for the first time. "You let Julien's wife venture into those gardens alone?"

Charles turned a bright shade of red. "She was rather determined." He took a large gulp from his own glass, then admitted the truth. "She fired her pistol over my team and sent them running when I refused to allow her to leave."

Both Giles and Webb looked at each other and then burst out laughing.

"I like her already, Julien," Webb said.

"I did my best," Charles said miserably, slinking back into his corner chair.

"I don't blame you, Charles. Maureen has a way about her," Julien admitted. "She can give new meaning to the word *stubborn*."

Giles's expression grew serious. "But she's missing?"

Julien nodded. He looked from one man to the other. He'd never been very close to his brothers-in-law, and what he was about to tell them would test all their loyalties.

Yet what choice did he have? He had little time left if he was to save Maureen.

"I'm about to ask you both to commit treason. To give aid to a known American spy and privateer. But it is a matter of life and death." He looked over the now deadly-serious faces studying him.

Webb tipped his head. "What are you telling us? That this Maureen is all these things?"

"No." Julien squared his shoulders. "I am."

*   *   *

"Who lives here?" Maureen demanded, planting her feet in the middle of the entryway and facing the Lord Admiral.

The Lord Admiral dismissed the guards and took Maureen by the arm. "Why, you do, my dear. As the Baroness Hawthorne, this is rightfully your home. Let me show you around before you have to depart."

Maureen stared at the man as if he'd gone mad. "Why do you keep calling me that?"

"Baroness? I thought you would enjoy it," he said, towing her down a long hallway, the walls decorated with portraits of Hawthorne family members. "Your great-great-grandparents, if I am not mistaken," he said, nodding toward a matched pair of portraits.

He leaned forward, running a finger over the frame and checking it for dust. Then he looked up at the handsome man in fashions at least eighty years old. "Poor man; has your father's weak chin about him. A weakness that has fortunately left the Hawthorne lines now."

Maureen stared at the Lord Admiral. "You not only tried to murder my father, you stole his house, his title—you took everything away from him because you couldn't have my mother."

He raised his fist as if he was going to strike her, but he paused in midair when she didn't cower or back down.

After a moment he lowered his arm, straightening his jacket and regarding her with the expression of an overtaxed parent.

"Your father was the one who stole everything from me." While his features maintained their control, his voice held a manic edge. "Ellen loved me. She was to be mine. Then your father tricked her, deluded her, turned her against me." The man's gaze finally turned as wild as his accusations. "He killed her."

Maureen shook her head. "You stole her life from her. As surely as you stole my father's title, his identity."

"I didn't steal a thing, you little fool." He caught her by the elbow and towed her farther into the house. "But imagine my surprise when the search for an heir turned out to be me. The next in line. Such a surprise. A fair trade for all I'd lost."

Hardly that, Maureen thought, seeing beyond the mock humility of a man who hadn't known a modest sentiment a day in his life. "So why did you bring me here?"

"So you could see what you've been working so hard for. Seemed a shame to have you die before you saw what you might have had. A glimpse of heaven, one might say, before you join your father in hell."

Maureen yanked her elbow out of his grip. "Take this place and the title. I don't care for any of it. Just let me and my son go, and we'll never set foot in England again."

The man laughed. "Your mother made nearly the identical plea when she came to me. Come, I will show you what I offered her."

He led her up a staircase and down a hall. He threw open a door to a beautiful room. A lady's room. Delicately striped wallpaper hung over the walls, lending a soft rosy hue to the room. A beautifully carved canopied bed, with lacy curtains and pink silk coverings, took up most of one wall. A dressing table sat ready and waiting before a gilt mirror, a selection of brushes and toiletries lined up as if their mistress had just arisen and left for her morning repast.

"Your mother's room. She could have kept it, you know. She could have been the mistress of this house. Been my wife." He turned from the untouched splendor of the room, his face twisted with ugliness. "She spurned my offer and left me."

"So let her daughter go and keep your title and lands."

He laughed. "I have the same answer for you as I did for her: never."

He pushed her out of the room and closed the door carefully. "You can't fool me that you don't want all this. That is why you're here, why you've been smuggling for all these years—to raise enough money to bribe your way back into my title and my home." His eyes narrowed. "You have your mother's cunning. But unfortunately, none of her charms."

He grabbed her again and hauled her back downstairs. Throwing open a door to a room off the entryway, he beckoned her to come in.

She approached cautiously but then entered the grand room. Models of ships were displayed on every wall. Old barques from the fifteenth century, Navy ships of all ratings, merchantmen, Dutch traders. Every kind of seagoing vessel imaginable.

She glanced up at the wide windows at the end of the room. The room afforded an unobstructed view of a small, private bay. From the lay of the land and the color of the water, she judged they weren't far from Sheerness, somewhere on the Kentish coast.

"You wouldn't even be here if your father had died the traitor's death he deserved," the Lord Admiral said from the middle of the room.

"My father was never a traitor," Maureen told him.

The Lord Admiral looked down his nose at her. "The Admiralty board disagreed. But they lost their nerve when it came to sentencing him. He should have died, but they granted him clemency. Life in prison. He should have died there. That was supposed to be how it would happen."

"Unfortunately for you," Maureen told him, "my mother prevented that. She loved my father and helped him escape. So despite all your efforts, they still had the life together you would have denied them."

"As I said, I underestimated your mother's cunning and intelligence. I have no doubts as to how she convinced that imbecile brother-in-law of hers, Will Johnston, to help her."

"Captain Johnston? He's not related to my mother."

He studied her for a moment. "You don't know. All this time in their house, and you never made the connection." He laughed as if it was the funniest thing he'd ever heard. "I can see that all the years I've kept Will on half pay have him sufficiently cowed. I told him I could have him court-martialed for aiding an escape, but I allowed him his freedom instead because I thought Ethan had died. As it turned out, Will was of more use to me in my debt and under my control."

He stepped closer to her. "Lady Mary is your

mother's younger sister. You've been living with your aunt and uncle all these weeks. Quite ironic, really, but brilliant on my part. I knew they'd watch you even closer, ensure that you wouldn't escape."

Maureen took a deep breath, her mind reeling. It was unbelievable and yet . . . it made sense. She remembered Lady Mary telling her about her sister.

*My sister eloped, and she and her husband were nearly caught by my father.*

All the times the lady had showered her with attentions that one would extend only to family rather than a prisoner.

Maureen didn't know what to believe anymore.

The Lord Admiral paced back and forth. "Imagine my surprise when I received an intelligence report that your father was still alive. And had turned to piracy." He clucked his tongue. "How dare he take your mother into such a life. It killed her. I knew right then and there, he deserved the death he'd escaped all those years before."

Maureen shook her head. "You ordered the destruction of the Alliance?"

"Of course. I had to ensure he would never return. That he and his daughter never saw the shores of England again."

"So you hired de Ryes," she whispered.

The man let out a sigh of disgust. "I should have taken care of that assignment myself instead of trusting one of my lesser captains to see to the removal of the Alliance. He assured me Captain de Ryes was not only eager for the gold I was offering for the destruction of the Alliance but quite capable of the deceit necessary to infiltrate their ranks."

"And he succeeded. You got what you wanted. The Alliance was finished that day."

"I wanted more than just the Alliance finished. If he had been the man I was promised, you would have died that day as well."

"He might as well have killed me, after my father died and your fleet sunk our ships."

"Yes, that might have been true, but the idiot had gone and married you first." Again the man's eyes glazed over. "He let you go when you were supposed to die."

Julien hadn't let her go, she'd fled his ship—not that the Lord Admiral would believe her.

"Little did I know he'd had time not only to marry you but to get a brat on you as well."

"Ethan," she whispered.

"Yes, Ethan. One of my agents followed you to Greenwich and witnessed that happy reunion. How sentimental of you to name the brat after your father. Did you think that would make his claim to my title that much stronger?"

"I told you, you can have the title and the house. I don't want any of it. Just let Ethan go."

"You expect me to believe you? Let this pretender to my title go free?" He stood up straight. "When I learned you were smuggling in this area, I knew you were plotting against me. What I didn't expect was that it would be so easy to capture you."

Maureen swung around. "You arranged for that cargo in Calais. You arranged all of it. The men on the beach, my arrest, the trial. Everything."

He bowed his head in acknowledgment. "Yes, and then what do I discover? You are only too willing to lead me to de Ryes. Trusting, foolish girl. So like your father." He crossed the room and caught her bound arms. He raised them up, sending hot pain through her trussed limbs. "You've unwittingly given me everything I need: de Ryes and the security of knowing the Hawthorne line will never be tainted by your father's blood again."

She laughed despite the pain. "You haven't got de Ryes. Not yet."

"But I do have you. And your son." He dragged her from the room. "He'll come for you. Just like your father chased after my Ellen. He'll come and find the same reward Ethan Hawthorne received for presuming to take what is *mine*."

"Mama!" Ethan cried, crossing the dark chamber like a whirling puppy. "You've come to rescue us!"

A guard shoved Maureen into the dank cellar vault and slammed the door shut behind her. Maureen fell to her knees, and immediately Ethan's arms wound around her neck. For a moment her son was content to just hold her.

"I wondered when you were going to arrive," her aunt's voice called out from a corner. "I've been promising Ethan you would come for us. I hated to think you were going to make a liar out of an old woman."

"Aunt Pettigrew," Maureen said, her eyes adjusting to the meager light falling from a narrow window high above them. She kissed Ethan's forehead and then went to her aunt's side. Even for all she had endured, the eighty-some-year-old woman looked more furious than frail.

"I will lodge a complaint with the authorities," her aunt declared. "I'll see that horrid Peter Cottwell get exactly what your parents should have given him all those years ago."

"You knew! You knew and you didn't tell me!" Maureen said. "I asked you directly if you knew anything about my father's family, and you told me you didn't. Not about the Lord Admiral . . ." She paused for a moment. "Or about Lady Mary."

Aunt Pettigrew reached over and patted Maureen's shoulder. "I couldn't tell you about Mary. If you'd have known you might have sought her out at some time during these years. Besides, I blame that spineless husband of hers for letting Ethan and Ellen down. He might have let slip about you and Ethan. You were better off not knowing, as were they."

Maureen frowned at her great-aunt. She didn't quite agree, but there was nothing she could do to erase the past.

"As for your father's side of the family," Aunt Pettigrew said, "you never asked about unethical cousins."

"Peter Cottwell," Maureen whispered. "He can't be related to my father."

"Sad to say, but it is true, though so distantly that I wouldn't worry overly much about his madness showing up in the bloodlines anytime soon. It happens even in the finest of families," her aunt said, looking over at the door that barred their freedom. "That wretched man stole your father's career as much as he stole his title."

Still, Maureen had questions. It was as if in the last twenty-four hours she'd had to rewrite her own history, changing everything she knew about her father and mother. "He never mentioned being a baron, having this house or lands. He always joked about being a poor Irishman."

"Probably because it pained him so much to lose it all. And he was telling you a half-truth about the Irish part. Your grandmother was Irish; married your grandfather against everyone's wishes. Oh, I remember the scandal all too well. He was a seafarer, like every Hawthorne has been down through the ages. He met her in Dublin. A wild lass with dark hair. It was from her untamed blood that you and your father got your coloring—and your dispositions."

"But how did the Lord Admiral lay claim to my father's title?"

"He was next in line. Everyone always thought your father was the last of his lineage, but after they declared your father dead and a search was conducted back through the family lines, there was Peter Cottwell, rightful heir to Hawthorne Hall and the title. I doubt even your father knew they were related before that."

"But he isn't the rightful heir," Maureen insisted.

"No, you are. The Hawthorne barony can pass through the female line, and as the legitimate daughter of Lord and Lady Hawthorne, you and your heirs are the rightful holders."

At this Ethan spoke up. "I'm a baron, Aunt Pettigrew?"

"Not yet," she told him, winking at Maureen. "You have to wait for your mother to die."

The boy's eyes widened with horror at the thought.

He moved closer to Maureen and put his hand on her shoulder. "Then I don't ever want to be a baron."

"You may not have to worry about that," she told her son, ruffling his hair. Maureen rose to her feet and stalked around the room, trying to gauge the best way to escape.

"Ethan and I have been over this room since we arrived. There is no way out," her aunt told her.

"Maybe, maybe not," Maureen said, bending over and sliding her dagger out of her boot.

"You see, Aunt Pettigrew," Ethan said. "If you let me have a knife, then we would have been able to escape."

"You with a knife?" The old lady snorted. "We'd be in a worse scrape than this! You leave those things in the hands of people who know how to use them." She turned to Maureen. "You do know how to use that wicked-looking thing, don't you?"

Maureen eyed the door and the lock. Smiling at her aunt, she nodded. "Oh, aye, Auntie. Now, let's see what trouble we can get into. Ethan, catch up that light and bring it closer," she said, pointing toward the lone candle in the cell.

"Do you know how to pick a lock?" she asked her son over her shoulder.

He shook his head.

"Then, watch carefully. 'Tis a skill everyone should master. Your grandfather taught me when I was about your age."

Even in the poor light of the candle, Ethan's eyes shone with delight.

"Maureen Hawthorne!" Aunt Pettigrew exclaimed.

"Whatever are you thinking, teaching your son petty larceny?"

"Can you think of a better skill to possess in a situation such as this, Auntie?"

Her aunt had no answer for that, other than a few muttered oaths, the likes of which even Maureen hadn't heard before.

But with no further complaints issuing from her aunt, Maureen set to work teaching her son the time-honored Hawthorne tradition of picking a lock.

# Chapter 26

Julien and his unlikely band of rescuers reached Hawthorne Hall just after noon. They considered waiting
until dusk, but they all feared giving the Lord Admiral
even another hour alone with Maureen and Ethan.

The sun rode high above head, so they made a slow,
undetected approach to the house, stopping at the stables to go over their plans one more time.

There was no sign of anyone about the house, no
guards about the grounds.

"It's too quiet," Julien said. "He's trying to lull us by
making it appear as normal as possible."

Webb and Giles nodded in agreement.

"How can we be sure they are here?" Charles
asked. "Seems a long way and a rather fancy place to
take her just to kill her."

Before anyone could answer Charles's tactless ob-
servation, Captain Johnston said, "He's here. Look
down in the bay. There's his schooner. He's always got

her nearby. He's like a rat, he is. Likes to have several escape routes. Besides, he knows we're here, or at least
that we will be soon enough." He nodded toward the
bay behind them.

Hawthorne Hall sat perched above a small private
bay. Seafaring had obviously been in the blood of
countless generations of Hawthornes. From the Hall's
vantage point, one could watch where the Thames
churned into the sea and the ships made their way
toward the London pool.

In the direction the captain pointed were two ships
poised just outside the rocky shoals ringing the narrow bay.

The *Destiny* and the *Retribution*.

By now the Admiralty would be sending out ships
from the pool to follow the *Retribution*, while messages
would have been flashed to the coast to be on the
watch for the renegade ship.

Julien kept a steady eye on the two vessels, gauging
how close the ships were so they could time their
rescue and be able to quickly row out and meet them.

As they were completing their final check of their
pistols and planned assault on the house, Giles gave
Julien a hard nudge in the shoulder. "I thought you
said your wife needed rescuing?"

Julien looked up and, to his amazement, spied
Maureen, Ethan, and Aunt Pettigrew sneaking along
the ivy-covered walls, headed directly toward them.

He couldn't shout at her for fear of alerting whatever hidden troops the Lord Admiral might have
waiting for them. But even without his help, a cry
came from the house, and in an instant the yard began

filling with soldiers. It seemed that a different squadron of marines poured out from every door, swarming after the trio.

"Maureen, this way," Julien shouted.

She turned toward his voice, her expression changing from one of fear to fierce pride.

With Ethan and Aunt Pettigrew in front of her, the threesome raced across the lawn, while the rescue party laid down a volley of gunfire to hold back their pursuers.

Ethan reached the safety of the stables first. He sped past the edge of the barn as if he wasn't going to stop until he reached the sea. But as he came alongside Julien, he came to a sudden halt and fell in behind him.

Maureen and her aunt arrived next. The old girl's eyes were alight with fire, and she tossed an "about time" over her shoulder as she ambled past Julien to safety.

As for his wife, she swooped into his arms. They kissed quickly, Julien only too relieved to have her back and safe.

Her clear blue gaze told him exactly what he needed to know.

She was his, and this time for good.

"I know you," Ethan said, tugging at Julien's sleeve. He glanced slyly from his mother to Julien. "And I guess you do too, Mama."

They both laughed, and Julien looked down at his son, an unfamiliar sting of tears blurring his vision for a moment. It would have been a good time to tell the boy the truth.

*I'm your father.*

But the Lord Admiral's troops had regained their footing and were sending a new volley of shots in their direction. He pulled Ethan back behind him and told him, "And I intend to get to know you as well, . . . Ethan." He turned to the Captain. "You and Charles lead them down to the shore. Get them into one of the longboats and out to the *Destiny*. We'll hold them off until we see you make it through the surf."

The Captain gave Maureen's aunt a supportive arm, while Charles caught Ethan by the hand.

"You have my hair," Ethan said to his cousin.

"And you have my eyes," Charles quipped back. "Come along, we've got an adventure to finish."

But Ethan wasn't budging. "Not without my mother."

The stubborn tilt of his chin and his squared shoulders brought laughs from Giles and Webb.

"He's a D'Artiers, all right. Right down to his bones," Webb said with a rueful shake of his head.

Julien turned to Maureen. "Go ahead. Get Ethan and your aunt to safety. We'll be right behind you." She looked only too ready to argue, so he hugged her close again. "I'm not about to lose you now," he whispered. "I promise."

"You'd better, or I'll have your hide," she told him.

Just as she turned to leave, he called after her. "Take this." He tossed her a pistol. "Just in case."

She nodded and started along with the Captain and Charles.

Julien, Giles, and Webb held off the Lord Admiral's men for as long as they could. In the bay behind them,

Julien could make out a longboat breaking through the surf. In the boat were four figures.

Everyone but Maureen.

He cursed and wondered what foolhardiness had stopped her from reaching safety. But there was no time to find out. Their attackers were closing in, and it was time to make their break for shore.

Then from behind them a shot rang out. It whizzed over their heads and took out a henchman who was about to breach their position. Julien spied Maureen, firing shots from a copse, aiding their escape.

"She's a brave woman," Giles said, as they started to run for Maureen. "Just don't have any daughters. With a mother like that, they'll be a handful. I know."

Julien kept one eye on his wife while he fired over his shoulder at their pursuers.

Giles and Webb made it to the trees first, and just before Julien reached the relative safety of Maureen's hiding spot, a bullet ripped through his shoulder.

He pitched forward, the force sending him reeling off balance. His arm and back burned with a hot fire, and for a moment he lurched and wavered until he fell hard to the ground.

"Julien, no!"

Maureen's cry echoed in his ringing ears. He felt her hands cradling his head, pulling at him to get up. He tried to reach for her, to tell her that he was alive, but he was no longer sure of that himself.

A widening void seemed to be overtaking him, erasing the pain now spreading down his arms and chest. It washed away the hot, sticky feeling of blood as it poured from his wound. And finally it robbed him of his senses until he saw and heard nothing.

"Julien, no!" Maureen cried, watching with horror as a bullet felled him. She rushed forward, ignoring the protests of his brothers-in-law or the bullets still buzzing around them.

Even in the few short seconds it took her to reach his side, blood was already soaking the back of his jacket.

"No! No! No!" she cried, clawing at his coat, trying to pull him up.

Lord Trahern came to her aid. "Take his arm," he told her.

Between them they dragged Julien to the cover of the trees, while Lord Weston fired wildly.

"He's out cold," Lord Trahern told her. "We'll have to carry him. It's the only way."

Maureen nodded and plucked the pistol still stuck in Julien's belt. She held out her hand for the Marquess's weapons. "I'll stay here. Give you and Lord Weston a head start."

Lord Trahern looked about to argue with her, but Lord Weston spoke up. "She's right, Giles. We can carry him faster. And she's a fine shot. Probably a better mark than either of us."

The other man nodded and handed over his pistols. "We'll wait for you there."

She shook her head. "No, make for the *Destiny*. Don't wait for me. It will take you some time to navigate the surf and get past the rocks. I can hold them off until then."

"But how will you—" Lord Trahern started to protest.

She leveled the pistol as his chest. "I'll swim. I'll make it. Just get Julien to the *Destiny*. Get him to the ship's surgeon before . . . before . . ." Maureen turned and took her position. "Get him to safety or you'll both answer to me."

They nodded, and she thought she detected a wry grin at the corners of Lord Trahern's mouth. With Julien between them, they set off for the beach.

Maureen took a deep breath and began to fire. She continued, taking aim and making every shot count. Near the house she saw the Lord Admiral gesturing to his men, shouting orders.

Glancing back, she saw three figures staggering across the beach. They'd made it!

Now all she had to do was get there herself. She'd fire everything she had, drive back the attackers, and then make for the beach.

She raised the two pistols and fired. The hammers clicked down, but nothing happened.

She was out of ammunition. And out of time.

There was only one thing left to do. Run.

But she didn't run in the direction of the shore. Instead, she ran directly at her attackers, screaming like an banshee and shaking her empty fists at them.

It stunned them momentarily, as she hoped it would. And it accomplished exactly what Maureen wanted: It kept them from the beach just that much longer.

For as they swarmed around her, binding her arms to her sides, she was still able to twist around and look toward the sea. The first longboat had made it to the *Destiny*, and the second one—the one that carried Julien and his brothers-in-law—had just passed the shoals.

Ethan and Julien would live.

And that was all that mattered.

She howled in victory, raising an ancient cry high to the heavens, until a fist crashed down on her head and she fell into the same oblivion that had overtaken Julien.

"Maureen," Julien called out. His head rolled from side to side, his eyes finally coming open. "Reenie?"

His blurry gaze focused on Giles. "Where is my wife?"

"She is following us."

Julien turned. He was aboard the *Destiny*, and from the feel of the ship, they were no longer anchored. They were underway.

He pulled himself up, fighting off the dizziness that threatened to overwhelm him.

Roger Hawley—the ship's surgeon, who had stood as Julien's best man—rushed forward, pushing him back down on his bunk. "Hold up there, Captain. You took a bullet. I've got to get it out."

Julien shook him off. He wasn't sure where the strength came from—maybe it was just the more frightening thought of continuing to live without Maureen, as he had for the last eight years, that pushed him to his feet. "Not until I have my wife aboard." He checked the wrap around his shoulder and then leveled a hard stare at his brother-in-law. "What happened?"

"After you were hit, your wife insisted we take you to the beach. She said she would follow." Giles shook his head. "I hate to sound like my son, but she put a pistol to my chest and ordered me to move."

"That's Reenie," Julien said, wishing his wife had a little less spirit. Damned if one of these days her willfulness wasn't going to get her killed.

If she wasn't dead already.

Outside, the echoing thunder of cannon rocked through the air.

The door to his cabin flung open. Ethan rushed in, with Charles right behind him. "They sent me down to tell you, sir," his son said in a wild rush. "There's a ship of the line bearing down on us."

Julien staggered to the door. He turned and looked at his brothers-in-law. "I'm sorry I involved you in this."

Giles shook his head. "I've always wanted to see life from the other side of the lines. Now's my chance. I doubt they can hang me if they shoot us out of the water first."

Julien snorted. "I don't intend to lose."

He continued his painful trip topside. If his men gave any notice to his injury, it was only a passing glance. They were too well trained to let anything distract them from their duties.

Across a narrow channel, the *Retribution* sailed alongside them. A Mr. Whitney, who had identified himself as the first mate, called over.

"What's our course, sir?"

Julien glanced up at the ship bearing down on them. They could more than likely outrun the heavier, bulkier ship, but that would mean leaving Maureen behind. He had no intention of doing that. "We attack," he shouted.

The man nodded and began calling out orders to the *Retribution*'s crew.

Julien turned his face to the wind and then gauged the distance between them and the British. The ship was looming larger and more menacing than it had at a distance.

A first-rater, with over a hundred cannon. Even with the added advantage of the *Retribution* at their side, they were still outgunned and outmanned.

At least they had the wind in their favor.

Giles moved to his side. "You could surrender. I could claim I was here on a diplomatic mission and that you were transporting me."

Julien laughed. "The *Destiny* on a diplomatic mission for His Majesty? It might bide us some time while they finish laughing. Then they will still blow us out of the water. You are forgetting there is a price on my head as well as on this ship. The crew who sinks the *Destiny* splits a prize of fifty thousand pounds. They wouldn't care if the entire royal family were aboard. Right now every man on that ship is spending his share."

Giles looked across the water at the ship bearing down on them. "I hope you have a plan."

"I do, but I doubt my wife would approve."

Just then there was a tug at his sleeve. "Father, where is my mother?" It was Ethan, his face brimming with pride. When Julien just stared at him, surprised to hear himself called by his rightful title, his son spoke up. "Cousin Charles told me."

"Remind me to talk to Cousin Charles after all this is over," Julien said, glancing across the deck to where the Earl of Hawksbury stood.

His nephew shrugged and then turned to aid a man who was adjusting the lines.

"Father, where is my mother?" his son repeated.

"She's still ashore."

Ethan nodded. "Will she be safe there?"

She damned well better be, he thought. Instead, he asked the boy, "What do you think?"

"I think she'll be safe."

"I do too. Now, since she isn't here, I have to ask your permission on something. Something I doubt she would like. But since you are most likely her second in command when it comes to the *Retribution*, I would like to ask your permission to captain her."

Ethan's face grew grave, as if he knew full well the weight of having to make this decision for his mother. "Are you a good captain?"

"One of the best."

He nodded. "Will you return her in good condition?"

"That's where I think your mother and I would disagree." Julien knelt down and explained his plan to his son. "You see, it is the only way. The *Destiny* is faster than the *Retribution*, and we'll need every sail to get away."

Ethan looked from the *Retribution* to the ship bearing down on them. "I don't think Mother is going to be happy with us, but I think you're right, sir. It is the best plan."

Julien grinned at his son and rose to his feet. "Start transferring every bit of powder we've got to the *Retribution*," he shouted to his men. "Leave us just enough to fight with, but we'll need every ounce over there if we are going to make this work."

As the men set to work, Ethan tugged on Julien's sleeve again. "Father, what can I do?"

If truth be told, he didn't want Ethan anywhere on the ship, but he couldn't turn down the lad's offer. "Where is your Aunt Pettigrew?"

"Helping Mr. Balton," Ethan said.

"Loading muskets?" Julien shook his head. Could he have heard his son correctly?

"Aye, sir. Mr. Balton says she has quite a hand for it. Should I go help?"

The ammunition stores, while dangerous in themselves, were well below the waterline and the least likely spot to be hit. Julien nodded to his son, and Ethan scampered down the nearest hatchway.

For a moment the pain in his shoulder rallied forth, leaving him nauseous and wavering on his feet, but he swallowed it back.

Cannon fire from the British ship cleared his senses, the balls landing close enough to send spray up over the sides of the *Destiny*.

The next ones would hit if he didn't change course.

Shouting more orders and stalking across the deck, he tamped down any thoughts but what was before him.

He had a fight on his hands, something he'd had countless times. Yet this time it was different. This time a fire burned within him that hadn't been present ever before.

This was one battle he couldn't afford to lose.

# Chapter 27

The icy dash of seawater brought Maureen awake. She sputtered and coughed, choking on the salt filling her mouth. Her fingers clawed at the decking beneath her, trying to find a handhold, something to hang on to.

Before she could catch her breath, a second bucket of water poured over her prone figure, this time sending the stinging, frigid water into her eyes and ears.

She shook like a wet, angry dog and reared back her head. "One more of those and I'll kill the son of a bitch."

Laughter followed, as cold and mean as the water running in rivers down her neck and back, streaming from her loose hair. "And you thought you could be a lady," the Lord Admiral's voice mocked from somewhere close by.

Maureen took low, steady breaths, bracing herself for the next round of water, but none came. Slowly, she raised her head and took in her surroundings.

She was aboard a schooner, more than likely the Lord Admiral's private vessel from the looks of the rich ornaments and other touches. They were sailing away from shore, Hawthorne Hall rising on the distant hill behind them like an ancient sentry. The men manning the ship regarded her warily, as if fearing to meet her gaze.

It occurred to her that one of them would have to kill her. The Lord Admiral hadn't brought her out here for a pleasure trip. The man did everything in a calculated, precise manner. He had his reasons, and she feared she'd find them out only too soon.

Her head pounded, leaving her unsteady and dizzy. But she could hardly protect herself lying on the ground, so she knew she needed to get up. She brought herself to a kneeling position, not wanting to stand too quickly and find her legs buckling beneath her. Her hand brushed over her boot.

Her dagger. She still had it. She almost grinned.

Whatever the Lord Admiral had planned for her, she was sure he would be more surprised by what she would give him in return.

In the distance a cannon boomed. Beside her the Lord Admiral laughed again.

"Get up, my dear Baroness. Get up. You'll miss the entertainment."

More cannon answered the first one, but this time with a different pitch. Two ships, maybe more, she estimated from the sounds.

Her gaze swung across the waves to where three ships were making their first maneuvers into engagement. She would have known the lines, the sails, of the first two anywhere.

The *Retribution* and the *Destiny*.

But it was the third ship that ran her blood as cold as the water they'd dashed over her head.

A first-rate. A hundred or more cannon strong. The largest of the British warships. A floating armory of firepower and unbeatable strength.

The Lord Admiral moved to her side, his fingers gripping her elbow as he dragged her to the railing. "Seems my best ship saw the signals from shore. Care to make a wager, *Baroness*? Your ships versus mine. I'll give you good odds, considering how outgunned and outmanned your side seems to be."

Maureen watched the movements between her ship and Julien's. She didn't even know if he was still alive. But one thing was for certain: Her family was aboard those ships, and she didn't want to just stand here and watch them die. "I'll take that wager. But forget the odds. My life for yours."

The Lord Admiral laughed. "Your life is already forfeit. If your husband continues to fight like that, you'll be a widow before you die."

The *Destiny* sent out a volley of shot, some hitting the British ship, most of it splashing harmlessly in the water.

It was obvious the frigate was playing target, darting in and out and taking the bulk of the shots, while the more maneuverable *Retribution* sailed in tight circles just outside the range of the warship.

Yet, it didn't make sense.

They should be working together to cripple the British so they could then make a run for the open sea. What was Mr. Whitney, her first mate, thinking? He should be helping the *Destiny*, not running scared.

"Would you like a closer look? It seems even the rats aboard your ship are deserting your husband," the Lord Admiral said, offering her a spyglass with the same mock gallantry one might use to offer a lady punch at Almack's.

She snatched the glass out of his hand and brought it to her eye. She scanned the decks of the *Destiny* but saw no sign of Julien. She swept it again and this time saw Mr. Whitney on the rear deck, shouting orders.

Mr. Whitney aboard the *Destiny*? Then who was manning the *Retribution*?

She turned toward her ship, but the Lord Admiral pulled the glass out of her hand before she could get it focused.

"As you can see, your husband is about to die."

"I wouldn't count out my husband just yet," she said. "De Ryes hasn't lost yet, and since he always wins against your poor fleet, I doubt today will be any different." At least she prayed it wouldn't be, for all their sakes. "And when he wins he'll sail straight for this bilge bucket of yours and send it straight to hell."

The Lord Admiral's mouth twisted with rage. "You arrogant bitch. Just like your mother. She was a fool as well."

Maureen stood her ground. "My mother had the good taste not to marry the likes of you. And she had the courage to save my father's life. Did any woman ever love you that much? For that matter, did anyone?"

His face mottled with an unholy fury and she braced herself for his retaliation, for she thought for sure he wouldn't let her live another minute. But even with his fist raised and ready to mete out his punishment, he suddenly stopped. His gaze turned toward the ships beyond them, his body stilled as if the sight before him left him in shock.

She swung around to the railing and climbed up to see the sight that had left the Lord Admiral gaping like a mackerel.

"Here, let me take that line," Charles said.

Julien looked over at his nephew in horror. "What the hell are you doing here?" He'd ordered everyone off the *Retribution*—at least he thought he had.

"You really didn't think you could run this ship single-handedly, did you?" his nephew said with a grin. Gone was the stylish young man-about-town, for Charles had stripped himself of his jacket and vest and now wore only a shirt and his breeches. Even his feet were bare, since it was obvious he knew what would come next. "I can sail and swim as well as anyone. You taught me."

"I didn't teach you to be foolhardy."

Charles shrugged. "Hardly that. I expect you want to live, considering Maureen is still out there."

"Your mother will kill me if she finds out."

"Never mind my mother." Charles laughed. "Your wife will have your hide when she finds out what you are going to do to her ship."

"I'll buy her another one," Julien quipped back, turning to watch the battle before them. He had to gauge their timing just right if he was to catch the British unawares. He needed them sure and cocky and so focused on sinking the *Destiny* that they would forget the smaller *Retribution* darting about them like an unseen gnat.

His shoulder throbbed, and he was having a hard time keeping the wheel steady. The currents from the ocean and the Thames were tricky, and with only the powder kegs on the deck, the empty holds left the ship tossing across the waves like a cork.

"Do you need a hand?" Charles called out.

Julien grit his teeth and shook his head.

Cannon fire blasted from the British warship. They both looked up to see how the *Destiny* fared.

It didn't look good. She smoked and faltered, and the British were tacking hard to move in for their final kill.

"Gads, how did they survive that?" Charles asked.

"Luck," Julien muttered, wondering at the wisdom of leaving Mr. Whitney to sail his ship. He was doing too good a job at appearing ready to go under. Julien turned his face to the wind to clear his eyes of the stinging smoke burning his vision.

"Isn't it about time?" Charles asked as another volley from the British cut through the battle haze toward the *Destiny*.

Julien nodded, suddenly glad to have Charles's able assistance. Between the two of them, they swiftly cut all the lines holding up the remaining sails. The cloth unfurled, catching the wind and sending the *Retribution* seething forward through the churning sea.

Pulling hard on the wheel, Julien maneuvered the sleek little schooner about, setting a course directly between the *Destiny* and the British.

The wind kept up, pushing them forward, driving them directly into the line of fire. The acrid smoke grew thicker, and it was hard for Julien to see where he was going, especially this close to the belching British cannons.

"Are the fuses ready?" he called out to Charles.

"Ready."

"After you are done lighting them, get overboard. Swim as hard as you can." Julien caught up the rope at his feet and began lashing the wheel in a set course. Currents and winds be damned. They were close enough now to the behemoth vessel to count the hairs on the gunner—the *Retribution* sailing directly alongside the gun ports of the stunned British.

"Light 'em," Julien ordered, running alongside the deck and tossing grappling hooks into the British ship, while Charles ran from powder line to powder line, touching off the fuses.

Smoke and fire filled the decks of the *Retribution*.

"That's the last one!" Charles yelled, heading to the side of the ship and diving for the water. Julien followed, but for a moment he paused on the railing, looking back at the British ship. The captain was shouting at his men to cut the schooner loose, but it was too late.

Too late to save his ship.

As the first keg exploded, Julien dove from the deck railing, hitting the icy water as flames leapt above him.

He swam as best he could underwater, the explosions above sending shock waves through the water.

First the *Retribution*, and then the second blast—the munitions on the now open and keeling warship.

As he came up for air, debris rained down around him, and he ducked down under to avoid being hit. When he surfaced again, the crippled warship was beginning to sink, its men calling out for help.

Ahead of him, Charles bobbed in the water, watching the sight before them. Julien swam slowly toward him, his one arm now useless. With his nephew's help they made their way to the *Destiny*.

The damage aboard was just as Julien hoped—minimal. The smoke pots on the decks and the false tattered lines and debris his men had pulled from the masts had only made it appear the British were winning their fight. It was a trick they'd used more than once in the last year.

He sank to his knees, blood running anew from his wounded shoulder, the salt from the seawater burning his open flesh. "Cut loose the longboats so those sailors out there have something to save themselves with," Julien ordered. His men nodded and set to work. Unlike their British counterparts, the American privateers maintained a strict code of conduct for prisoners. Too many of them had lived under the British lash at some time in their lives and had no stomach for the brutality that ruled His Majesty's Navy.

Their war was one of honor and reputation.

Roger stepped forward. "I've got to get that bullet out."

"Not until I've found Maureen."

Ethan rushed forward, a spyglass in his hand. "I saw her, Father. I saw Mother. She's on that schooner." He pointed to the west of their position. "I saw her on the deck."

Julien rose and took the offered glass from his son. It didn't take but a moment to spy Maureen. She stood on a railing, her hands clinging to the lines. Her dark hair whipped and flowed in the wind.

As if she sensed him watching her, she saluted him.

"Go after them. Stop them before they hit the river," he ordered.

The Lord Admiral's schooner, with its four carronade on deck, was no match for the *Destiny*. In minutes they were bearing down on it, the privateer's cannon already reloaded and primed for its next battle.

As they drew alongside, every man aboard stilled at the sight before them.

For on the deck of the schooner, the Lord Admiral stood with a pistol to Maureen's temple.

"Back off," the man ordered. "Or watch her die."

"If you harm her you won't live a minute longer," Julien said, his hands gripping the railing.

He couldn't watch her die, not a second time.

His men held their muskets steady, every one trained on a member of the Lord Admiral's crew, and half a dozen aimed directly at the man himself.

Maureen's gaze caught and held Julien's. Her face was a mask of courage and bravery. She wasn't about to die, not if the proud tilt of her shoulders indicated anything.

And then she glanced down at her feet.

Julien's gaze followed, and there he saw it. The hilt of her dagger sticking out of her boot. The one she'd taken from the *Destiny* all those years ago.

Then she glanced up at the railing, as if telling him what she had planned.

The scene, one he'd played in his mind over and over since that day eight years ago, returned.

*Maureen standing on the deck of the* Destiny, *a bloody knife in her hand.*

But there was one difference. Unlike the madman grasping her now, he hadn't been holding a gun to her head and he would rather have shot himself than her.

"Please, no," she wailed. "Don't shoot me."

The helpless feminine pitch of her cry almost made Julien laugh.

Almost.

"I'm so frightened, Julien. Do as he says. Please don't let me die." Her wailing theatrics were starting to take on a flavor rarely seen even in the melodramas of Covent Garden.

Julien nodded to his men, and they started to move the *Destiny* off.

The Lord Admiral smiled, his finger cocking back the trigger. Maureen slumped into his arms as if in a deep faint. The man let her fall to the deck. But instead of the prone figure he likely expected, she rolled like a cat, pulling her dagger out of her boot and sending it sailing through the air, directly into the Lord Admiral's heart.

The man stood for a moment, wavering in disbelief, while a red blossom of blood spilled down his chest. The pistol in his hand fired, sending the bullet crashing toward where Maureen had stood.

But she was no longer there. She hadn't even stopped to see if her dagger had hit the mark, but instead had flung herself headlong over the railing.

Even as she splashed into the water, the Lord Admiral crashed to the deck of his ship, dead.

"Get her aboard," Julien called out. Then he turned to the crew on the schooner. "Get away from my ship, or you'll join your master in hell."

The Lord Admiral's men dropped whatever weapons they possessed and set to work turning their ship back to shore. Not one of them saw to the man's body, still staining the deck with his blood.

As Julien watched Maureen climb aboard, he finally succumbed to his own injuries. It was his turn to fall to the deck, the strident cries of his beloved wife echoing through his ears as he fell into a spinning abyss.

"What in bloody hell were you thinking? Blowing up my ship!"

He grinned and closed his eyes to the pain.

Maureen followed Giles and Webb as they carried Julien to his cabin.

Roger Hawley brought up the rear, having finished helping the few men who had been wounded in their fight with the British.

Now, with the threat of the Lord Admiral gone, Maureen had simply given Mr. Whitney's plan—get them as far out into the Channel as they could sail—a passing nod of agreement.

Julien was still out cold when they rolled him over

and Roger began the process of cutting his shirt away. Maureen helped strip it, leaving Julien's back bared to clean the gaping wound. His injury looked terrible, but it wasn't the hole in his shoulder that caught her attention.

It was the *T* branded on his other shoulder.

"What is that?" she gasped, shocked at the hideous mark burned into his flesh. She'd felt that scar the night they made love, but he had told her it was nothing.

Now she saw how "nothing" it was.

"The brand?" Roger said, rather too nonchalantly. From the looks of the way the man worked, he was used to sewing up the wounds from battle. "He's had that for some time. I thought you knew."

She shook her head. "Who did this to him?"

"The bloody Brits," he said. Looking up at the two British noblemen still in the room, he made a rude noise in the back of his throat. "Beggin' your pardon, my lords."

Webb nodded at the man, obviously as transfixed by the ugly scar as Maureen was.

The wound looked old, as if it had been there for some time, but he hadn't had it when they married. She was almost afraid to ask, but her desire for the truth drove her further toward her suspicions. "Where did he get this? He's not a criminal; he's never lost a fight."

"Only one." The man reached for the basin Aunt Pettigrew had brought in and then opened his case to take out a probe. Without looking up he began the slow, laborious work of pulling out the bullet.

"How . . . Where did this happen?"

He didn't look up but answered in his usual gruff tones. "With a British branding iron. As to where this happened, the same place we all received one. Jamaica."

"All of you?" she asked.

Julien's men, several of whom had poked their heads in to see how their captain fared, nodded.

She looked at Lord Trahern and Lord Weston for an explanation, but they both shrugged, obviously as puzzled by this as she. "Whatever for?" she persisted. "Why would any of you be branded traitors?"

Roger snorted and looked up from his work. "For you. Because he married you. When he married you and took his vow with the Alliance, he broke the agreement he had with the British. We all did."

Even though she'd told Julien she believed that he had tried to stop the British slaughter of the Alliance, she hadn't really let go of her memories. It seemed to her impossible to reconcile what she'd seen that day with Julien's assertions that he'd tried to stop the slaughter.

"You and I were both there," Maureen said to Roger. "The *Destiny* fought the Alliance. Julien sent the British word, brought them to the cay. Helped them destroy the Alliance."

Roger shook his head. "If you had stayed on the deck a little longer that day, you would have seen that our cannons were not aimed at your father's ship or any of the other Alliance ships. We moved in line with the British to get in close enough to cripple them. Not unlike what we did today with your ship."

She shook her head. It couldn't be true. All these years she'd clung to her mistaken beliefs, her anger, and now it was starting to dawn on her that she'd been wrong.

Terribly wrong.

"I was there. I saw the battle," she whispered. At least she thought she had. "How can what you say be true?"

The man shrugged and went back to his work. "Tell that to the men of this ship. When Julien came to us and asked us if we were willing to switch sides, everyone agreed. The Alliance offered us a better chance of growing rich than the paltry blood money the British had offered for your father's head."

She still couldn't fathom it. Julien hadn't betrayed her father; instead, he'd tried to save him. Just as he'd told her—aboard the *Destiny* and here in London.

Why had she been so willing to ignore the truth? Even now she tried to make sense of it. "But they came. The English. I saw a man row out to inform them."

"You saw a traitor," Roger spat. His brow furrowed, and then with a sucking sound and rush of fresh blood, he pulled out the lead ball. He held it up for all to see and sat back, letting the wound clean itself. "The one man who betrayed us. All of us. What Julien didn't know when he'd joined on was that he was actually a British officer, placed on the *Destiny* to ensure we completed our mission. He volunteered that night to take false information to the awaiting ships."

"And instead he told his superiors where we were."

"Aye." Roger reached for his needle and thread and began stitching up the wound. "They came in at dawn.

And you know what happened next." He knotted the thread and began closing the ragged flesh.

Aunt Pettigrew, ever the perfectionist when it came to needlework, leaned over his shoulder and then nodded with approval at the dark, even stitches.

"After the battle was over, they surrounded us." Roger clipped the thread and leaned back in his chair, studying his work with a practiced eye. "Threatened to blow the *Destiny* out of the water. We'd been able to cripple the frigates, but we were no match for the others. Julien struck our colors rather than allow any more bloodshed." The man paused. "I think if he'd known the hell we were in for, he might have tried to fight it out. We spent six months in a Jamaica prison for treason. Each one of us was branded so we'd never forget what we did. We escaped two days before we were to be transported to Botany Bay."

Roger took the basin and strode across the room. Tossing the contents out the window, he looked back at Maureen. "He'll probably be out for some time. Watch him for any signs of fever. I need to check on my other patients."

Then the brusque man left, leaving Maureen as shocked and stunned as if she'd just had a bullet plucked from her body. From her heart.

The others, obviously sensing her need to be alone with her husband after this revelation, followed the doctor out of the cabin. Charles, the last to leave, closed the door behind him.

She gazed down at the man she'd thought she knew and realized how wrong she had been. For all these years. Wrong about Julien, wrong about everything.

Her fingers reached out and traced the *T* on Julien's back.

The mark of a traitor.

She was the only traitor in the room, for not trusting him. For not believing him. For not following her vows, for believing with her eyes and not her heart.

She retraced her memories of that long-lost day and saw it as Roger had described it.

If only she'd stopped and let Julien explain. If only she'd had her mother's courage to see past the insurmountable evidence of a court-martial.

She laid her head down on his branded shoulder and wept.

Julien gauged it was early morning when he opened his eyes and saw light streaming in from the windows of his cabin. His shoulder ached, but given that he was undressed and in his own bed, he had a feeling the pain in his shoulder was just the remains of Roger's work.

The ship rolled softly, as if it were moored near shore. He wondered how long he'd been out and where they were.

The door slid open, and soft footsteps trod over the floor. He closed his eyes so it appeared he was still asleep. The person worked about the room, and when he peered between his shuttered lashes, he saw the unmistakable form of Maureen bent over one of his chests, pulling out maps and charts.

"So you didn't slit my throat last night."

She jumped and turned around. Her face looked as pale as if she'd seen a ghost. "Julien," she whispered.

The tenderness and love in her voice were tinged

with something else. Something he couldn't quite discern.

"Where are we?" he asked.

"A harbor near Dover. I've used it a time or two for smuggling." She laughed, though again there was something in her voice that marred the humor. "I never thought I'd be smuggling into England three of its peers. They are just about to go ashore."

Relief swept through him. Webb, Giles, and Charles would be safe now. And though he wondered when he would ever be able to see his family again, at least he could rest easy knowing they were home.

"Your nephew is being a regular blood about going ashore." Maureen leaned closer. "He'd heard some of the men discussing the *Bodiel* and decided he wanted to try his hand at privateering. I've threatened to send him off in irons if he doesn't set a better example for Ethan." She smiled at the memory and then reached out to touch his face.

Her fingers stopped just short of his jaw, and in her hesitation he finally found his answer.

*Regret.*

Her eyes were filled with regret.

The gaze that had haunted him for so long, the color of which he'd seen only in the waters off the West Indies, now looked down at him with understanding that at first he didn't comprehend.

Then he realized. With his shirt gone she'd seen more than just his wound. "You know."

She closed her eyes and nodded. "I saw the brand when Roger was tending you. He told me everything."

Julien turned away. "I didn't want you to find out.

Not until we'd come to an understanding. I wanted you to love me because you wanted to. Not because you felt you had to." He let out an exasperated breath and glanced back at her. "I know that sounds odd, but what I am trying to say is that I know you. You're an incredible woman, Reenie, but you are stubborn. I knew given time you'd love me again. At least I hoped you would. And if you could find it in your heart to love me again, I wanted you to come to that on your own. Then I knew you'd be willing to listen to the truth and forgive me for my mistakes."

She nodded. She wouldn't have believed him, trusted him. She'd been so set in her ways. But he'd tackled her hatreds, her misperceptions, in the only way he knew how.

A steady course through the turbulent seas of her heart.

He reached for her, and she came to him, her lips eagerly touching his. For a time they kissed and allowed the world around them to drift away. They murmured promises that they knew this time would last forever, and when it seemed they couldn't get enough of each other, the door to Julien's cabin swung open.

"Mother!" Ethan's shocked voice reverberated through the room.

Obviously, his son had never seen his mother kiss a man before. That pleased Julien more than he cared to admit.

"I came to say good-bye," Ethan said, this time shyly, as he crossed the room, his curious gaze flitting between his two parents as if he was still unconvinced about this notion of having both a mother *and* a father.

"You're going with your uncles?" Julien asked, sitting up abruptly, his gaze swinging to Maureen for confirmation. He wasn't about to let Ethan leave, not just yet. Not when he finally had the chance to get to know the lad.

But one glance at Maureen told him this was the only way.

"It's for the best," she said softly. "At least until the war is over. Until we can guarantee his safety with us."

"And where are you off to, son?" he asked Ethan.

"To Uncle Giles's house. And Aunt Pettigrew is coming as well," the boy said, climbing between his two parents. "Cousin Charles says he'll teach me to ride this summer and how to sail." He grinned at both parents. "You should come with me," he said hopefully.

Julien shook his head. "We can't. Not just yet. But we'll be with you soon. As soon as we can."

"Yes, very soon," Maureen told him. "We'll miss you every day." She turned her gaze to Julien. "It is for the best," she said, as if trying to convince herself. "Especially given that he will someday inherit so much more than I ever thought he would."

"Hawthorne Hall." Ethan grimaced. "What do I want with some old pile like that?"

"You'll want it for your wife," Julien told him.

At this Ethan looked horror-stricken. "A wife? I'm not going to ever get married. When I grow up I'm going to be a smuggler and a privateer."

Maureen laughed and ruffled his hair. "Oh, you might find something else you like better."

"Don't be so sure," Julien told her. "I made the same vow when I was about his age."

Charles appeared at the doorway. "Ethan, it's time."

Julien struggled to get up, and ignoring the irate looks Maureen sent him for rising from his sickbed without her permission, he caught up a shirt and tugged it on.

Above-deck the day had dawned bright. After one last hug and kiss from Ethan and strong, heartfelt handshakes from his brothers-in-law and nephew, he watched them row ashore. He reached out and took Maureen's hand, squeezing it gently.

"We'll have him back with us soon," he promised. "If I have to negotiate a peace treaty myself."

She nodded, her eyes brimming with tears. He wrapped his arm around her shoulder and drew her close. They stood on the deck and watched their son until he was safely to shore and bounding up the beachhead, his small hand tucked into that of his newfound cousin.

As soon as the longboat returned, Julien started issuing orders.

The wind was freshening, and down the coast was Portsmouth.

And the Halifax-bound *Bodiel*.

"Do you think we still have time to catch her?" Maureen said, sidling up to him as he stood by the rail, looking out toward the open sea.

"We have to. I need that gold. I have a ship to buy. To replace my wife's."

Maureen laughed. "You don't owe me another ship. What do I need one for? I have no intention of ever setting foot on anything other than the *Destiny*." She looked up at him. "That is, if you'll have me?"

He gazed into those azure eyes and knew this time he wouldn't have to worry what the fates would bring them as he made his vows to her for a second time.

"Aye, Reenie. I'll have you. From this day forth . . ."

# Epilogue

The Kent Coast
1838

The dark shadows of the moonless night hid everything. Clouds masked even the stars. The wind had picked up in the last hour, bringing the waves crashing up on the small beach, muffling the sounds of the men working to off-load the kegs of brandy and the bales of tea from the longboats onto the waiting wagons.

'Twas a night made for smuggling.

"I didn't expect you so soon," Maureen said, wrapping her cashmere shawl tighter around her neck. She squinted into the night at the ship anchored in the private harbor of Hawthorne Hall. "She's a fine one, Ethan. Fleet and quick, just like you said she would be."

Her son beamed at her as he strode up the beach. A partner in D'Artiers Shipyard, Ethan was known for designing some of the most innovative and fastest ships in the world.

"I used some of the clipper lines from our American ships but added some of the old lines from the *Retribution*." He wiped at the chestnut lock falling over his forehead. "I think we set a Channel record. Too bad I can't tell Father."

Maureen nodded in agreement. "I don't think that would be wise. He might start asking questions, and if he found out . . ."

They both knew what Julien D'Artiers would say if he found out his wife and son were involved in one of the areas richest smuggling operations.

He'd have both their heads.

It wasn't that Maureen liked hiding this fact from her husband, but . . . well, Julien had become so respectable of late that he made it impossible for her to tell him the truth.

He had taken to life at Hawthorne Hall like a man born to the manor, a man who'd never set foot to sea. But for her the adjustment hadn't been as easy.

Even now, with Ethan and their three other children grown and married, Maureen could not shake the sea from her soul. Not that she'd meant to get back into the smuggling business, but once she'd done some digging into her family history, she learned it was a Hawthorne tradition.

And as the Baroness Hawthorne, she felt some traditions were worth continuing. Even if you had to keep them secret from your husband.

As for her son's involvement—that had been accidental. But once he'd discovered his mother's side business, he'd given her little choice but to let him help.

The stubborn determination he'd inherited from his D'Artiers relatives, coupled with his pirate Hawthorne blood, made him a natural smuggler.

"See the kegs to town," she ordered the men. "And the tea to the cellars. We'll send it out next week with the regular shipments." She tousled Ethan's hair, knowing how much he hated it.

But not tonight. He looked to be in far too good a mood at the success of his new ship. He only nodded and went back to work, helping the local men move the goods that added extra money to all their pockets.

Maureen turned and started up the beach, regretful that she couldn't stay and help.

There were times, like tonight, when she missed the life she and Julien had led after they'd rediscovered their love for each other. They'd sailed the *Destiny* out into the war-torn seas and taken prize after prize together.

Including the gold-laden *Bodiel*.

Then the war had ended, and they'd been able to return to England to be with their son. No one in society seemed the wiser that the very handsome Julien D'Artiers and his beautiful wife, the former Miss Fenwick, were in actuality Captain de Ryes and his privateer bride.

And after a few months in London, Julien convinced his wife that for Ethan's sake and in memory of her father they should seek to have the Hawthorne title returned to its rightful holder.

An announcement that immediately divided the scandal-happy *ton* of London.

Eustacia Bennett, née Cottwell, the current Lady Hawthorne, was a proper young matron, married with a child on the way. The old guard rallied to her defense, looking with a skeptical eye at the possibility of having to acknowledge the dashing and just a bit unseemly Mrs. Julien D'Artiers.

It had taken Giles's and Webb's considerable pull to have the case of Ethan Hawthorne reopened, and with the testimony of Lady Mary and Aunt Pettigrew as to Maureen's rightful paternity, it was obvious there had been a grievous mistake.

Still, Eustacia was not her father's daughter for nothing, and she started a vicious gossip campaign to undermine Maureen's case and reputation.

Rather than use such public tactics, Maureen and Julien presented the Lord Admiral's haughty and arrogant daughter with an impressive and irrefutable ledger of information about her father's less than honorable acts as Lord Admiral—the likes of which, if made known, would keep her from polite society for the rest of her life.

Rather than have her father's memory sullied, Eustacia acknowledged the error in inheritance, surrendered the Hawthorne title to Maureen, and quietly retired to her mother's Welton dower lands in the north country.

Maureen strolled across the dark lawns of her home and entered the house by a side door she'd left unlocked.

The servants knew better than to latch that door on a moonless night. Having been raised on Hawthorne lands, each and every one of them, they knew enough to turn a blind eye to such goings on.

Julien would be incensed at her taking such risks, she thought as she passed his portrait hanging in the long gallery. While the likeness captured him standing on the bow of one of his ships, she knew the dashing man done in oil was lost to her—having become as stuffy and rigid as the rest of England.

A new queen and a growing prosperity in the country had ushered in a more proper and decorous society. Maureen felt as out of tune with her peers as she did with her husband.

When had it happened? When had they drifted apart?

She didn't know. All she knew was that she missed him. Missed the excitement they once shared.

As she passed Julien's office, she noticed a light shimmering in the shadows.

How odd, she thought. Julien was up in London, as he often was each month. Which turned out to be quite convenient, since she could then go about her smuggling activities without his knowledge.

She opened the door and crossed the room toward the single candle on his desk. As she leaned over to blow it out, his chair swung around and she found herself eye to eye with her husband.

His eyes glittered with an old fire she hadn't seen in years. "There you are, Reenie. I wondered where you were. Odd that none of the servants seemed to be able to tell me where you'd gone on such a wild night."

*Reenie.*

He hadn't called her that in years. The sound of her old nickname thrilled her, as did the dangerous challenge behind his words.

"I needed some air," she told him, her gaze locked with his.

"And that was all?"

She nodded.

He caught her arm and pulled her closer. "Isn't the beach path rather dangerous in this weather? You never know what sorts may wash ashore. Villains, blackguards . . . *smugglers*."

Maureen's next breath caught in her chest.

*He knew.* He'd been there, watching her.

Still she tried to brazen it out. "Smugglers? Blackguards?" She laughed. "Julien, you've been reading your old log books to the grandchildren again, haven't you?"

"Reenie," he said, his tone low and dangerous.

"Oh, Julien, it was just one load of brandy."

He stared at her, one brow cocked upward.

"And some tea," she admitted. "Just this once. It was a lark, just a chance to try out Ethan's new ship."

He coughed and shook his head.

"Well, maybe more than once," she told him.

"Try every month for the last year," he corrected.

She bit her lip. Oh, she'd done it now. He was probably furious with her. He would probably leave her. A respected shipbuilder with ties to the government couldn't very well have a smuggler for a wife.

But instead, he swept aside the papers on his desk, blew out the candle, and pushed it aside as well. He caught her in his arms and pinned her down on the cherry-wood desk top. "You wild, untamed lass. What am I ever going to do with you?"

His mouth swooped down on hers and kissed her with an abandon that she had thought lost between them. His mouth claimed hers, teasing her lips, begging her to open up to his hunger.

She answered with a deep sign of longing. "Julien."

For some time they kissed, as if they'd never before met, as if all their years of marriage and raising children and sharing the same bed had been erased.

"Reenie, oh, Reenie, I'm so sorry," Julien whispered into her ear.

She leaned back and looked at him. "Whatever for? I was the one who risked so much. Smuggling, and at my age!"

"You aren't of an age. To me you are timeless. And it is I who should be apologizing. I'd forgotten what it was like. I became so embroiled in the ships and the yard and cargoes that I forgot." He kissed her again, this time slowly and tenderly.

"I thought you'd be so angry," she told him. "If you found out."

"I have to admit, I wasn't all that pleased when I discovered the midnight ventures of you and Ethan, but then as I investigated it I found myself tempted to join in your misdeeds. The cargoes, the signals, the cover of night. I hadn't felt that alive since we left the *Destiny*. And it struck me hard that I've let myself become landlocked."

She smiled. The pride and regret in his voice were like manna, feeding her soul anew.

"And then, as I found myself waiting each month

for the moon to wane, waiting for your night to arrive, I realized what you'd been missing all these years. What we'd lost."

Tears filled her eyes. "What do we do now?"

He rose from the desk and held out his hand to her. His fingers wound around hers with a familiar warmth and strength. He led her upstairs to the room they'd shared all these years. Candles glowed from the mantel, while a low bed of glowing embers lay banked in the fireplace.

She entered the room sensing something was different. And there on the bed she saw why.

Gracing the expensive satin counterpane were her old clothes. Her shirt, her breeches, and her dagger.

And beside them, a model of a clipper. The most beautiful ship she'd ever seen.

"I don't understand," she said to him.

"Wear them again, Reenie. Come sail with me. We'll explore the world." He picked up the model and handed it to her.

She held it in her hands and gazed at the fine vessel. On the bow was inscribed the ship's name.

The *Temptress.*

"She's yours. I had her built for you. We'll take her around the world; just say the word." He grinned at her, that boyish charm alive in his eyes as if it had never been lost. "We'll go down around the Horn, to India, to the China seas. and eventually we'll find our way to this cay I once visited in the West Indies, where the water is so blue . . . well, let me show you how blue."

He caught her hand and pulled her toward the mirror over the mantel. Gently, he pulled the stray tendrils of hair back from her face, and from behind her he nodded toward their reflection. "Like your eyes. I want to swim in that water again. I want to see you on that beach." He kissed her again, the kind that said he wanted to do more than just walk hand in hand along that sand strand.

When he released her he knelt by the bed and started pulling out charts hidden beneath it, spreading them out at her feet. "We'll live like we used to, barefoot and happy. Just tell me that you'll come with me."

Maureen's lips trembled, her vision awash with tears. "You'd go to sea again? With me?"

"Oh, yes, Reenie, my love. I want nothing more. I was a fool to ever make you leave it."

At this she shook her head. "No, Julien. Don't say that. We made the right choice, regaining the Hall, giving Ethan his heritage, raising a family. We've done what we were supposed to do."

"And now?"

She took a deep breath. "We'll shock everyone. Including the children."

"Aye, I'm counting on it. I want them to see their mother as I first beheld her. A siren calling me from across the waves. You still are, Reenie. My tempting siren."

"Oh, go on," she said with a wave of her hand.

Julien's eyes lit with a passion that left her knees weak. "I will," he vowed.

And with that, he swept his wife into his arms and showed her just how tempting she still was.